# MUSIC FROM ELSEWHERE

*Music From Elsewhere*
by Doug Skinner

FIRST PUBLISHED BY
Strange Attractor Press in 2024,
in an unlimited paperback edition
& a hardback edition of 300 copies.



LAYOUT & DESIGN BY
Tihana Šare and Baphorock

ISBN: 9781913689216



A CIP CATALOGUE RECORD for this book is available from the British Library.

DISTRIBUTED BY The MIT Press, Cambridge, Massachusetts. And London, England.

PRINTED AND BOUND IN Estonia by
Tallinna Raamatutrükikoda.

STRANGE ATTRACTOR PRESS
BM SAP, London, WC1N 3XX UK,
www.strangeattractor.co.uk

# MUSIC FROM ELSEWHERE

## Haunting Tunes From Mythical Beings, Hidden Worlds, and Other Curious Sources

Doug Skinner

*THIS BOOK developed from many concerts and lecture demonstrations I've given over the years. I'd like to thank the people and institutions who presented them: Ellie Covan of Dixon Place, Geoff and Lynette Wiley of Jalopy Theatre, the late Phyllis Benjamin of the International Fortean Organization, Joanna Ebenstein and Laetitia Barbier of Morbid Anatomy, and Bob Rickard and Paul Sieveking of the Fortean Times UnConvention. And I owe particular debts to Shannon Taggart, who booked me for an unforgettable concert for the Spiritualist community in Lily Dale, NY, and to Mark Pilkington of Strange Attractor Press, who urged me to write this.*

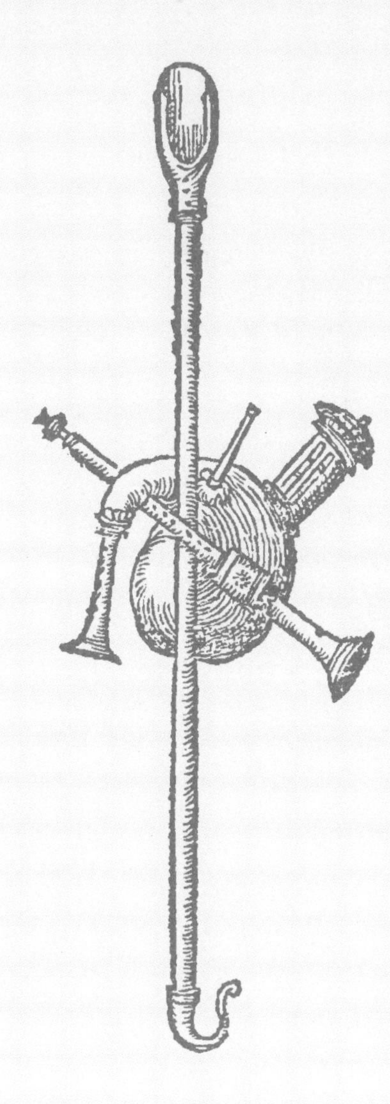

# INTRODUCTION

This book is a collection of anomalous music: that is, music that falls outside the usual practices of composition or social use.

I'll define the former, loosely, as conscious composition, which has used many techniques over the centuries and over the globe: writing by formal rules (dance forms, counterpoint, serialism, and aleatoric techniques), improvisation (including improvisation within conventional parameters, like jazz, blues, and ragas), or setting tunes to verses, to name a few.

Music's social uses include courtship, dance, military display, religious ceremony, background music (such as music for meals), storytelling (including narrative ballads and scores for plays and films), and the more recent form of concerts (in which a seated audience listens to performers), none of which is exclusive. And we can add commerce, since, after all, music is often made for money.

For the purposes of this book, I've established several categories of anomalous music — all rigorously and unavoidably imprecise.

We open with music that doesn't exist. This includes silent music, lost music, mythological music, imaginary instruments, and fictional composers.

Once the introductory silence subsides, I propose seven further categories.

*The first is music attributed to the elusive but earthbound people of folklore*: fairies, trows, trolls, piskeys, banshees, and other shadowy beings.

*The second is reserved for the music of the sky people*: of angels and aliens.

*The third is music attributed to the dead.* This includes pieces by ghosts, spirits, and channeled composers from the past, as well as a few practitioners of trance and spirit possession.

*Number four is the musical cipher*: the various methods for using music linguistically, such as musical codes and constructed languages.

*The fifth category is speculative music*: which uses musical materials as hermetic and cosmological metaphors.

*The sixth category is music based on birds and other animals*, with a look at methods of notating and appropriating it, as well as our complementary impulse to teach birds human tunes.

*The seventh, and last, category is music from dreams*. Hearing music in dreams and trances is common, but it does often seem to the hearer to come from elsewhere. It may also account for some of the music in the other chapters.

I should clarify as soon as possible some of the things that this book is not.

It's not a collection of 'weird music'; in fact, the common forms of composition often produce stranger material.

It doesn't mock unusual ideas; I'm more inclined to enjoy them.

It also neither endorses claims of the 'paranormal', which I clothe in quotes because the definition is so slippery, nor debunks them. This is due less to principled neutrality than to the subjectivity of the reports, which makes all explanations tricky to falsify. And although the music comes from 'elsewhere', I've mostly stuck to the European tradition, where I can read the texts and music, rather than blundering through unfamiliar cultures like a clueless tourist. I urge those steeped in different traditions to compile more delightful works like this one.

What this *is* is primarily a collection of music: after all, if someone hears a fairy tune, I want to know the tune. So, I give notations whenever possible. If you don't read music, which seems to be all the rage nowadays, perhaps you can ask some cute musician friend of yours for help.

Much of what follows comes from brain activity not usually classed as rational: hallucinations, visions, séances, interactions with imaginary beings. The classification, though, is all too often arbitrary, since the rational and irrational defy separation. Nor can our instincts be dismissed: just as pareidolia showed Hamlet camels in clouds, or Christians Jesus in tacos, we inevitably hear patterns in the most random noises. The rational, irrational, and instinctual are firmly intertwined, which I hope makes everything more interesting.

One of my favorite collectors of anomalies was Charles Fort, the early twentieth century American author who stockpiled data he considered to be 'damned' by orthodoxy and compiled them into books, most famously *The Book of the Damned* (1919). Before I head into Chapter 0, then, I'll consider the possibility of Fortean music.

And what would that be? Fort himself was mostly mum on the subject, although he did consider Kepler's version of the music of the spheres (see Chapter V below for details) in his book *New Lands* (1923). You could argue that perennial sonic puzzles like mystery hums and ringing rocks are Fortean music, or indeed some of the categories presented in our book.

The most clear-cut examples, though, are the songs that Fort himself sang. We know from a letter he wrote to Theodore Dreiser in 1921, shortly after he and his wife Anna had moved to London, that one evening they sang their favorite songs in the kitchen, fueled by numerous bottles of Bass Ale:

> I said, we'll have another, and we did. And we began to sing, 'Oh, Elsie, kind and true,' and I haven't been so happy in years and years, and there were four black bottles on the table.
>
> We sang 'Juanita,' ☞ and there's a dip in it when I bring in the bass in a way that moves me more than the profoundest of metaphysical discoveries ever could. And there were six big black bottles on the table. FIG 1 p. 162
>
> And we sang 'On the Banks of the Wabash,' ☞ and I almost cried because it made me think of the dear, horrible, delightful, humble days of our greatest poverty, when we always had two or three pots of beer a night, and sang and scrapped and were happy. And there were eight or nine black bottles on the table. FIG 2 p. 163–165

So, let's take a look at those three songs.

I suspect the first one is not 'Elsie', but 'Ella Ree' ☞, a 'New Ethiopian Melody', by Charles E. Stewart and James M. Porter, published in 1852. The first line is 'Oh, Ella Ree, so kind and true.' Septimus Winner borrowed FIG 3 p. 166–168 it, to use the polite term, for an 1865 song called 'Ellie Rhee', changing the narrator to a freed slave returning to his beloved in Tennessee. It was then taken up by folk singers, who sometimes changed it to 'Sweet Allalee'. In around 1889, the South African songwriter Jacobus Toerien heard American workers sing it in the Transvaal gold mines, and translated it into Afrikaans as 'Sarie Marijs'. It became so popular that it inspired the first South African talkie, in 1931, a 10-minute short called *Sarie Marais.*

'Juanita' was first published in 1853, as part of a collection called *Songs of Affection*, and was once quite popular. The lyrics are by Caroline Norton, a notable poet, novelist, and social reformer. She's often credited as the composer as well, and 'Juanita' is sometimes cited as the first commercially successful ballad by a woman. The original sheet music bore the byline 'Arranged by T. G. May', and the first four measures of the melody are identical to *Lascia ch'io pianga*, from Handel's *Rinaldo.* Oddly enough, I can find no trace of any other music credited to T. G. May. Perhaps Norton sang her lyrics to her own tune, unwittingly channeling Handel, and called on a friend to arrange it for her.

'On the Banks of the Wabash, Far Away' was written by Theodore Dreiser's brother, known professionally as Paul Dresser, which is what prompted Fort to write the letter. It was published in 1897, became his most successful song, and was chosen as the state song of Indiana in 1913. And it was partly written by Theodore, as he explained:

> After a little urging — I think the fineness of the morning had as much to do with it as anything — I took a piece of paper and after meditating a while scribbled in the most tentative manner imaginable the first verse and chorus of that song almost as it was published. I think one or two lines were too long or didn't rhyme, but eventually either he or I hammered them into shape, but before that I rather shamefacedly turned them over to him, for somehow I was convinced that this work was not for me and that I was rather loftily and cynically attempting what my good brother would do in all faith and feeling.

> He read it, insisted that it was fine and that I should do a second verse, something with a story in it, a girl perhaps — a task which I solemnly rejected.

The song prompted a copyright battle in 1917, eleven years after Dresser's death, when two songwriters, Ballard McDonald and James Hanley, obtained permission from Dresser's publisher to quote it in their song 'Back Home Again in Indiana'. They agreed to use two measures, and then took 26. Dresser's estate sued for plagiarism, but the case was never settled. Now, the two songs are often confused, and 'Back Home in Indiana' is sometimes played as the state song.

Fort's songs are not particularly anomalous, but they do have colorful and convoluted histories. And I hope this establishes the canon of Fortean music once and for all.

0

# On Music That Isn't There

There's a large body of music that's silent, lost, destroyed, imaginary, or fictional.

Nevertheless, it does exist. A null set is still a set; the nothingness within it separated from the nothingness outside it. Non-existent music appears throughout history, folklore, and literature; silent pieces are notated and published.

## SILENT MUSIC

Silence has long been a part of musical practice. Just as music is organized sound, silent music is organized silence. It's used in ceremonies and social occasions: Quaker meetings, memorials, and sitting zazen, among others. There have been many silent pieces, all different, even though they all sound the same.

Perhaps the first notated silent piece was written by Alphonse Allais in 1884.

Allais was a prolific and inventive comic writer, with a taste for fantasy, formal precision, and cruelty; his 'anthumous works', as he called them, remain in print, and have been championed by Surrealists, Pataphysicians, and Oulipians. His silent piece was written for the 1884 *Arts Incohérents*, an exhibition of comic artworks organized by the journalist Jules Lévy. The year before, Allais had contributed a sheet of white paper entitled *'Première communion de jeunes filles chlorotiques par un temps de neige'* (First communion of chlorotic girls in the snow). Monochromes were a common comic trope at the time; specimens include Paul Bilhaud's black painting 'Negroes Fighting in a Tunnel' (1882), Paul de Bouillant's 'Opaque window to decorate a room for the blind' (1884), and Jules Moy's 1897 monologue 'The Unicolorist'. Allais extended the premise with a sheet of music paper with several empty measures. He called it 'Great sorrows are mute. — Incoherent funeral march'. It was marked *'Silentio doloroso'*, and, he informed Lévy, marked the death of the Coherents.

In 1897, Allais published a booklet called *Album primo-avrilesque* (April-Foolish Album), which collected several other monochromes and the silent piece. This second version was called *'Marche funèbre*

MARCHE FUNÈBRE

COMPOSÉE POUR LES

*FUNÉRAILLES D'UN GRAND HOMME SOURD*

Lento rigolando.

T. S. V. P.

*Marche Funebre*

*composée pour les funérailles d'un grand homme sourd'* (Funeral march composed for the funeral of a great deaf man) and its marking changed to *'Lento rigolando'*. It took up two pages, one with nine measures and one with fifteen, and bore a brief 'witty preface':

> The creator of this Funeral March was inspired in its composition by this principle, admitted by everyone, that great sorrows are mute. These great sorrows being mute, the performers will confine themselves to counting the measures, instead of indulging in that indecent racket that removes the noble character from the best funerals. ☜

There's a literary silent genre too, comprising such works as Elbert Hubbard's 1905 *Essay on Silence*, numerous joke blank books (like the 1880 classic *Political Achievements of the Earl of Dalkeith*, or later favorites like *Actors I Have Met and Liked* and *Reasons to Vote Republican*) and the blank, black, and marbled pages in *Tristram Shandy*. If brevity is the soul of wit, silence must be wittier. A set is defined which, by its own definition, must be null.

*Il Silenzio*

The first silent piece to be published was probably *Il Silenzio: Pezzo Caratteristico e Descrittivo* (Silence: Characteristic and Descriptive Piece), which appeared in *La Nuova Musica*, on November 30, 1896. It was credited to Samuel, the pseudonym of Edgardo del Valle de Paz, and consists of one page, with 21 measures, for 'any instrument' and piano. Unlike Allais's blank staff, it's adorned with nonsensical key signatures, frequent changes of meter, and elaborate expressive markings, all applied to complex combinations of rests. Paz, a composer and teacher of somewhat conservative tastes, was apparently using his alter ego to satirize the excesses of new music.

Erwin Schulhoff's *In Futurum*, from 1919, resembles *Il Silenzio*, but seems to spring from a different impulse.

Schulhoff was a brilliant composer whose career ended at the age of 48, in the Wülzburg concentration camp. He had a particular fondness for jazz. Around 1919 and 1920, he also wrote several exuberant Dada pieces, including *Bassnachtigall* (Bass Nightingale, for solo contrabassoon) and *Sonata Erotika* (a notated orgasm for soprano, complete with post-coital piss).

His piano suite *Fünf Pittoresken* quoted popular genres, with a Foxtrott [sic], Ragtime, One-Step, and Maxixe. The third movement, *In Futurum* is not like the others: a single page with thirty measures of rests, fermatas, question marks, exclamation points, and smiling and frowning faces. It's marked *'Zeitmaß-zeitlos'* (tempo-timeless), and the performer is directed to play *'tutto il canzone con espressione e sentimento ad libitum, sempre, sin al fine!'* (the whole song with expression and sentiment *ad libitum*, always, until the end!). ☞ FIG 1 *p. 170*

In context, Schulhoff's piece seems more like exuberant Dada than criticism. The silences in these three pieces are as different as Parisian wit, Italian satire, and Czech buffoonery, all of which have their own rich traditions.

However, all three can be seen as graphic parodies of sheet music, which has its own tradition, including such gems as Arthur Goldstein's burlesque method books, the *Complete Method für der Waldhorn oder der Ventilhorn* by Professor Eric von Schmutzig (1949}, and its sequels for woodwinds and strings; and the unplayable compositions of John Stump: *Prelude and the Last Hope in C and C-sharp Minor* (1971), *Faerie's Aire and Death Waltz* (1980), and *String Quartet No. 556(b) for Strings* (1997).

The silent pieces of Allais, Paz, and Schulhoff remained on the page. The American bandleader Raymond Scott took the step of bringing silent music before an audience in 1940, introducing a piece called 'Silent Music' into his shows. A performance at the Strand movie theater in Manhattan in 1941 was mentioned in the March 3 issue of *Time*. From it, we learn that there were 13 musicians, that they energetically mimed playing, and that it made the audience 'fidget and giggle.' And it seems to have been not entirely silent: 'The band was going through all the motions: the swart, longish-haired leader led away; the brasses, the saxophones, the clarinets made a great show of fingering and blowing, but the only sound from the stage was a rhythmic swish-swish from the trap-drummer, a froggy slap-slap from the bull-fiddler, a soft plunk-plunk from the pianist.'

The French artist Yves Klein, who seems to have based most of his output on one page from Allais's *Album Primo-Avrilesque (Stupeur de jeunes recrues apercevant pour la première fois ton azur, O Méditerranée* (Stupor of young recruits [i.e., 'blues'] on first beholding your azure, O Mediterranean!)) wrote his *Symphonie Monoton-Silence* in 1947: a D major chord sustained for 20 minutes, followed by 20 minutes of silence. It remained unperformed until March 6, 1960, when it accompanied nude women rolling in paint at the Maurice d'Arquian gallery in Paris. Curiously, Klein's original score, which scrupulously notates the chord for 42 players, specifies that it should last 5 or 7 minutes, followed by 44 seconds of silence; he must have expanded it later. Whatever the duration, it may be the first silent piece not meant as a joke; he called it 'the exact transposition of the articulation between the visible and the invisible', which was probably serious.

The best-known silent piece is, incontestably, John Cage's *4'33"*.

He first considered it in 1948, as a silent Muzak disk called 'Silent Prayer', four and a half minutes long, like other Muzak disks. Under its new title, *4'33"*, it was premiered by the pianist David Tudor in Woodstock, NY, on August 29, 1952. It was the first silence to be divided into movements, listed on that first program as *30'*, *2'23"*, and *1'40"*.

Cage tried different notations, including empty measures (as in the Allais, which he later said he'd never seen) and a proportional score in which lines represent time. The definitive score, published by Peters, simplifies the piece into three movements each marked *Tacet*. In a note, Cage acknowledges the original timings (and, oddly, gets them wrong), but says they can be any length.

Its simplicity, as well as its place in Cage's ebullient career as composer, provocateur, zen sage, theorist, and raconteur, have made *4'33"* famous. It has a remarkable power to enrage audiences, even though it's essentially no different from the silent ceremonies mentioned above. The fact that it's defined as music, and not framed as a joke, seems to upset its detractors.

It inevitably inspired tributes and parodies, and soon mere emptiness was loosed upon the world. Pop and rock albums especially teemed with silent tracks. There are several brief pieces with joke names, in the Allais tradition, like John Denver's 6-second 'Ballad of Richard Nixon' (1969), or John Lennon's 4-second 'Nutopian International Anthem' (1973). Others have purely descriptive titles, in the Cage tradition, like Brian Eno's 'Silence' (2011) or Wilco's '23 Seconds of Silence' (1999). Among providers of blank recordings are Soundgarden, Sly Stone, The Kaiser Chiefs, Afrika Bambaataa, Korn, and The Melvins; nor should we forget the 1970 MGM album *The Best of Marcel Marceao* [sic] and the 1980 Stiff album *The Wit and Wisdom of Ronald Reagan*, both firmly in the null-set camp.

One of the best-publicized examples was 'A One Minute Silence', on *Classical Graffiti*, a 2002 album by Mike Batt and The Planets. It was credited to Batt/Cage, prompting a lawsuit from Peters, Cage's publisher. The press dutifully reported that Batt settled out of court for an unspecified six figures. Eight years later, Batt admitted it was a publicity stunt, and that he actually donated a thousand pounds to the John Cage trust — the six figures included the pence.

And perhaps the most respectable silence was published on December 28, 2000, when the US Congress passed Public Law 106–579, establishing the National Moment of Remembrance: a minute of silence to be observed every year at 3:00 pm on Memorial Day, the last Monday in May. A White House Commission on the National Moment of Remembrance was also established, with a budget of $500,000 for the fiscal year 2001, and $250,000 for each fiscal year from 2002 to 2009. That seems cheap by governmental standards, but still expensive for one minute of silence, especially with no donation to the John Cage trust. It's not enforced, so the official intentional silence is mixed with unofficial intentional silence, unintentional silence, intentional sound, and unintentional sound.

## LOST MUSIC

Music that's lost is also silent now. Most music is lost, since so little was notated throughout history, and nothing was recorded until we had gramophones. It's regrettable, since a lot of it was probably pretty good.

The earliest musical instrument may be the Divje Babe flute, found by Ivan Turk in Slovenia in 1995. It's part of a cave bear femur, about 43,100 years old, and pierced with two holes. Turk proclaimed it a Neanderthal flute, and it's now displayed as such in the National Museum of Slovenia. Some scholars, however, think it was just gnawed by a hyena. If so, the many attempts to reconstruct and play it are recreations of music that never existed. Nevertheless, its flutiness is now supported by national pride.

The earliest undisputed instrument is the Hohle Fels flute, found in the German cave of that name in 2008. It's roughly 35,000 years old, made from a vulture's wing bone, and has five finger holes. Other bits of ivory flutes (for which I propose the term 'flutesherds') in the area may be even older. Sadly, we have no idea what Paleolithic flutists played; they may have used it as a bird call rather than a flute.

By definition, we don't know the history of prehistoric music, and preliterate cultures left no literature. When people started writing, we do have some records, but more is lost than saved. Mesopotamia left cuneiform notations as early as 2000 BCE, but reading it takes guesswork. In India, the Samaveda preserved notation from around 1200 BCE. But not all literate cultures wrote music; the Olmecs, Incas, Mayans, Aztecs, and Hittites left lovely pictures and sculptures of musicians, but no pieces. China's classical court music, yayue, started in the 11th century BCE, but nothing was written until the 7th century CE; the sixth Confucian classic, the *Classic of Music*, might have been informative, but was either destroyed or never existed to begin with. Arabic music remained unwritten until about 800 CE.

The music of the Hebrews may have sounded Egyptian, particularly if Freud and his apostles are correct in conflating Moses and Akhenaten. We know surprisingly little about it. It was obviously important, since musical instruments pop up throughout the Bible; the first are the *kinnor* and *ugab* in Genesis 4:21.

But what were they? King James's scholars translated them as 'harp' and 'organ', which may be wrong. The *kinnor* was David's instrument, and is assumed to be a lyre, although the number and tuning of the strings is unknown. The *ugab* is more of an enigma. Saadia Gaon (10th c.) and Jonah Ibn Janah (11th c.) call it a 'kitar'; Solomon ben Abraham Ibn Parhon (12th c.) identifies it as a bowed stringed instrument; and Abraham di Porta Leone (17th c.) says it was a viola da gamba, which is unlikely.

Many other biblical instruments are unidentified, and the ban on images precluded illustrations, leaving the poor translators to guesswork. Even worse, several are hapaxes. The shalishim of 1 Samuel 18:6 are translated simply as 'instruments of music.' The *shiddah* of Ecclesiastes 2:8, rendered in the KJV as 'musical instruments, and that of all sorts', have been variously interpreted also as cups, cup-bearers, baths, litters, and wives. All of which, admittedly, do make noise.

Perhaps the most baffling lost instrument is found not in the Bible, but the Talmud. This is the fearsome *magrepha*, which first appears in the Mishnaic tractate Tamid, written shortly after the destruction of the Second Temple in 70 CE, and is mentioned later in the Gemara. The Mishnah describes it as a shovel to sweep ashes from sacrifices, but so loud that it could be heard for miles, and the Gemara identifies it as an elaborate musical instrument. It's been suggested it was a gong, bell, drum, percussion machine, siren, or hydraulic organ. Perhaps the simplest solution is that the word had many meanings; future musicologists, after all, may be puzzled that we both toot horns and put on shoes with them. The 16th century Shiltei Giborim describes it as a sort of harmonium, with a chest containing ten pipes, each with ten holes. It had a keyboard, which controlled small pieces of metal that stopped the pipe holes, permitting 100 pitches, and bellows to sound the pipes. In 1960, Joseph Yosser proposed another design in the *Journal of the American Musicological Society*: a box with the bellows inside, worked by a hollow handle outfitted with 100 pipes and the requisite shovel. Whatever it was, it's now gone.

As is all the joyful noise in the Bible, all of David's *kinnor* tunes and the original settings of the Psalms.

We do have clues, though, since the Masoretic Text sports traditional cantillation accents, which provide indications for chanting. Each accent stands for a melismatic sequence, although the interpretation varies from country to country, and even from book to book. The tradition for the three poetic books (Job, Proverbs, and Psalms) is lost entirely.

Inevitably, eager scholars have found the 'original' meaning of the accents. The 1906 *Jewish Encyclopedia* cites several — J. C. Speidel (1740), C. G. Anton (1790), L. Haupt (1854), and L. Ardens (1867) — adding 'the fanciful in their conclusions outweighs the probable.'

Which might also be a fair summation of the more recent work of Suzanne Haïk-Vantoura, a French organist and composer who argued that the accents represented pitches, rather than phrases. She identified eight that she matched to the diatonic scale: Darga was C, Tevir D, Silluq E, and so on. Since she relied on intuition more than evidence, most scholars dismiss her. Undaunted, she spent decades deciphering her melodies (like those Baconians who found acrostics in Shakespeare's First

Folio), and revealed them in her 1976 book *La Musique de la Bible révelée* (The Music of the Bible Revealed). Once again, nationalism guides belief; just as Slovenians rally around the Neanderthal flute, the French are the keenest Haïk-Vantourians.

We know more about the music of ancient Greece, but still too little. We can study musical treatises and scraps of notation, notably a chorus from Euripides's *Orestes*, but reconstruction is still chancy. We've lost the soundtracks of the tragedies, and can only wonder how Homer was chanted, or what Socrates strummed on his lyre or Sappho on her barbitos.

It comes as a surprise, to me anyway, that Ancient Rome is so silent. We have sheafs of their literature, much of it enthusing about music, but not a single tune. Apparently that poetry-mad society never wrote down its songs.

As we thread our way through more modern times, I'll note a few tantalizing losses from European history. I find it unfortunate, for example, that we've lost the music of three brilliant figures of the Italian Renaissance: Marsilio Ficino, Vincenzo Galilei, and Leonardo da Vinci.

Ficino helped launch the Renaissance by reviving Plato's Academy and translating Plato and the *Corpus Hermeticum*. But he also played the lyre, sang his own reconstructions of the Orphic Hymns, and practiced a sort of musical healing. In the third book of his *De Vita Triplici* (Three Books on Life), he devoted a couple of chapters to music as a sort of corrective for astrological imbalance. He laid down three rules for fitting songs to the stars:

> the first is, to discover what powers these have in themselves, which star, planet, and aspect has what effect on them... The second rule is to consider which star, planet, and aspect has what effect on them... The third rule is, pay attention every day to the location and aspects of the stars...

No doubt, he called on the traditional correspondences between planets and pitches that we'll puzzle over in Chapter V of this book. But, unfortunately, he left no scores.

Some time around 1580, Vincenzo Galilei, father of Galileo, created the first stirrings of opera, experimenting with what he called 'monody' to recreate Greek tragedy. He set a passage from Dante, the lamentation of Count Ugolino, for solo voice and viol. He followed it with the Lamentations of Jeremiah. Both are lost; they may have been partially improvised.

Leonardo da Vinci was popular with his contemporaries not only for his art and inventions, but for his extemporaneous songs. Apparently he never bothered to notate them. According to Giorgio Vasari, who should know, Leonardo entertained Ludovico Sforza, the Duke of Milan, on a silver *lira da braccio* shaped like a horse's skull. That too has vanished.

Many of Monteverdi's and Handel's operas are gone; major works by Bach, including two Passions, are gone; 'cello concerti' by Mozart, Haydn, and Mendelssohn have all disappeared. An oboe concerto by Beethoven is also gone. Stacks of Chopin's waltzes, polonaises, mazurkas, and écossaises have vanished, attested only by contemporary references.

Some missing music sounds particularly intriguing. I regret, for example, the silence of Jean-François Rameau, the nephew of Jean-Philippe Rameau, memorably portrayed in Diderot's *Rameau's Nephew*.He was known as *Rameau le fou*, and, true to his name, ended in an asylum. Two brief songs and a poem, *Le Raméide*, have survived, but his 1757 collection *Nouvelles Pièces de clavecin* (New Pieces for Harpsichord) is known only from descriptions. Judging by Élie Catherine Fréron's review, in his *Année littéraire* for October/December 1757, it must have been lively.

It included a programmatic battle scene, pastoral dances, a ballet on Cupid and Psyche, and, intriguingly, *Les Trois Rameau:* a portrait of Jean-Philippe, his brother Claude, and Jean-François himself. Fréron, no fan of the Encyclopedists, relished *L'Encyclopédique: Menuet intra ou ultramontain* (The Encyclopedic: Intra or Ultramontane Minuet) which he noted was 'bizarre in character.' Later editions added a 'vaudeville' on the tiff between Lully and Rameau, and something called *La Voltaire.* All of it, alas, has evaporated, while mountains of formulaic fluff have been scrupulously preserved. I would gladly trade a bale of forgettable operettas and pop songs for Rameau's collection.

# IMAGINARY MUSIC

Robert Benchley wrote an essay called 'Mind's Eye Trouble', in which he described his habit of imagining everything he read as taking place where he grew up, in Worcester, Massachusetts: Caesar was stabbed at the corner of May and Woodland, Dickens's novels unfolded on Shepard Street, and all Western battles were fought in his Aunt Mary Elizabeth's side yard. No amount of travel, he confessed, could override those early imprints.

I'm curious about what music, if any, we imagine when we think about those pieces that don't exist. But, already, we run afoul of our scattershot language, because the very word 'imagine' implies images. The related words are also visual: picture, visualize, envisage. There was really no term for hearing music in the mind until the music educator Edwin Gordon coined the word 'audiate.' We apparently talk more about the mind's eye than the mind's ear. At any rate, I gratefully acknowledge Gordon's neologism.

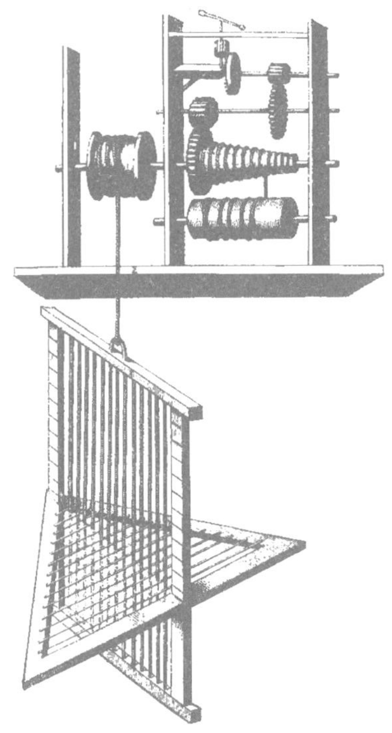

*Fludd's music box*

And just as we can only imagine something we've never seen by mixing our memories, we can't audiate something we never heard. We may be able to audiate Francis Drake's ghostly drum sounding the alarm for England, because it would just go 'bang bang bang', but the music of the Sirens would be harder, since it has melody and harmony.

There's another problem with mythological music: it's meant to be suprahuman. If we could actually audiate those Sirens, we too would go mad. If we knew the Pied Piper's tune, we too could lure rodents and children from Hamelin. Stage and film realizations always disappoint, since the tunes don't work as advertised. Mythological music needs to be silent. We're spared wondering if the Sirens sang the same song in the *Odyssey* and the *Argonautica*.

Here, for example, is a litany of legendary instruments that defy audiation: the aulos with which Marsyas challenged Apollo, the biwa that Benzaiten is always holding, the conch that Triton blew to control the waves, the damaru that Shiva plays for the Tandava, the three gongs with which Sang Hyang Guru invented the gamelan, the Gjallarhorn blown by Heimdallr, Bragi's harp, the horn that Gabriel and/or Israfil will blow on the day of judgment, the kantele that Väinämöinen made from the jawbone of a giant pike, Apollo's kithara, the lyre with which Heracles killed Linus of Thrace, the lyre with which Orpheus charmed beasts and stones, the olifant that burst Roland's temples, the Panchajanya that Vishnu blew to begin the *Mahabharata*, the pipa Mo-Li Hai plucked to affect the four elements, Ling Lun's bamboo pipe tuned to the cry of the phoenix, Pan's pipes, the salpinx that Tyrsenos invented, Ihy's sistrum, the harp called Uaithne with which the Dagda marshaled the seasons, Saraswati's veena, Krishna's venu.

Many instruments have been invented, but never realized. Leonardo da Vinci not only failed to notate his improvisations, but never built his viola organista (a sort of combination harpsichord and hurdy-gurdy), or the mechanized drums, graduated tympani, tunable bells, glissando recorders, bellows bagpipes, and other devices that fill his sketchbooks.

The physician and Rosicrucian apologist, Robert Fludd, whose more metaphorical instruments we'll get to in Chapter V, published a nominally feasible device in his book *Utriusque Cosmi, Maioris scilicet et Minoris, metaphysica, physica, atque technica Historia* (vol.1, 1618). He called it *Instrumentum nostrum Magnum*: gears and pulleys lowered a vertical frame studded with quills and dampers through a horizontal harp. Unfortunately, it probably wouldn't work.

There are also literary instruments never meant to be built, which also resist audiation.

We may as well bring back Alphonse Allais. In his 1894 story *Dressage* (Training), he introduces a man who plays wickerwork trombone, reading notes provided by birds sitting on telegraph wires.

We also have this squib by his fellow Honfleurais Erik Satie; it was transcribed by Pierre-Daniel Templier sometime around 1930, from a manuscript later lost in World War 2:

> 2 piston flutes (F sharp)
> 1 alto overcoat (C)
> 1 door handle (E)
> 2 slide clarinets (B-flat)
> 1 siphon in C
> 3 keyboard trombones
> 1 leather double bass (C)
> Chromatic bucket in B
> Instruments in the marvelous family of cephalophones, with a range of thirty octaves, absolutely unplayable. An amateur in Vienna (Austria) tried, in 1875, to use a siphon in C; following the execution of a trill, the instrument burst, broke his vertebral column, and scalped him completely. Since then, no one has dared use the powerful resources of the cephalophones, and the State has been obliged to forbid the teaching of these instruments in the municipal schools.

Some of these are hybrids, like the creatures of Greek myth, such as the flute with a trumpet's pistons, others are pitched versions of non-resonant bodies, such as the overcoat in C. The guiding principle is they can't be audiated.

Of similar unplayable inspiration is the Pianocktail, in Boris Vian's 1947 novel *L'Écume des jours* (The Scum of the Days), which mixed cocktails when played. Each key added a different alcohol, the loud pedal egg whites, and the soft pedal ice. Models were made for the two film adaptations, but the true Pianocktail is an unattainable ideal.

The Moog corporation contributed to the genre with a series of non-existent instruments released on April 1: a Polyphonic Theremin, with ten theremins, one for each finger; an Auto-De-Tuner, which reverses autotune; the MF-433, which silences audio output for four minutes and thirty-three seconds. With that, we reach a sort of apotheosis:

an imaginary instrument playing a silent piece, thereby giving us an imaginary silence.

Not all literary instruments are comic. In Francis Bacon's *The New Atlantis* (published posthumously in 1627), he suggested 'sound-houses', where diligent scholars experiment with quarter-tones, new instruments 'some sweeter than any you have', hearing aids, 'strange and artificial echoes', and 'means to convey sounds in trunks and pipes.' Cyrano de Bergerac proposed 'books made wholly for the ears' in his 1657 lunar fantasy, *L'Autre Monde* (The Other World). Dane Rudhyar invented the Cosmophonon for his 1953 novel *Return from No Return*: this marvelous contraption, stored on a planet in Sagittarius, was made of 'a field of forces surrounded by myriads of glowing crystals of many shapes and colors.'

The creations of Raymond Roussel pose special audiation challenges. Although best known for his hallucinatory novels and poems, he was more than a casual musician, having studied piano seriously at the Conservatoire, and taken up the tuba in his military service. Many of the inventions in his books are musical, such as the insects, concealed in tarot cards, that play 'The Bluebells of Scotland' in *Locus Solus.*

But it's the *Gala des Incomparables*, the show performed by the castaways in *Impressions d'Afrique*, that poses more serious problems. Roussel describes a remarkable variety show, including a quadruple amputee one-man band, a tenor who sings a four-part round with himself, and a talking horse. All are firmly set in an artificial world, free from physics. To make things more complicated, he also produced a stage show based on the novel. The poster promised twelve of the acts, four of them musical: Skarioffsky's giant trained worm, which played Hungarian melodies by dripping a mysterious dense liquid onto a zither; Lelgonalch's solo on a flute made from his amputated leg; Bex's musical machine, outfitted with strings, flutes, and drums made of a material called Bexium, which responded to changes in temperature; and Stéphane Alcott, who imitated a choir by bouncing echoes from the chests of his six emaciated sons. The only surviving script is an early draft, with no indication of how the acts were staged. The original music is imaginary, and its realization lost. I assume our audiation of both sets will be different — the former ideal, the latter a theatrical simulation of the ideal.

Fictional composers also appear in novels. Some are only nominally fictional, such as E. T. A. Hoffmann's excitable Johannes Kreisler (*Kreisleriana*, 1813–15, *Johannes Kreisler*, 1815, and *Lebens-Ansichten des Katers Murr*, 1819–1821), who is transparently Hoffmann himself. Chevalier Seraphael, in Elizabeth Sara Sheppard's 1853 novel *Charles Auchester*, is simply Mendelssohn with a silly name. To audiate their works, we can just listen to their models.

Some fictional composers are tragic heroes, their music secondary to their struggles and triumphs. Wilhelm Wackenroder's 1796 novella, *Das merkwürdige musikalische Leben des Tonkünstlers Joseph Berglinger* (The Strange Musical Life of the Composer Joseph Berglinger) presents Berglinger as a tortured soul. Romain Rolland's voluminous partwork *Jean-Christophe* (1904–1912) casts its hero as a modern Beethoven, but doesn't describe his music much. Thomas Mann's *Doktor Faustus* (1947), as the title telegraphs, features Adrian Leverkühn as a genius inspired by the devil, or at least by syphilis. The descriptions of his compositions were written with Theodor Adorno, so Adorno's music may be the best guide to audiation.

Other fictional composers are purely didactic, like poor old Paolo Gambara, in Balzac's 1837 novella *Gambara*. Balzac uses him to argue that one should write sentimental music when drunk rather than intellectual music when sober. The reader's inner ear is given a workout: Gambara plays his fictional opera *Mahomet*, all three acts of it, with precise musical descriptions, and later plays selections from Meyerbeer's real opera *Robert le diable*, again in great detail. To add an extra challenge, *Mahomet* is ugly when played sober on the piano, but beautiful when played drunk on Gambara's invention, the Panharmonicon.

Later novelists were more interested in mocking modernism. Gottfried Rosenbaum, in Randall Jarrell's *Pictures from an Institution* (1954), is a clownish professor; one of his pieces is an homage to Bach using only instruments beginning with B, A, C, or H. Christopher Miller's *Simon Silber: Works for Solo Piano* (2002) stars a pretentious fraud who writes pieces based on wind chimes, touchtone phones, and, in the Allais tradition, crows on power lines.

Like mythological music, fictional music is most affecting when unaudiated. When Proust wanted a piece of music for *À la recherche du temps perdu*, he considered a Saint-Saëns violin sonata, but substituted a sonata by the imaginary Vinteuil as more suitable for fiction, and was astute enough to even deprive his character of a first name. As the equally astute Keats noted, 'Heard melodies are sweet, but those unheard are sweeter.'

## SURVIVING MUSIC

As a sonic coda to this prolonged hush, I'll turn to two pieces that can be heard, both notable as sole survivors of lost genres.

The first is '*Quan lou bouyé*', 'When the Herdsman', a folksong sometimes cited as the only remaining song of the Cathars.

According to their pious inquisitors, the Cathars sang defiantly on their way to the stake. We don't know what they sang, since their music was destroyed along with the rest of their culture.

'*Quan lou bouyé*', however, is traditionally credited to them, particularly in Southern France, where they're still revered. There are several versions, in both French and Provençal. ☞ FIG 2 p. 171

Here's one of the Provençal versions, the first verse of nine:

*Quan lou bouyé ben de laura (bis)*
*Planto soun agulhado,*
*A, E, I, O, U,*
*Planto soun agulhado.*

When the herdsman returns from his labor (bis)
He puts up his cattle prod,
A, E, I, O, U,
He puts up his cattle prod.

In the following verses, he finds his wife ill and disconsolate by the fire, and offers to make a soup of lark, turnip, and cabbage. She replies that when she dies, she wants to be buried in the cellar, with her feet by the wall and her head under the fountain; pilgrims will ask whose grave it is, and be told that it's poor Joana, gone to heaven with her goats.

The herdsman has been identified as the constellation Boötes, and sometimes as the Vatican. Joana becomes the Cathar church, dying by the fire because Cathars were burned, disconsolate (*descounsoulado*) because she needs the *Consolamentum*, the last rites. The vowels have been variously glossed as a call of alarm, a sacred chant, and, unconvincingly, as the motto of Friedrich III of Austria (usually given as *Aquila ejus iuste omnia vincet*, 'our eagle justly triumphs over all', although inventing other acronyms is a national pastime). The soup is curious: the Cathar priests, the Perfects, ate no meat, milk, or eggs, since they were all products of copulation. The *Consolamentum* made the dying patient a Perfect, so a dead bird seems an unlikely last meal.

Although '*Quan lou bouyé*' is considered the only known Cathar song, it may not be unique. The troubadours were also a product of Southern France, so some may have been Cathars, although there's little to suggest it in the poetry.

Cathar or not, they left another singularity: one surviving song by a trobairitz, a female troubadour.

The trobairitz in question is the Comtessa de Dià, who left five songs, one with music. Not much is known about her. She lived in the late 12th or early 13th century, may have been named Beatritz, and may have known one of the earliest troubadours, Raimbaut d'Aurenga.

The song, *A chantar m'er*, is found in only one manuscript, *Le manuscript di roi* (The King's Manuscript), compiled for Louis IX's brother, Charles d'Anjou, in 1270. ☞ FIG 3 *p. 171*

There are five verses, plus a concluding couplet. Here's the first:

*A chantar m'er de so qu'eu no volria,*
*tant me rancur de lui cui sui amia;*
*car eu l'am mais que nuilla ren que sia:*
*vas lui nom val merces ni cortezia,*
*ni ma beltatz ni mos pretz ni mos sens;*
*c'atressim sui enganad' e trahia*
*Com degr'esser, s'eu fos dezavinens.*

I must sing what I would not have wanted to;
So angry am I with the one I love;
For I love him more than all that is;
Mercy and courtesy are of no avail with him,
Nor my beauty, nor my worthiness, nor my good sense;
For I am deceived and betrayed
As I would be, were I unpleasing.

With those exceptions as overture, we can now turn to the mythology we can hear: the music of the ultraterrestrials.

# I

# On the Music of the Ultraterrestrials

We turn now to music that we can hear, but which is credited to nonhuman creatures: fairies, banshees, trowies, gnomes, and other shadowy beings.

The word 'ultraterrestrial' comes from the late writer John A. Keel, who defined it as 'Related to this earth but set apart from it by unusual physical characteristics. Neither superior or inferior to the human race, but different.' My use of the term here acknowledges the similarity of reports about different sorts of paranormal beings. As both Keel and another researcher, Jacques Vallee, noted, the more recent stories of aliens often resemble older tales of fairies. Witnesses of both report missing time, stolen babies and fetuses, attempts by the victims to steal objects to prove that their experience was real, and the little people's obsession with our water, metal, and salt. However, here I'll confine myself to those traditionally confined to the earth, and save the sky people for the next chapter.

Again, let me remind you that reporting folktales doesn't imply belief; the fossil record yields few pixie skulls. My only conviction here is that some of this music was not consciously composed by its witnesses.

We'll start with the fairies. Descriptions of these elusive races vary from region to region, but they were usually said to be about two or three feet tall, usually dressed in drab browns or greens. They were mischievous, elusive, and often hostile to humans. There have many attempts to explain them, including drunk witnesses and vivid dreams. In Margaret Murray's engaging but dubious books, *The Witch-Cult in Western Europe* (1921) and *The God of the Witches* (1931), she argues that fairies were a reclusive tribe of dwarfish humans, perhaps stunted by poor diet.

Most of the music I've found comes from the British Isles, particularly those lively Celtic parts, and Scandinavia. Other cultures do have musical ultraterrestrials. Arabic djinn dictated poetry and music; the orang bunian in Indonesia and Malaysia filled the forests with their singing and whistling. The tunes, though, seem not to have been notated. Fairies in other places have little interest in music. I've searched in vain for the music of the Menehune of Hawaii, or the many Pukwudgies, Kiwolatomuhsisok, Gahongas, Paissa, and other beings that bedevil Native Americans. I've found songs about them, but not attributed to them. I assume there's a lot of material I haven't unearthed, and only hope someone more steeped in those traditions can plug up the gaps.

I'll start with some music from Cornwall. In 1921, a composer named Thomas Wood was camping on Dartmoor when he heard music in the air. He described it in his 1936 autobiography, *True Thomas*:

> And then I heard the last thing I could have expected to hear — music in the air as faint as breath. It died away; came back louder, hung over me swaying like a censer that dips and swings, and is withdrawn. In all it lasted twenty minutes... Portable wireless sets were unknown in 1921; heather-covered moss will not carry sound far and the day was a roaster; my field glasses again assured me that no picnicker was in sight, still less a gramophone, and what I heard could not possibly have been music of the mind extraverted into music for the ear. Nor was it music that resembled in the least the music that I had just written or even music that I wanted to write... It was not a melody, an 'air.' It sounded like the weaving together of various tenuous fairy strands.

He notated what he heard, and scored it for four violins, adding 'I am prepared to say on oath that what I wrote down is so close to the original that the authors themselves would not know the difference.'

As Wood says, his own music was very different. He wrote hearty choral songs, with titles like 'Forty Singing Seamen' and 'Salt Beef', and arrangements of folk songs, including many versions of 'Waltzing Matilda'. The fairy snippet is unusual for him, but does sound like much European music of the time, with its parallel fifths and pandiatonic harmonies.

In Cornish folklore, his example would be attributed to the pixies, or, as they're usually known there, the 'piskies'. Cornwall has other fairies, like the malevolent spriggans, and the knockers who lurk in the mines, but the piskies are the ones most associated with music. They were described as little old men, often with red hair, lurking near stone circles. Many stories follow the familiar fairy narrative of a young man

*Thomas Wood Fairy Music*

lured by music into a cave, where the piskies are dancing and feasting. The tradition had been waning by the time Wood went camping. In 1824, Samuel Drew noted 'But the age of piskays, like that of chivalry, is gone... Their music is rarely heard; and they appear to have forgotten to attend their ancient midnight dance.'

And, in fact, this is the only reputed music I've been able to find.

Moving north into Wales, we find a long tradition of the little people, also called the Tylwyth Teg, Gwyllian, and Ellyan. One of the best-known stories of fairy music comes, oddly enough, from a book about Ireland: *Fairy Legends and Traditions of the South of Ireland*, written in 1828 by Thomas Crofton Croker. He included a few Welsh stories, including one similar to Thomas Wood's.

*Morgan Gwillim tune*

It comes from a certain Morgan Gwillim, who said that he saw and heard fairies by Cylepsta Waterfall. He said:

> I could at that moment see them distinctly, glittering in all the colors of the rainbow, and hear their music softly blending with the murmur of the waterfall... then they ascended the rock, and frisked away; the sound of their melodious harps dying away among the mountains, whither they had fled; and the last strain I heard sounded something like this but the falling cadence I could not catch for the life of me, it was so faint.

I could find nothing more about Morgan Gwillim, and, perhaps not incidentally, no other mention of Cylepsta.

The 1880 book *British Goblins: Welsh folklore, fairy mythology, legends, and traditions*, by Wirt Sikes, offers more musical tidbits. Sikes retells Gwillim's story, and changes the eighth notes in his tune to quarter notes, for some reason known only to himself and his conscience. He mentions that fairy music was often heard in the area: 'Many heard their music, and said that it was low and pleasant; but that it had this peculiarity: no one could ever learn the tune.' He claims some witnesses were able to retain some of the words, and gives a bit of verse, beginning *'Dowch, dowch, gyfeillon mân'*, which he refused to translate into 'bald English.'

He also presents a tune with an elaborate backstory. A crwth player named Iolo ap Hugh (the crwth being a sort of six-string fiddle) went to a cave in North Wales on Halloween, carrying a large supply of bread and cheese and seven pounds of candles. He never returned, but long afterwards, an old shepherd saw him at the opening, frolicking around with his crwth, with a lantern around his neck, until he was dragged back inside. Later still, one cold December, music was heard coming from under the local church. The shepherd recognized it as the tune Hugh was playing, and the parson notated it from his whistling. Sikes then gives this tune. ☞ FIG 1 p. 174

In other versions of the story, the crwth player is called Ned Pugh, and other versions of the tune are called *'Ffarwel Ned Puw'* (Farewell Ned Puw). One was collected by Edward Jones in 1794, in his *Musical and Poetical Relicks of the Welsh Bards*; another was arranged by Beethoven for voice and piano trio in his collection of Welsh folk songs. ☞ FIG 2 p. 175

Wirt Sikes also prints another scrap of fairy melody, explaining, 'Then the fairies would come at midnight, continue their revels till daybreak, sing the well-known strain of *"Toriad y Dydd,"* or "The Dawn," leave a piece of money on the hob, and disappear.' The tune may not be as well known today, so here it is. ☞ FIG 3 p. 176

I can't leave Wales without mentioning the tune 'Largo's Fairy Reel'. It was either composed or collected by Nathaniel Gow in 1802, and included in his 1809 compilation *Fifth Collection of Strathspey Reels*. Since then, it has entered the folk repertory, and is known by many names, including *'Dawns y Tylwyth Teg'*, 'Dance of the Fairies', and, on the Isle of Man, *'Daunse ny Farishyn'*. And is, inevitably, accepted as a typical fairy tune. ☞ FIG 4 *p. 176*

And with that, we cross into Ireland. The Irish have an elaborate tradition of fairies, the *aes sidhe*, whose membership includes Leprechauns, Clurichauns (who may just be drunk Leprechauns), mermaids called the Merrow, headless horsemen called the Dullahan, goblinish Pookas, even a miniature Sasquatch called a Grogach. Many are musical.

It's noteworthy that one of Ireland's most popular composers, the 17th century blind harpist Turlough O'Carolan, claimed fairy inspiration. He was said to sleep on a fairy mound, and receive music in his dreams. None of his compositions, however, is attributed directly to fairies, and only two refer to them: 'The Fairy Queen' and '*Sí Bheag, Sí Mhor*'. The latter translates as 'Small Fairy Mound, Big Fairy Mound', and is based on a legendary battle between fairies. The fact that the subject was suggested by O'Carolan's patron, Squire George Reynolds, suggests human, rather than ultraterrestrial, inspiration.

So we turn instead to a tune attributed, with purely anecdotal evidence, to the fairies. It can be found in the 1888 book *Irish Wonders*, by D. R. McAnally, Jr. He merely identifies it as a 'Fairy Dance', and adds 'As played by a Connaught Piper, who learned it from "The Good People".' ☞ FIG 5 *p. 177*

Many of the Irish accounts are somewhat vague on provenance. Among them are numerous folktales that incorporate music from the fairies. Unlike the unaudiated mythological music, there are specific tunes. There's the story of Lusmore, for example, so called because he wore a sprig of foxglove (lusmore) in his hat. He was a hunchback, who one day was resting on the slopes of the old fairy fort of Knockgrafton. He heard the fairies singing *'Dé Luain, Dé Máirt'* (Monday, Tuesday). He listened awhile, and then chimed in with *'Agus Dé Céadaoin'* (and Wednesday). The fairies were so delighted with this addition, which somehow had never occurred to them, that they took him into the fort, and feasted with him all night. The next morning, he awoke with his hump gone. Another hunchback, Jack Madden, heard about this, and hurried off to Knockgrafton. He too heard the fairies singing, and shouted out '*Agus Déardaoin, Agus Dé hAoine*' (and Thursday and Friday). But the fairies didn't like his lyrics, so they punished him by adding Lusmore's hump to his own. ☞ FIG 6 p. 178

'The Gold Ring' has a similar plot. A piper hid to hear the fairy's music, and found a gold ring after they left. He returned the next night, and returned the ring in exchange for the tune. In another version, a farmer surprised a fairy gathering, and picked up the ring when they ran off. Again, he traded it for the tune. ☞ FIG 7 p. 179

One more unsettling type of Irish Ultraterrestrial is the Banshee, who appears to announce a death. She's described sometimes as old, sometimes as young, often dressed in white or gray, with long hair. Traditionally, only five families were visited by the Banshee: the O'Neills, the O'Briens, the O'Connors, the O'Gradys, and the Kavanaghs.

Surprisingly (to me, anyway), there are a few transcriptions of the banshee's cry. Here's one from McAnally's *Irish Wonders*, cited previously. Unfortunately, he doesn't say who noted it, or how, just that he heard it from a 'Kerry pishogue'. ☞ FIG 8 p. 180

And here's an earlier one, from *Ireland: Its Scenery, Character, &c.*, by Samuel Carter Hall and Anna Maria Hall, from 1843. Curiously, it's similar to the first one, and even in the same key. And again, no source is given. ☞ FIG 9 p. 180

We even have a third example, notated by William Butler Yeats in his 1892 book *Irish Fairy Tales*. Oddly enough, it was collected not in Ireland, but in Colombia. As Yeats explains:

> A distinguished writer on anthropology assures me that he has heard her on 1st December 1867, in Pital, near Libertad, Central America, as he rode through a deep forest. She was dressed in pale yellow, and raised a cry like the cry of a bat. She came to announce the death of his father. This is her cry, written down by him with the help of a Frenchman and a violin. ☞ FIG 10 p. 180

He saw and heard her again on February 5 1871, at 16 Devonshire Street, Queen's Square, London. She came this time to announce the death of his eldest child; and in 1884 he again saw and heard her at 28 East Street, Queen's Square, the death of his mother being the cause.

And with that, we cross into Scotland. One of the most compelling Scots fairy tunes comes from the MacLeod clan, headquartered in Dunvegan Castle, on the Isle of Skye. The family carefully preserves a tattered scrap of silk known for centuries as the Fairy Flag, although its origin is decidedly murky. And as part of this fairy tradition, they also claim a lullaby.

The story is that one day, centuries ago, a woman entered the castle without invitation, and went directly to the infant heir in his cradle. She sang him a lullaby, and then left the castle and disappeared over the moor. The lullaby was preserved by the family in the succeeding generations, as an enchantment to protect the heir.

There are many variations of the tune, under as many titles, such as 'Fairy Lullaby' or 'Cradle Spell of Dunvegan'. This is the closest we can come to the original tradition, sung by Neil MacLeod, who had learned it from his father. It was transcribed by the Skye folklorist Frances Tolmie in 1908, as *'Oran Talaidh na Mna-Sidhe'*, 'The Lullaby of the Fairy-Woman'. ☞

FIG 11
*p. 182–183*

Skye is also home to a curious little genre of water-horse lullabies. Some are attributed to the kelpie, a shape-shifting water spirit that appears as either a horse or human; some to the similar but fiercer eich-uisge. Both were fond of devouring passersby and seducing young women. The lullabies present the water-horse singing a lullaby to his son, after the mother has spotted the father's hooves and abandoned both husband and child. They probably belong in the category of songs about, rather than by, ultraterrestrials, but the tradition is ambiguous.

I'll give here two *eich-uisge* lullabies that Tolmie collected in 1897, *'Oran Tàlaidh an Eich-Uige'* and *'Caoidh an Eich-Uisge'*, both from a singer named Mary Ross. ☞

FIG 12
*p. 183*

The richest tradition of fairy music, for some reason, comes from the Shetland Islands, way up in the northeast. The local little people are called the trows, and, as the name suggests, are similar to trolls.

According to fairy folklorist Thomas Keightley, 'The Trows are of a diminutive stature, and they are usually dressed in gay green garments. When travelling from one place to another they may be seen mounted on bulrushes and riding through the air.' They also love music, and have inspired a repertory of fiddle tunes called 'trowie tunes'.

One intriguing thing about the trowie tunes is that they often have more specific origin stories than other fairy music.

Here, for example, is 'Winyadepla'. In the winter of 1803, Gibbie Laurenson of Norderhoos, Gruting, set out to grind a load of corn at Fir Vaa. At the mill, he sat on a stool and pretended to sleep. The trows came in, and drank all of his braand, a type of fermented milk. One of the trows, named Shanko, played a tune while the others danced on a nearby green. After the music stopped, Gibbie looked out and saw the trows heading up a hill toward Stackaberg. He later whistled the tune for his son, who was a fiddler and wrote it down. This is unusually specific. We have not only the name of the witness, but the name of the trow. Here's the tune. ☞ FIG 13 p. 184

There are many trowie tunes, so I'll limit myself to a couple more. 'Hylta Dance' comes from Fetlar. A man was returning home just before dawn, and saw a circle of trows dancing, with the fiddler and his wife in the center. The sun's rays turned them to stone. The stone circle, known as Haltadans (fairy ring), with two stones in its center, can still be seen in Fetlar. And the poor man could only learn half of the tune. ☞ FIG 14 p. 184

'Aith Rant' has a more specific date than most. Around 1790, a Cunningsburgh carpenter was returning home after celebrating the completion of a sixareen, a small fishing boat. Looking through a crack in a rock, he saw trows dancing in the moonlight. He wrote down the tune, and played it later on the fiddle. ☞ FIG 15 p. 185

'Garster's Dream' also has a named witness, a certain Garster, although he wasn't said to have seen any trows. The story is that he was returning from a wedding in Fetlar, stopped to rest on a trow's mound, and heard the tune in a dream. As is only appropriate, the categories blend and blur; a trowie tune can also be classed as music from a dream. It's also notable as being one of the first Shetland fiddle tunes to be notated, one of fourteen written down by a J. T. Hoseason in December 1862. ☞ FIG 16 p. 185

There are many more trowie tunes, and the tradition is by no means dead. Shetlanders are still collecting them, and now post them on the muses' latest arena, YouTube.

We've had examples from England, Wales, Ireland, and Scotland, and now we'll turn to the Isle of Man. The Manx fairies are called the *mooinjer veggey*, and are just as musical as the others. Two Manx fairy tunes are both called *'Bollan Bane'*, that is, mugwort, which is considered a protection against enchantment. In both, a fiddler heard fairies as he was returning home late at night. He had to backtrack a couple of times to learn the tune properly, and didn't get home until morning. His wife was furious, but was mollified when she heard the tune. These versions were collected by the Manx historian Arthur William Moore, who provided them with inappropriate piano accompaniments. ☞

FIG 17
*p. 186–188*

We leave the British Isles now, to consider an odd bit of music from Norway. I suppose we should consider it the music of the gnomes, or dwarves: the *Underjordiske* (underground people).

In 1740, the German composer Johann Mattheson published a pamphlet in Hamburg, called *Etwas Neues unter den Sonnen! Das unterirdische Klippen-Konzert in Norwegen* (Something new under the sun! The underground cliff concert in Norway).

It related a story from a certain Heinrich Meyer, leader of the town band in Christiana. He claimed that on Christmas Eve, 1695, he and three other musicians followed a local farmer to a mountain near Bergen. There they heard a concert that seemed to come from within the mountain, played on organ, voices, trumpets, trombones, violins, and other instruments. He added 'I annex here a melody which I myself have heard in the cliffs near Bergen', which I suppose means it wasn't the same one. At any rate, here it is. ☞

FIG 18
*p. 189*

The story is delightful; the tune sounds like a simple fiddle tune. I have to note that Mattheson may be an unreliable narrator. He wrote a number of theoretical works noted for their burlesque pomposity and mock erudition. His sense of humor is evident in his Sonata for Harpsichord in G, dedicated 'to whoever will play it best.' And, since we consider celestial music in the next chapter, I'll also note that he wrote a treatise on the scriptural evidence for music in heaven: *Behauptung der himmlischen Musik* (Assertion of Heavenly Music, 1747).

Whatever its provenance, the tune has entered folklore as a tune of the trolls. Here are two versions from later collections of Norwegian folk tunes. Each harmonizes it differently, but both keep it in A, which must be the favorite key of the trolls. ☞ FIG 19 *p. 190–191*

The *hulder* are another variety of Norse ultraterrestrial. Turning to Keightley again, we find: 'The Norwegians call the Elves Huldrafolk, and their music Huldrasalaat: it is in the minor key, and of a dull and mournful sound. The mountaineers sometimes play it, and pretend they have learned it by listening to the underground people among the hills and rocks.' Ludvig Mathias Lindeman also presents a *Hulder-Laatt*. He gives no details, but does provide a nice arrangement of the tune, which doesn't sound particularly dull or mournful to me. ☞ FIG 20 *p. 192–193*

For an example from Sweden, I turn to Elard Hugo Meyer, who in 1891 attributed this tune to the little people, adding 'In Sweden about a hundred years ago, the peasants danced in their graceful way to this.' ☞ FIG 21 *p. 194*

It's probably fruitless to speculate about the origins of these tunes, since no theory could be verified, but I will anyway. The brevity and simplicity of some reports lead me to suspect candor. My guess is that Morgan Gwillim would have invented something fancier if he were just spinning tales, and that he heard some natural sound, like water, or the birds that will warble for us in Chapter VI, and passed it through his internal piskie filter. Many witnesses meet their ultraterrestrials late at night or in a doze, when groggy brains brew illusions. Dreams can also be influenced by natural sounds, or can transform human music. Some tunes may have been composed in the usual way, and later attributed to fairies when passed to friends of friends. Then too, lies can't be ruled out. Life is mostly nasty, brutal, and proverbial, and lies are a cheap and soothing form of entertainment, the comfort food of social intercourse.

II

# On the Music of the Sky People

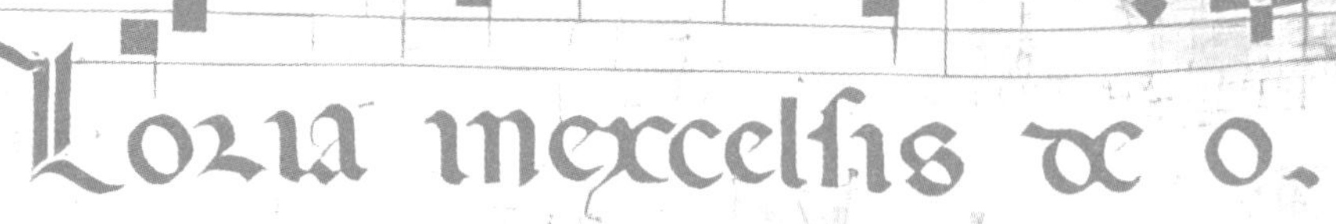

Musical nonhumans are not found exclusively on earth. Angels, those mysterious functionaries of the celestial hierarchy, have also sung to us. Although there are plenty of angels in Judaism, sometimes depicted as singing around the throne of God (in the Midrash, for example, in Genesis Rabbah 8), musical angels are more commonly Christian. Some standard Gregorian chants are even attributed to them.

The first reported Christian angel song was the one heard by the shepherds in Luke 2:13–14. Despite its familiarity, and its commemoration in carols, the story is missing from the other gospels, and the text says that the angels 'praised' or 'said', rather than 'sang'. Perhaps it's more appealing to audiate angels singing in chorus, rather than speaking in unison like the 'mic checks' at political demonstrations.

An early example is mentioned in *Musica Disciplina*, a treatise by the 9th century monk Aurelian of Rhéôme. With the introductory waffle 'If my memory of the past does not fail me', he tells the story of a monk from the monastery of St. Victor near the city of the Cenomani (that is, Le Mans), who kept an all-night vigil outside the basilica of the Archangel Michael on Mt. Gargano. He heard a choir of angels singing, and reported it to the clerics of Rome. The piece they sang, *Cives apostolorum et domestici*, was incorporated into the responsory sung at the Nativity of the Apostles. It's worth noting that the clerics changed one of the lines: *In omnem terram exivit sonus eorum* replaced something that must have been too angelic for their taste. It's also worth noting that the story doesn't specify if the angels sang the text now used in the liturgy, which is taken from Ephesians 2:19–20 and Psalm 18:5. ☞ FIG 1 *p. 196*

Another part of the liturgy, *Regina caeli laetare*, sung from Easter Sunday to Pentecost, is also traditionally ascribed to angels. Around 600, Pope Gregory I, the Gregory of Gregorian chant, heard angels singing the first three lines. He promptly added the fourth; again, angels needed human editing. ☞ *next page*

Other angelic choirs were not notated. One reportedly announced the death of the third or fourth century saint, Julian of Le Mans. Bede, in his *Ecclesiastical History of the English People*, notes that in 672, St. Chad's death was preceded by angelic singing. He specified that it came from the south-east, but, unfortunately, didn't provide the tune.

*Regina caeli laetare*

Nor did Felix, whose 8th century *Life of Saint Guthrac* claims angels marked the death of that saint as well.

Celestial choruses have not abated with the centuries, but the music is still seldom specified. D. Scott Rogo, in *NAD: A Study of Some Unusual 'Other World' Experiences*, collected 101 reports of music heard at near-death experiences, trances, séances, and deathbeds: most witnesses simply remembered the music as beautiful; four identified it as 'hymns', and one thought it might have been Wagner, but didn't say which piece.

We do, however, have the music for a few cases. One of the more curious is the angelic 'Audition' of Chrétien Urhan.

Urhan, born in Germany, was already a precocious violinist when he was sent to Paris at 14. He eventually became concertmaster at the Opera, and also took up the viola and viola d'amore. The viola d'amore solo in Meyerbeer's *Les Huguenots* was written for him, and he premiered Berlioz's *Harold in Italy*, for viola and orchestra. He also played the organ at Saint-Vincent de Paul, and became extremely devout, living ascetically, and giving most of his income to the poor. His friend Ernest Legouvé described him as a 14th century monk who had somehow ended up at the Opera. Wary of temptation from saucy soubrettes, Urhan kept his eyes fixed on his music, never looking at the stage.

His angelic encounter occurred in the Bois de Boulogne, on August 20, 1835. He was thinking of setting a poem called 'The Angel and the Child', by Jean Reboul. As Legouvé wrote, 'Suddenly, he hears a sound in the air that makes him tremble, he lifts his head; at the sound another follows; a melody begins; it seems to him that a voice is singing the words of the angel and the child to another melody than his.' He also heard an accompaniment, for 'Aeolian harp.' A voice then told him 'My friend, write what I sang to you.'

Urhan did as he was told, and added two piano pieces to make a sort of suite. He called it *Auditions*, and it was duly published and performed.

The music is certainly unusual. The poem, a sentimental verse about an angel and a dying child, is set as a simple chant of 84 measures. The accompaniment, which Urhan marks as 'Aeolian harp', consists of repeated A-flat chords, with an occasional added seventh; the first seven and last eight measures are unaccompanied. The austerity must have been effective, despite the bathetic lyrics. The two piano pieces are *Les Larmes* (Tears), two pages of arpeggios, and a longer piece called *Le Désir du ciel* (The Desire of Heaven), which is more conventionally bombastic. The performance was received well, although some thought Urhan should have let the angelic music stand alone. ☞ FIG 2 *p. 197–205*

As I've mentioned before, and may have to again, some reports may be due to mental illness. Hearing voices, even angelic ones, is not a good sign. That seems to have been true for Urhan, who became increasingly depressive, and starved himself to death in 1845.

It was also the case with Robert Schumann, who ended his life in a mental hospital in Endenich. Before that, he was plagued with hallucinations, both of angels and devils. On the night of February 17, 1854, 'angelic voices' dictated a theme to him; it was one he had already written, but he didn't recognize it at the time. It inspired his last work, the *Ghost Variations*, whose composition was interrupted by a suicide attempt. ☞ FIG 3 *p. 206*

Aliens are a recent addition to the folkloric pantheon, although many of their characteristics are similar to earlier beings. As already mentioned, they have much in common with fairies. They've also been conflated with angels, in such books as *UFO and the Bible* (Morris K. Jessup, 1956), *Les extraterrestres* (Paul Misraki, 1962), *Flying Saucers in the Bible* (Virginia Brasington, 1963), and the memorable *God Drives a Flying Saucer* (Robert Dione, 1969); Ezekiel's Wheel and the Star of Bethlehem are favorite topics in the genre. The connection was also made explicit in the Raëlian books of Claude Vorilhon, like *Le Livre qui dit la verité* (1974); in the earlier editions, his naive drawings of the Elohim look like the little grays of UFO lore with rabbinical beards.

Those who claim interaction with aliens fall roughly into two camps: abductees, who suffer unpleasant medical procedures from bug-eyed humanoids, and contactees, who receive spiritual teaching from charismatic space brothers. The former, not surprisingly, seldom hear music, but the latter often do.

For some reason, musical aliens tend to come from Venus. An early example comes from Guy Ballard, alias Godfré Ray King, who led the I AM Movement with his wife Edna, alias Lotus Ray King, and their son Donald. His 1934 book *Unveiled Mysteries* describes a visit to a Venusian retreat under the Grand Teton, in Wyoming. In another conflation of mythologies, his guide is none other than a Venusian version of the Count of Saint Germain, whose own terrestrial music will be considered in Chapter V. The obliging count introduces Ballard to some of his musical instruments:

> This seems to be a pipeless organ but the pipes, which are much smaller than ordinary, are placed within the case. The tone of the whole instrument is superior to anything the earth has ever known before in music. These organs will come into use in the outer world as the incoming Golden Age moves forward.

> Next we examined four magnificent harps, slightly larger than those in ordinary use in the musical world today. Saint Germain seated himself at one of these and played several chords to give me some idea of their tone. It was the most wonderful music, I have ever heard.

Later in the book, Ballard himself participates in a concert:

> Saint Germain played the first number on the great organ, a composition he called 'Hearts of the Future.' It seemed to me the most delicate, colorful, yet powerful music that ever came from an organ on earth. While he played, the most beautiful colors, gorgeous past description, poured through the atmosphere of the enormous room.
>
> A group played the next number. The Master Saint Germain at the organ, three of the Lady Masters from Venus, and Lotus played four harps, two of the Brothers from Venus, our son, and I played four violins... The volume and power swelled into such magnitude, it seemed as though the beauty and glory of that joy must send forth enough God-Consciousness to lift all mankind, yes, even the earth itself, into Everlasting Perfection.

In the 1935 sequel, *The Magic Presence*, Godfré and his mining partner Daniel Rayborn visit several Retreats, Temples, and Chambers with Saint Germain and other Ascended Masters of the Great White Brotherhood. They attend several concerts, and hear a number of songs, usually credited to Daniel's wife Nada and their children, Rex and Nada: 'The Arabic Love-Song', 'Love's Light Eternal', 'Light of Life We Look to Thee', 'Master Jesus We Follow Thee,' 'In the Light I Rest Secure', 'I Come on the Wings of Light', 'I Love You', 'In the Name of Christ We Reign', and 'Holy Night'. The only one of these I could find any other trace of is 'I Come on the Wings of Light', which was included in a 1938 songbook, where it was attributed to Catherine Rogers.

Music was an important part of the I AM organization, since Edna Ballard played the harp, and made several recordings with the group's organist, Frederick Landwehr. She also occasionally channeled the Goddess of Music, who told her audience that there were 'Eternal Invincible Legions of Angels of Music', and warned them, 'Do not try to create melodies down here according to man-made rules of harmony; because that would not even resemble the Music of the Spheres.' And she informed them, 'Your Beloved Saint Germain is no small musician!'

*Vivenus with guitar*

Despite these revelations, none of the musical output of I AM seems to have been channeled. Songs were credited to the Ballards and Landwehr, or written to existing tunes; I note with satisfaction that the song 'Beloved Leto' used Charles Fort's favorite tune, 'Juanita'. In earlier years, the pianist Virginia LaFerrera and the singer Catherine Rogers also wrote and recorded many songs. They eventually left the organization, and testified against Edna and Donald when the latter two were tried for mail fraud in 1940. And the question of musical channeling was addressed in their testimony: LaFerrera said that she wrote the song 'Call to Light', but that George Ballard told his flock that she received it from the Goddess of Light, whom, she insisted, she had never met. In later songbooks and catalogues, works by LaFerrera and Rogers were either expunged or reattributed: in the 2014 edition of the *'I AM' Songbook*, 'Call to Light' is credited to Godfré Ray King.

A couple of decades later, another musical Venusian enlivened the UFO community. Vivenus claimed to be a Venusian who had taken over a suicidal woman in 1960. She traveled throughout the US, distributing her 12-page journal *Feelings... The Venusian Way*, and appearing at UFO conventions. I have been unable to learn her real name, or what eventually happened to her. She claimed that the woman she took over had been a singer, and, not surprisingly, she too wrote songs. In 1980, she recorded

'It's Not Odd to Vote for God', a message she also promoted with brochures, buttons, and matchbooks, all of which seem to have vanished into the ether. The song too is apparently lost, but an article in the *Oakland Tribune* (July 13, 1980) describes it as a 'mournful tune', and quotes some lyrics: 'It's God for President! So go become a resident! Write him in and we can win! And come election day we'll say, "Oh, it's not odd to vote for God"'.

One of the iconic contactees of the 1950s, Howard Menger, also claimed contact with Venus, but credited his piano playing to Saturn. He claimed he had visited a cabin in the woods in the fall of 1956, where he met two Venusians, who introduced him to a Saturnian they called 'our own private Liberace.' The Saturnian encouraged Menger to play his unusual keyboard:

> I looked down at the keyboard. It was entirely different from a conventional piano keyboard. This one was much longer and contained many more keys, which were narrower and had strange symbols on them which I did not understand. The entire instrument was much lower and closer to the floor.
>
> I almost automatically reached down to touch the keys, suddenly knowing which to strike to correspond with the sounds of the melody running through my mind. Although I had never been able to play before, it all seemed natural and delightfully simple.

The Saturnian told him, 'You're going to play this melody on the piano, Howard, and thousands of people of Earth will hear it.'

Menger later did perform the tune around the country, and recorded it on an LP called *Authentic Music From Another Planet*, released in 1957 by Slate Enterprises. The first side contains Menger's narration, and two instrumentals, 'Marla' and 'Theme from the Song from Saturn', which sound like Italianate pop tunes played on accordion or Hammond organ. The second side is devoted to Menger's 'Song from Saturn', tranquil piano noodling in D-flat, with an arpeggiated bass. Menger said that he never played it the same way twice. I suppose it was an improvisation on an original melody, perhaps in a trance state, perhaps not.

Another musical contactee, Eugenio Siragusa, may be less familiar to anglophones. He was born in Catania, in Sicily, and started receiving telepathic messages from an alien named Bahrat in 1952. They came in three ways: by interpenetration (*conpenetrazione*), by Telex-Sens (which he defined as a system of extrasensory perception), and by Solex-Mal (the astral language). Like Menger, he also met aliens in the flesh: the space brothers Ithacar and Asthar, from Mars and Metaria, respectively, introduced themselves on Mt. Etna in 1962. Like Ballard, he also met the Count of Saint Germain, who gave him an autographed card from Voltaire in Paris in 1972.

He also channeled alien music, usually on the organ. In 1976, he released a 45 in Barcelona: the A side, *'Musica Terapeutica Astrale'*, consists of pentatonic tunes over a drone and electronic percussion; the B side, *'Paso Glorioso de Cristo'* (Glorious Passage of Christ) removes the percussion and adds a few tone clusters. Both, he claimed, were channeled from an alien being known as Adoniesis, whose eerie photo adorns the cover. An EP was also released in Italy, but I can't determine the year: the A side, *'Una Lacrima e un Sorriso'* (A Tear and a Smile) features Siragusa reading Kahlil Gibran to organ accompaniment; the B side, *'In Cammino Verso il Signore Armonia di Shangra-Lah'* (On the Way to Lord Harmony of Shangri-La) is another instrumental for organ and electronic percussion. Like Menger, he favored the black keys.

Many professional musicians have claimed UFO sightings, but without channeling. The roster includes David Bowie, John Lennon, Olivia Newton-John, Keith Richards, Robbie Williams, Elvis Presley, Kesha, Russell Crowe, and a host of others. The remarkable Sun Ra claimed to be from Saturn, which I suppose classes him with Vivenus, but his large and elaborate body of work, combined with his enigmatic persona, make it satisfyingly impossible to specify if or how he was channeling.

Like Edna Ballard, Claude Vorilhon, founder of the Raëlians, was a musician before his professed contacts. As Claude Celler, he recorded seven pop tunes in the Jacques Brel vein between 1966 and 1971, and had a hit with *'Le Miel et la canelle'* (Honey and Cinnamon). According to his website, he's gone on to write some 200 songs, and still records. I assume even such Raëlian numbers as the rousing singalong *'C'est une secte'* (It's a cult) were composed by the usual terrestrial methods.

Philip Rodgers produced a different kind of celestial music. He lived in Grindleford, near Sheffield, in England. He had poor vision, and eventually went blind; he played the recorder, and wrote several compositions and method books for it. When flying saucers became popular in the '50s, Rodgers was as interested as everyone else. He couldn't watch the sky, so he set up a tape recorder to catch transmissions from outer space. He received voices, as well as sounds like beeps and clicking. But he did also tape some music, which he described as 'a fantastic series of musical signals, mostly of instruments unknown on earth.' Among these were a 'strange harplike instrument, improvising on strings, tuned to a somewhat modernistic chord' and 'an unidentified trumpetlike instrument, playing a modernistic musical phrase, quite unlike any fanfare I have heard on earth.'

Only one of his tapes has survived, which picked up voices but no music. However, he did transcribe one of the pieces he heard.

An internet search turned up an article in the November 30, 1967 *Wellington (Texas) Leader*, reporting that at a meeting of the Wellington Music Club, 15-year-old Sidney Duncan performed Philip Rodgers's 'Music from Outer Space in G Minor' on the clarinet. I suspect it was the same piece.

Other researchers went on to experiment with Electronic Voice Phenomena — tuning radios to blank areas on the radio frequency spectrum to receive mysterious transient sounds — but they usually captured fleeting spoken phrases, which their critics dismissed as meaningful only with a heaping spoonful of pareidolia. The dogged experimenter Marcello Bacci caught some brief choral fragments, but the EVP praxis seldom produces music, and radio broadcasts may well be to blame.

But we do have Philip Rodgers's curious little tune. I suspect there was more to it than this page, but if so, it may be lost in the mists of British ufology. ☞ FIG 4 p. 207

Rodgers was not the only enthusiast tuning in extraterrestrial signals. In 1952, the ufologist and archaeologist George Hunt Williamson (also known as Michel d'Obrenovic and Brother Philip) was trying to contact aliens. Working with a ham radio operator, Lyman H. Streeter, he claimed to have communicated with a number of entities on different planets. He also experimented with automatic writing, often with his wife Betty and their friends Alfred and Betty Bailey. On August 30, 1952, a message from Uffa of Uranus told them about a language called Solex Mal, 'the Mother or Solar or Mother Tongue', spoken by 'all men of other worlds.' This was, as you may recall, the same language Siragusa said his aliens used.

Neither the radio nor the writing generated any music, although Zo from Neptune did reveal that the word for 'musical instruments' is 'tonas.' A decade later, however, songs in Solex Mal were channeled by a nearly forgotten colleague of Philip Rodgers, Bernard Byron. I say 'nearly', because he made a memorable appearance on the BBC show *One Pair of Eyes: Can You Speak Venusian?* on November 8, 1969, speaking fluent Venusian and Plutonian for Sir Patrick Moore.

A few years before that, he had been active in the STAR Fellowship, founded by Rodgers and Tony Wedd in 1961. The Fellowship's principal objective was distributing badges bearing a white star on a blue field, as a sign of welcome to the aliens. One of its unrealized projects was to produce recordings of Byron channeling songs in what he called 'Solexmar.' He said they often came to him while he was singing in the bath. Only two songs seem to have survived. The music to one of them, beginning *'Laya seminaya limi issi laya nasa laya'*, has been lost, but the other, 'Anya Ray', was recorded and transcribed, some time in December 1962. I don't know if the recording is still extant, but the transcription follows.

The lyrics begin *'Muz Anya Ray uzzo ayen ovanyi ooya gaba yesto vay'*, which he translated as 'Merrily we are traveling through Space and Heavens.' And the music, a jaunty tune in C major, could not be more fitting. ☞ FIG 5 *p. 208*

Pabst Kaiser Kaiserin Cardinal König

Herzog Abt Ritter Carthäuser Burgermeister Do

Doctor Wucherer Kapellan Amtmann

# III

# On the Music of the Dear Departed

Once again, our categories are fluid, for the sky people are inevitably conflated with the dead. According to some traditions, angels are just dead humans (or at least virtuous ones), who have floated upwards to learn the *kinnor*. But in other traditions, the dead become earthbound spirits, and can either play music or channel it through mediums. In some of the reports to follow, the music comes through a medium, but it's unclear whether the spirit is a former human or a being from some ethereal realm.

For many centuries, the standard method of calling the dead was necromancy. Curiously, though, I can find no music in the annals of that unsavory art. Sorcerers usually hoped to contact kings and generals, to get some saleable bit of prophecy. Perhaps the ceremonies were too difficult and grisly for just a tune.

But we do have an early musical ghost in the Drummer of Tedworth. In 1681, in the Wiltshire, England town of Tedworth (now Tidworth), a certain John Mompesson prosecuted a wandering drummer named William Drury, for carrying a forged pass and collecting money under false pretenses. Drury was jailed, and Mompesson got the drum. Mompesson was then plagued by nocturnal drumming, as well as lights, thrown objects, moving furniture, knocks and raps, and sulfurous odors. This sounds like a classic poltergeist, but Mompesson blamed witchcraft, and accused Drury of summoning a spirit. It's also been suggested that Gypsies, or Mompesson's own children, were to blame. Other suggestions followed: In Joseph Addison's 1716 play *The Drummer*, the phantom drummer was a hoax, and Edith Sitwell made it a demon in her 1930 poem 'The Drum'.

Mompesson didn't say whether he thought the spirit was human, but he did think its music was. In a letter to William Creed (December 6, 1662), he noted that 'the Drum beat the same point of Warre that is usually beaten when guards breake up', as well as 'the Tattoo and severall other points of Warre.' I assume these were standard military drum beats. It also played 'the tune called "Roundheads and Cuckolds goe digge, goe digge"', sometimes for hours on end. Phantom drummers have annoyed people in many places (Cortachy Castle in Kirriemuir, Angus, and Herstmonceux Castle, in Hailsham, East Sussex, to name but a couple), but the music is rarely specified. Unfortunately, nobody has identified 'Roundheads and Cuckolds'. A tune can't be played on an unpitched instrument, so it must have had a distinctive rhythm. Whatever it was, Mompesson apparently recognized it.

In the 1830s, necromancy, in the form of music channeled from the dead, enjoyed an odd and passionate flowering in the US. The United Society of Believers in Christ's Second Appearance, known informally as the Shakers, had been founded in England in 1747; one of the leaders, Ann Lee, established a church in New York in 1747, and by 1807 Shaker communities had spread westward into Ohio and Kentucky. They became known for their industry, herbalism, lively ceremonies, and celibacy.

On August 16, 1837, in Watervliet, New York, a 14-year-old Shaker, Anna Maria Goff, fell into a trance, and sang a song beginning 'Where the pretty angels dwell, heaven'. The music, unfortunately, was not notated. But she started a rage for channeled music that lasted for decades in the Shaker church. The songs were scrupulously documented, often with music, but seldom published in the Shaker hymnals.

I filed the Shaker 'vision songs' in this chapter, since they were often attributed to the spirits of the dead, including Ann Lee, other early leaders of the church, and historical figures like George Washington and William Penn. But they defy strict classification, being also credited to angels, the Heavenly Father, Holy Mother Wisdom (Shakers recognized two Gods, male and female), Jesus, and various saints. Many songs were also channeled in gibberish identified as Chinese, Hottentot, Persian, Turkish, and other tongues, as well as in Black and Native American dialects that make for uncomfortable reading today. It was never clear if these various nationalities were also among the dead.

Here's an example of a song channeled from Ann Lee, 'Mother Ann's Song', received by 'O. W.' on September 22, 1844. ☞ FIG 1 *p. 210*

Even extraterrestrials were sometimes credited, as in this song from c. 1838, 'learned in vision by one of the sisters at Groveland while visiting the moon'. ☞ FIG 2 *p. 210*

Shaker channeling waned in the late 1860s, and by 1870 what was later called the 'Era of Manifestations' had run its course.

But another strain of necromancy had emerged in New York in 1848, when the Fox sisters, Margaretta and Catherine, started producing eerie raps and knocks in Hydesville. This domestic pastime grew into public demonstrations, and then into the Spiritualist movement.

One of the earliest pieces of Spiritualist music was written by their older sister Leah, who was less active as a medium, but quickly became their manager. In 1851, the Boston firm G. P. Reed published 'The Haunted Ground', 'as sung by the Fox family', with lyrics by the popular poet Felicia Hemans and 'Music dictated to Mrs. Fish [Leah] through the medium of the Rappings, while sitting at the piano.' A spirit, the Foxes explained, could not only rap for 'yes' and 'no', but give longer messages by 'calling for the alphabet': it rapped five times, and then once for each letter it wanted as the alphabet was recited. Here's Leah's explanation:

> The following is a beautiful and curious experience which came one evening at Rochester, in the early days of our mediumship: Maggie and I were sitting alone in my cozy little parlor in Troup Street, enjoying ourselves by a warm fire while the pouring rain and howling winds outside assured us that we should not be interrupted by callers. I was reading *Memoirs of the Wesley Family*, when the alphabet was called for by the usual signal. I repeated the letters as they came through the alphabet, and wrote them as designated successively by the Spirit, viz.:
>
> 'GAGCBAGAGEFEFAGFEFGFEDAGGCEDGGCBAGCCDBC.'
>
> These letters could not, of course, be construed into words, and I cast them aside saying, 'This must be the Spirit of Johnny Story', a simple boy whom we had known when living, who could never be taught to read. The alphabet was again called for and the message given by the Spirit was, 'Apply the letters to your piano.'
>
> On doing so I recognized in them, to my surprise and delight, a sweet and tender melody. I was then told to set the music to 'Haunted Ground' in Mrs. Hemans's Poems, but with the variation of changing 'Haunted' to 'Hallowed' in the last verse.

'The Haunted Ground'

Margaretta later confessed that her entire mediumistic career had been a fraud, and publicly demonstrated how she made loud noises by snapping the tendons in her feet. With that in mind, we should probably be suspicious of this little song, and assume either that the story is fake, or that Margaretta hoaxed her sister. But here it is, the first alleged channeled music of the Spiritualist movement, and the only one I know supposedly written by those famous Fox knocks.

The 1851 edition credits Jesse Hutchinson, a composer and singer who led the popular and progressive Hutchinson Singers; he must have written the piano part. *The Missing Link* gives two simpler arrangements, one for piano and one for organ, by the songwriter J. Jay Watson. ☞ FIG 3 *p. 210*

The distinction between a real and fraudulent séance was not only vague, but deliberately ambiguous. It was, in fact, central to the praxis, as both believers and scoffers flocked to mediums hoping either to validate or debunk them. For hoaxers, music could not only misdirect attention, but cover the sounds of confederates. Trick séance instruments were available from magic suppliers. For example, *Gambols with the Ghosts*, a 1901 catalog from Sylvestre, offered a self-playing guitar: 'Indispensable for mediums. Finely finished Guitar. In dark séances they play without medium's hands touching them. Price $25.00.' Sylvestre didn't say how it worked, but the psychic investigator Hereward Carrington explained further in his book *The Physical Phenomena of Spiritualism*: 'the secret being that it contained a music-box, which, when wound up and set going, would play a tune without necessitating any fingering of the strings by the medium.' A music box doesn't sound much like a guitar, so I can only wonder how effective it was. Fabric and other props could also be stashed in it, which must have been handy. Unfortunately, no specimens seem to have survived.

*Davenport Brothers with musical instruments*

There are many reports of music from mediums, but most of it was either unspecified, or an already familiar tune. The Fox sisters' channeling method was apparently unique.

Two of the busiest early practitioners, William and Ira Davenport, often played music in their demonstrations. In one of their famous set pieces, they were tied securely inside a large crate, with a number of instruments between them. When the crate was closed, the instruments played; when it was opened, the brothers were still bound. Houdini claimed the brothers told him the knots they used, but I can find no record of what they played.

If reports are to be believed (note the if), they also produced music from unseen musicians. Paschal Beverly Randolph, whom we'll meet again in Chapter V, wrote a biography of the Davenports; in it, he described 'nightly concerts of vocal music by amateur singers, accompanied by *post mortem* instrumentation on horns, trumpets, banjos, violins, guitars, bells, and tambourines', but, again, didn't mention what that interesting orchestra played. He also reported unfamiliar whistling:

> Occasionally these *port mortem soirées* were varied by whistling concerts; and no wind instruments could equal their strangely wild and mournful melody. The only unsatisfactory circumstance about the affair was that nobody could remember the music, and no provision was made for writing it down, as ought to have been done.

I can only nod numbly; if there was indeed wild whistling, I'm sorry we have no score.

In the 1850s, two Ohio farmers, Jonathan Koons and John Tippie, in Millfield Township, Athens County, also caused a stir for the music in their 'spirit rooms'. Another prominent Spiritualist, Emma Hardinge Britten (whom we'll get to in a moment), described them in some detail in her 1870 book *Modern American Spiritualism.*

Koons and Tippie lived a few miles apart, and put on similar shows. Each had a small cabin (Koons's was 12 by 15 feet) that housed a curious device:

> In each room was a 'spirit machine,' which consisted of a somewhat complex arrangement of zinc and copper, serving the purpose, as the spirits alleged, of collecting and focalizing the magnetic aura used in the manifestations. This novel battery was placed upon a long wooden table, by the side of several instruments, provided according to direction, and consisting of a harp, guitar, violin, accordion, tambourine, triangle, several bells, a tin trumpet, and a variety of toys.

The trumpet, it should be noted, was a 'spirit trumpet', a megaphone used by mediums. 'Two drums of different sizes were slung up on a high frame, and a round-table was so placed as to come in contact with the square wooden one supporting the instruments.'

A drawing of the machine was published in the *Cleveland Plain Dealer* (November 4, 1854), and reprinted in *Scientific American* (Feb. 3, 1855). It had a framework about four feet high, adorned with plates, wires, and glass knobs, and must have been used somehow to play the two drums. The *Scientific American* was unhappy with it: 'It is a wonder that any

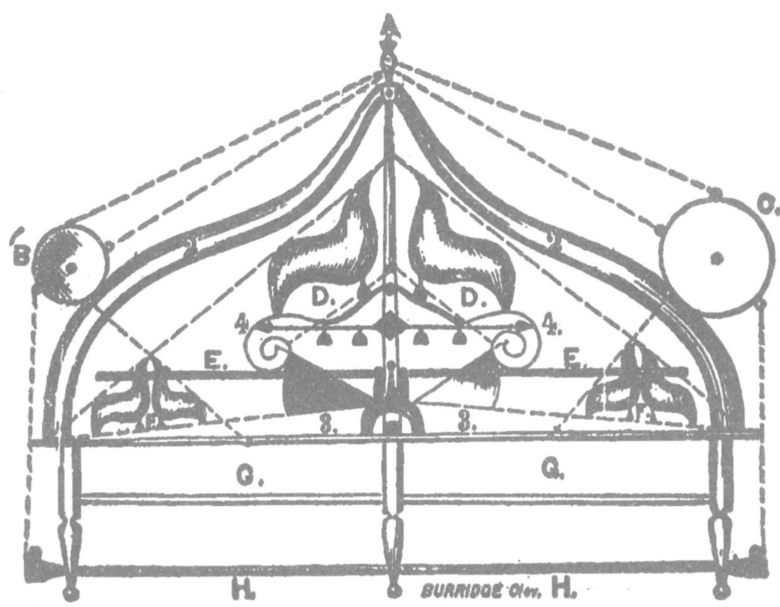


*The Koons Spirit Machine*

grown-up men and women in our country, where we boast so much intelligence, can suffer themselves to be deluded with such nonsense.'

As was customary, the room was darkened, and the spirits assembled, holding conversations, orating through the trumpet, and materializing phosphorescent hands to write messages. The music, however, was the main attraction. Koons usually started by playing the violin himself, and 'the various instruments made to join in occasionally, playing solo and chorus alternately, produced a most pleasing effect.' The instruments often flew around the cabin, again held by those luminous hands.

Tippie's evenings were much the same, except that he didn't play the violin. 'At Tippie's room, however, the music is all produced by spirits, and is more varied and interesting than at Koons's.'

Koons had eight children, and Tippie ten, which to believers meant more spiritual power and to scoffers more confederates. The music was often praised, but, as usual, nobody thought to identify or notate it. And again, it was unclear what the spirits were supposed to be. A personality called 'King', who appeared to other contemporary mediums, sometimes showed up, but his origin was left unexplained. As was that of the musicians, who sound more like elementals than dead relatives. By 1859, both Koons and Tippie had moved, and given up their performances.

We know more about the music of Daniel Dunglas Home, who began his career in 1851, and attracted both believers and debunkers until his death in 1886. He was most famous for his levitations, but also often worked with an accordion. Sometimes he played it while it was in a cage, and sometimes it too levitated. His only selections were 'The Last Rose of Summer' and 'Home Sweet Home'; since both have only an octave range, one explanation is that he hid a harmonica under his dashing mustache. Whatever his technique, the music itself was strictly terrestrial.

Emma Hardinge Britten, whom we mentioned earlier, produced some channeled music, but apparently not by the Fox Sisters' elegant method. She was not only a medium and an advocate for Spiritualism, but a professional musician, having worked as singer, pianist, music teacher, and choral director. In fact, she began as a singer, appearing in opera in London, Paris, and New York in the 1840s and 1850s. In 1856, her setting of Tennyson's 'Footsteps of Angels' was published by Horace Watson in New York, but I've been unable to trace a copy. In 1857, she started giving trance lectures, and, naturally, soon started combining her two avocations.

On April 24, 1857, her cantata 'The Song of the Stars' was performed at Academy Hall in Manhattan. She had written both words and music, but hinted they were channeled, or at least partly beyond her control:

> Both were written or composed by a power that worked through my organization, such as it is or was, according to the limitations of the instrument that organization afforded... As to the music, it was composed and set down in far too much haste to satisfy my own instructed taste.

The evening also included her song 'Passed Away', and another choral piece, 'Forest Days'. The *New York Herald* was suspicious of the Spiritualism, but liked the music: 'whoever the Spirits that controlled Emma Hardinge might be, they could at least make good music.'

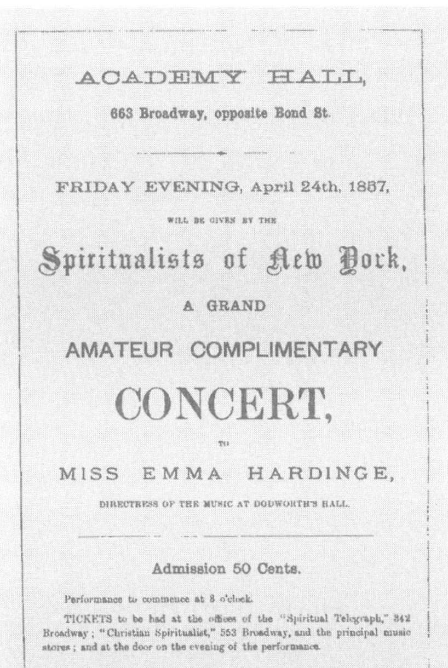

ACADEMY HALL,

663 Broadway, opposite Bond St.

FRIDAY EVENING, April 24th, 1857,

WILL BE GIVEN BY THE

Spiritualists of New York,

A GRAND

AMATEUR COMPLIMENTARY

CONCERT,

TO

MISS EMMA HARDINGE,

DIRECTRESS OF THE MUSIC AT DODWORTH'S HALL.

Admission 50 Cents.

Performance to commence at 8 o'clock.

TICKETS to be had at the offices of the "Spiritual Telegraph," 342 Broadway; "Christian Spiritualist," 553 Broadway, and the principal music stores; and at the door on the evening of the performance.

Mann, Stearns & Beale, Stationers, 141 Fulton St., N.Y.

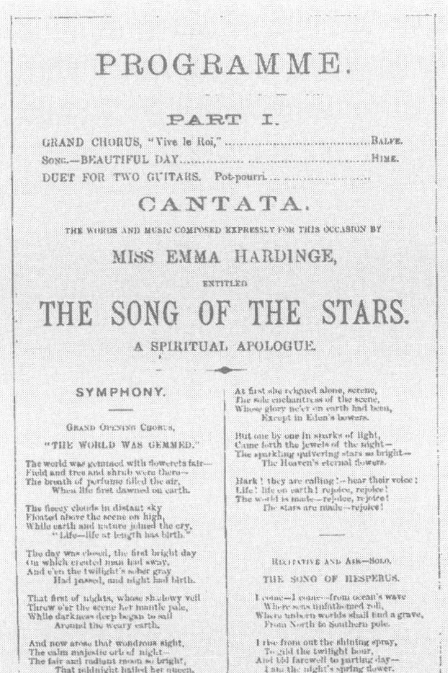

PROGRAMME.

PART I.

GRAND CHORUS, "Vive le Roi," ........................................ BALFE.
SONG.—BEAUTIFUL DAY.................................................. HIME.
DUET FOR TWO GUITARS. Pot-pourri..........................

CANTATA.

THE WORDS AND MUSIC COMPOSED EXPRESSLY FOR THIS OCCASION BY

MISS EMMA HARDINGE,

ENTITLED

THE SONG OF THE STARS.

A SPIRITUAL APOLOGUE.

SYMPHONY.

GRAND OPENING CHORUS,

"THE WORLD WAS GEMMED."

The world was gemmed with flowerets fair—
Field and tree and shrub were there—
The breath of perfume filled the air,
When life first dawned on earth.

The fleecy clouds in distant sky
Floated above the scene on high,
While earth and nature joined the cry,
"Life—life at length has birth."

The day was closed, the first bright day
On which created man had sway,
And e'en the twilight's sober gray
Had passed, and night had birth.

That first of nights, whose shadowy veil
Threw o'er the scene her mantle pale,
While darkness deep began to sail
Around the weary earth.

And now arose that wondrous sight,
The calm majestic orb of night—
The fair and radiant moon so bright,
That midnight hailed her queen.

At first she reigned alone, serene,
The sole enchantress of the scene,
Whose glory ne'er on earth had been,
Except in Eden's bowers.

But one by one in sparks of light,
Came forth the jewels of the night—
The sparkling quivering stars so bright—
The Heaven's eternal flowers.

Hark! they are calling!—hear their voice;
Life! life on earth! rejoice, rejoice!
The world is made—rejoice, rejoice!
The stars are made—rejoice!

RECITATIVE AND AIR—SOLO.

THE SONG OF HESPERUS.

I come—I come—from ocean's wave
Where seas unfathomed roll,
Where unborn worlds shall find a grave,
From North to Southern pole.

I rise from out the shining spray,
To gild the twilight hour,
And bid farewell to parting day—
I am the night's spring flower.

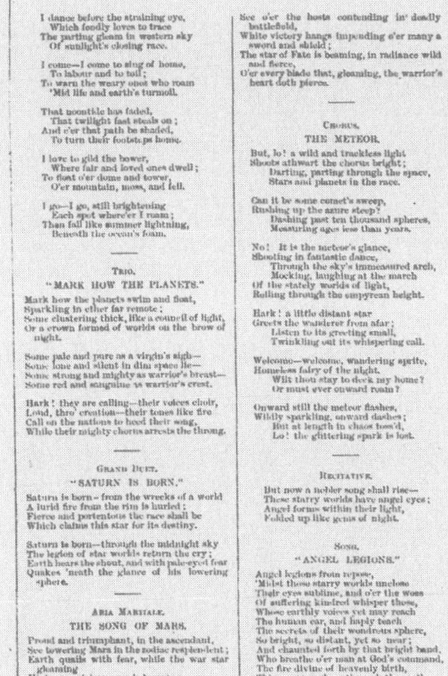

I dance before the straining eye,
Which fondly loves to trace
The parting gleam in western sky
Of sunlight's closing race.

I come—I come to sing of home,
To labour and to toil;
To warn the weary ones who roam
'Mid life and earth's turmoil.

That noontide has faded,
That twilight fast steals on;
And o'er that path be shaded,
To turn their footsteps home.

I love to gild the bower,
Where fair and loved ones dwell;
To float o'er dome and tower,
O'er mountain, moss, and fell.

I go—I go, still brightening
Each spot where'er I roam;
Then fall like summer lightning,
Beneath the ocean's foam.

TRIO.

"MARK HOW THE PLANETS."

Mark how the planets swim and float,
Sparkling in ether far remote;
Some clustering thick, like a council of light,
Or a crown formed of worlds on the brow of night.

Some pale and pure as a virgin's sigh—
Some lone and silent in dim space lie—
Some strong and mighty as warrior's breast—
Some red and sanguine as warrior's crest.

Hark! they are calling—their voices choir,
Loud, thro' creation—their tones like fire
Call on the nations to heed their song,
While their mighty chorus arrests the throng.

GRAND DUET.

"SATURN IS BORN."

Saturn is born—from the wrecks of a world
A lurid fire from the rim is hurled;
Fierce and portentous the race shall be
Which claims this star for its destiny.

Saturn is born—through the midnight sky
The legion of star worlds return the cry;
Earth hears the shout, and with pale-eyed fear
Quakes 'neath the glance of his lowering sphere.

ARIA MARTIALE.

THE SONG OF MARS.

Proud and triumphant, in the ascendant,
See towering Mars in the zodiac resplendent;
Earth quails with fear, while the war star gleaming
High over victory ever is beaming.

See o'er the hosts contending in deadly battlefield,
White victory hangs impending o'er many a sword and shield;
The star of Fate is beaming, in radiance wild and fierce,
O'er every blade that, gleaming, the warrior's heart doth pierce.

CHORUS.

THE METEOR.

But, lo! a wild and trackless light
Shoots athwart the chorus bright;
Darting, parting through the space,
Stars and planets in the race.

Can it be some comet's sweep,
Rushing up the azure steep?
Dashing past ten thousand spheres,
Measuring ages less than years.

No! It is the meteor's glance,
Shooting in fantastic dance,
Through the sky's immeasured arch,
Mocking, laughing at the march
Of the stately worlds of light,
Rolling through the empyrean height.

Hark! a little distant star
Greets the wanderer from afar;
Listen to its greeting small,
Twinkling out its whispering call.

Welcome—welcome, wandering sprite,
Homeless fairy of the night.
Wilt thou stay to deck my home?
Or must ever onward roam?

Onward still the meteor flashes,
Wildly sparkling, onward dashes;
But at length in chaos toss'd,
Lo! the glittering spark is lost.

RECITATIVE.

But now a nobler song shall rise—
These starry worlds have angel eyes;
Angel forms within their light,
Folded up like gems of night.

SONG.

"ANGEL LEGIONS."

Angel legions from repose,
'Midst those starry worlds unclose
Their eyes sublime, and o'er the woes
Of suffering kindred whisper those,
Whose earthly voices yet may reach
The human ear, and haply teach
The secrets of their wondrous sphere,
So bright, so distant, yet so near;
And chaunted forth by that bright band,
Who breathe o'er man at God's command,
The fire divine of heavenly birth,
This song re-echoes through the earth.

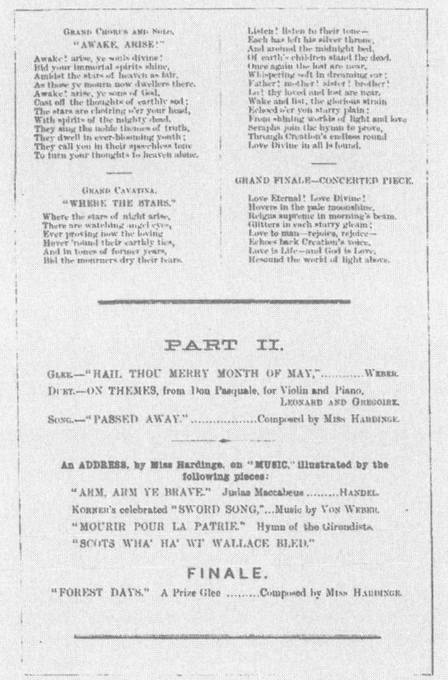

GRAND CHORUS AND SOLO.

"AWAKE, ARISE!"

Awake! arise, ye souls divine!
Bid your immortal spirits shine,
Amidst the stars of heaven as fair,
As those ye mourn now dwellers there.
Awake! arise, ye sons of God,
Cast off the thoughts of earthly sod;
The stars are choiring o'er your head,
With spirits of the mighty dead.
They sing the noble themes of truth,
They dwell in ever-blooming youth;
They call you in their speechless tone
To turn your thoughts to heaven alone.

GRAND CAVATINA.

"WHERE THE STARS."

Where the stars of night arise,
There are watching angel eyes,
Ever proving now the loving
Hover 'round their earthly ties,
And in tones of former years,
Bid the mourners dry their tears.

Listen! listen to their tone—
Each has left his silver throne,
And around the midnight bed,
Of earth's children stand the dead.
Once again the lost are near,
Whispering soft in dreaming ear;
Father! mother! sister! brother!
Lo! thy loved and lost are near.
Wake and list, the glorious strain
Echoed o'er yon starry plain;
From shining worlds of light and love
Seraphs join the hymn to prove,
Through Creation's endless round
Love Divine in all is found.

GRAND FINALE—CONCERTED PIECE.

Love Eternal! Love Divine!
Hovers in the pale moonshine,
Reigns supreme in morning's beam,
Glitters in each starry gleam;
Love to man—rejoice, rejoice—
Echoes back Creation's voice,
Love is Life—and God is Love,
Resound the world of light above.

PART II.

GLEE.—"HAIL THOU MERRY MONTH OF MAY,"............ WEBER.
DUET.—ON THEMES, from Don Pasquale, for Violin and Piano, LEONARD AND GREGOIRE.
SONG.—"PASSED AWAY."..................Composed by MISS HARDINGE.

An ADDRESS, by Miss Hardinge, on "MUSIC," illustrated by the following pieces:

"ARM, ARM YE BRAVE." Judas Maccabeus.........HANDEL.
KORNER'S celebrated "SWORD SONG,"...Music by VON WEBER.
"MOURIR POUR LA PATRIE." Hymn of the Girondists.
"SCOTS WHA' HA' WI' WALLACE BLED."

FINALE.

"FOREST DAYS." A Prize Glee .........Composed by MISS HARDINGE.

*Program and libretto to 'The Song of the Stars'*

We're again frustrated, since all of her music seems to be lost. We can only read the program and libretto.

I can note another mediumistic tune from around that time, though. It's the 'Dirge of Hardworking Prime Numbers', transmitted to Gustav Brabbée by 'Bandmaster No. 59' at a séance in the home of Johann Heinrich Stratil in Austria, on January 10, 1858. Brabbée was a Freemason, best known for publishing his grandfather's masonic and alchemical papers; Stratil was an official who led some of the first Spiritualist circles in Austria; Bandmaster No. 59 remains elusive. ☞ FIG 4 p. 212

Groups of fellow believers like to sing together. My shelves are stocked with songbooks from religious sects, lodges, fraternal organizations, temperance unions, Esperantists, and many other organizations. Spiritualists also liked to sing, and published hymnals similar to more conventional Protestant collections of the time.

One of the first Spiritualist hymnals was *The Spirit Harp: A Gift Presenting the Poetical Beauties of the Harmonial Philosophy*, compiled by Maria F. Chandler in 1851. Both Chandler and her twin sister Mary Ann were poets, although Mary Ann seems to have been more active. Maria's collection contained verses by her and her fellow Spiritualists, as well as poets they liked (Longfellow, for example). None was channeled. There was no music, but the verses were fitted to familiar hymn tunes.

It was followed in 1853 by *Spirit Voices: Odes, Dictated by Spirits of the Second Sphere, for the Use of Harmonial Circles*, by Esther C. Henck, who led the First Spiritualist Circle in Philadelphia. These verses were indeed channeled, obtained from the 'Spirits of the Second Sphere', who used to visit her 'Circle A.' Again, no music was given, but the spirits obligingly provided lyrics for familiar tunes like 'Auld Lang Syne' or 'The Canadian Boat Song'.

However, there was clearly a need for a fully-fledged Spiritualist hymnal, so in 1856 J. B. Packard and J. S. Loveland published *The Spirit Minstrel; A Collection of Hymns and Music for the use of Spiritualists, in their circles and public meetings*. Packard, as far as I can tell, was a composer and bass singer, and Loveland wrote several books on Spiritualism. As they say in the introduction: 'The Spirit Harp and Spirit Voices furnish us some beautiful poetry... but we have no music, and hence are obliged to use the cumbersome works of common church music.' Packard did write most of the music, apparently without spiritual assistance, but added a few selections of 'common church music', as was probably expected. Here, to satisfy your curiosity, or to intone at your next meeting, is one of his songs, 'Light'. ☞ FIG 5 p. 213

Many other hymnals followed, one of the most popular being the 1911 *Spiritualist Hymnal*, published by the National Spiritualist Association.

These were all crucial to the movement, and I presume uplifted the assembled, but offered no anomalous music; Leah Fox's alphabetic procedure remained unique.

*Mérovak*

We're luckier with the flamboyant French musical medium Mérovak, since one of his channeled pieces was preserved.

Mérovak was born Gabriel Robuchon in 1874, and by the late 1890s had assumed his pseudonym, after the legendary founder of the Merovingian dynasty, grown a flowing beard, and taken to wearing elaborate medieval costumes. He called himself 'The Man of the Cathedrals', and told the curious, 'I date from the reign of Louis XI, and knew Joan of Arc quite well.' For a while, he stayed in the belfry of Notre-Dame, befriended by the bell-ringer Auguste Herbet and the resident cat Quasimodo.

In addition to all this flamboyant cosplay, he was a skilled draftsman, whose drawings and watercolors of cathedrals are still prized. And he also gave concerts on the piano and organ, which some listeners assumed were channeled from spirits.

*L'Écho du merveilleux* (*The Echo of the Marvelous*), a journal of all things occultish edited by Gaston Méry, took a particular interest in him. In the August 15, 1897 issue, an article by Dr. Corneille, 'A Case of

Musical Mediumship', proclaimed Mérovak a musical medium. Méry, on a front-page piece on January 1, 1898, took special notice of his keyboard technique: 'It is enough to follow his playing, to examine his fingering, to realize immediately his absolute ignorance of what is usually taught by piano teachers. His playing and fingering are disconcerting, absurd, impossible to reproduce.'

For Méry, the crucial question was whether Mérovak had musical training, and therefore played pieces he'd written, or was untaught, and therefore channeled spirits. He considered the matter in an article in the next issue, 'The Improvisations of Mérovak':

> I have already remarked one of the reasons that, in my opinion, weakens *a priori* this judgment of the skeptics: the eccentricity of his fingering. To cite only one example, I will note the exclusive use, on the arpeggios, of the thumb, the index, and the little finger.
>
> To this first reason I could add many others: the absolute absence of diatonic passages, a somewhat childish overuse of tremolo, the almost continual execution of the theme, the melody, by the left hand.
>
> But above all I will call attention to the fact that Mérovak plays constantly in the same key, C-flat.

Since Mérovak didn't notate his music, there's no reason to call the key C-flat (7 flats), rather than B (5 sharps). But like Howard Menger and Eugenio Siragusa, our alien channelers, he did like the black keys.

He had several pieces in his repertory, including 'The March of the Immortals', 'Farewells to Life', and 'The Swing of Life'. To determine if they were the same for each performance, Méry sat Mérovak at an *enregistreur Rivoire*, a piano that notated what was played. Méry then assembled musicians to compare the score with another performance, and verified that they weren't identical. This convinced Méry that the music was channeled. He compared the process to different scholars translating Horace: the ideas were the same, but the details varied.

There are, as you may already have been objecting, other explanations. Mérovak simply could have been an untutored improviser, shuffling a few set ideas. We should note his own description, from a later issue (March 1, 1898):

> I played a melody of which it would be impossible for me to repeat a note. When I am placed before the instrument, everything sings: the stones, the woodwork, the pillars, the vaults, the clouds of incense, the images on the windows. I listen and I transcribe.

Fortunately, the *Rivoire* gave us '*Chant des Immortels: Marche triomphale*' ('Song of the Immortals: Triumphant March'), which apparently was also known as '*Marche des Immortels*'. It's 82 measures long, and is not really in C-flat, but the relative minor, A-flat. It's also, not surprisingly, naive and improvisational. It's innocent of melody or structure, consisting of reiterated chords, scalar passages in doubled octaves, and *tremoli*. The rhythm is repetitive, and the harmony relies on a few chords, never straying far from A-flat minor. To my ears, it seems banal and bombastic, but his showmanship must have carried it: another journalist, Adolphe Brisson, described his playing as 'All of it without order, without method, but not without charm, with an instinct for rhythm, a sense of harmony, and an incontestable virtuosity.' ☞ FIG 6 *p. 214–217*

Mérovak later turned to giving multi-media presentations, with a magic lantern and gramophone. He showed up playing the carillon in *Vieux Paris*, a reconstructed medieval village built for the 1900 Paris Exposition, where, true to his method, he 'improvises vague chants' rather than playing the standard repertory. After that, I lose sight of him.

Another notable piece of mediumistic music was not channeled, but heard. On August 10 1901, the Principal and Vice-Principal of St. Hugh's Hall, Oxford, Charlotte Moberly and Eleanor Jourdain, visited the Petit Trianon in Versailles, and believed they had been whisked back in time. They reported seeing buildings and bridges that were long gone, and chatting with people from the past. They then researched the history of the park, and in 1911 published *An Adventure*, in which they suggested they had entered the mind of Marie Antoinette on August 10 1792, the last day of the monarchy.

A few months later, on January 2 1902, Ms. Jourdain revisited the park, and once again felt she had visited the past. Among other things, she reported music: 'faint music, as of a band not far off, was audible. It was playing very light music with a good deal of repetition in it. Both voices and music were diminished in tone, as in a phonograph, unnaturally. The pitch of the band was lower than usual.' Later in the book, she added that the instruments were violins.

Fortunately, she notated it, or at least eleven measures of it, although 'without all the inner harmonies.' For some reason, it was not printed in the five editions of *An Adventure*, but was finally published in a booklet by the Welsh composer Ian Parrott in 1966, although copies had apparently circulated privately before that. Another, slightly different, version is also extant. ☞ FIG 7 *p. 218*

The sixth measure, at least to my eyes, doesn't make much sense. Ms. Jourdain and Ms. Moberly paged through many eighteenth century scores, and found similar passages in Sacchini, Philidor, Monsigny, Grétry, and Pergolesi. In 1961, the journalist James Edward Holroyd noted 'The last three bars are identical with the final bars of the well-known nineteenth-century revivalist hymn "Count Your Blessings".' I'll add that they're a descending scale, which can be found in many pieces.

Ms. Jourdain's statement that the pitch was 'lower than usual' is puzzling, and provoked a debate in the *Journal of the Society of Psychic Research* after the publication of Parrott's booklet. Rollo Myers argued that she couldn't have heard the pitch as lower unless she already knew the piece, J. P. Hill suggested that she was referring to the key, since A-flat is unusual for violins, and J. H. M. Whiteman noted that A was tuned lower in the 18th century. I'll add that she also could have meant the overall range of the ensemble, and thought the violins played more on the lower strings, but we'll never know.

The most popular explanation is that the two women had wandered into a masquerade party thrown by Robert de Montesquiou, the extravagant dandy who inspired both Huysmans and Proust. A dark pockmarked man the women met has even been identified as Montesquiou himself. He did throw similar parties in the area, although there's no record he did on either of the dates in question. It's also been suggested that Ms. Jourdain heard distant military music, although she did specify violins.

We're left, then, with those odd eleven measures, which Eleanor Jourdain insisted came to her from the past. She and Ms. Moberly thought their first 'adventure' came from the mind of Marie Antoinette, but she gave no explanation for the second one, several months later.

Many mediums claimed to channel music from specific composers from the past, but left no record of it. I'll acknowledge them, but briefly, since their music is gone.

*Jesse Shepard*

Jesse Shepard was one of the more active and certainly one of the more flamboyant. Born in England in 1848, he was raised in Illinois, and by the 1860s was touring Europe. He was said to be an exceptional pianist, with hands that spanned an octave and a half. He was an equally impressive singer, able to sing duets with himself, alternating bass and soprano, like the later *virtuosi* Candy Candido and Tiny Tim. Like Mérovak before him, he adopted a flamboyant persona: a wig, rouged cheeks, a dyed mustache, and, on occasion, a voluminous Russian squirrel-skin coat.

He channeled several composers, including Mozart, Chopin, Thalberg, and, once they were dead, Liszt and Berlioz, but refused to notate or record his performances. In his later years, he turned to writing books on mystical subjects under the name of Francis Grierson, and died in 1927, shortly after playing his 'Grand Egyptian March' for a circle of admirers.

Around 1870, a Connecticut teenager named Catherine Mettle attracted attention by evoking Mozart, Beethoven, and Weber. And around 1900, a French medium, George Aubert, cheerfully demonstrated his ability to summon Chopin, Schumann, Méhul, Rubinstein, Mozart, Glinka, Liszt, Schubert, Beethoven, and Mendelssohn. In the absence of musical documentation, we can only speculate that they, like Mérovak, were essentially improvising, perhaps in some kind of trance, and will note that only famous composers were summoned.

Among more recent mediums, the Brazilian Jorge Rizzini was particularly industrious, and had no qualms about notation and recordings. He was a devotee of the French Spiritist Allan Kardec, who, for reasons unknown to me, is more popular in Brazil than in France. Rizzini channeled many Brazilian composers, including Noel Rosa, Ataulfo Alves, Ary Barroso, and Lamartine Babo, but also called on Verdi, Puccini, and Ellington, among others. Perhaps my favorite work of his is *'Glória a Kardec'*, a lively march transmitted by John Philip Sousa. ☞ FIG 8 *p. 218*

No musical medium, however, was as prolific as Rosemary Brown.

She was born in London in 1916; her family was poor, and neither religious nor musical, although her mother and grandmother had some psychic experiences. She married a freelance journalist, Charles Brown, in 1950, and had two children. After both he and her mother died in 1961, she began receiving ghostly visits from both of them.

She had, she said, seen spirits all her life. Franz Liszt, for example, had visited when she was seven. And after her husband died, Liszt began appearing more often. He not only dictated his new compositions, but introduced her to his colleagues. Eventually, she received pieces from Bach, Beethoven, Berlioz, Brahms, Chopin, Debussy, Delius, Grieg, Handel, Monteverdi, Mozart, Poulenc, Rachmaninov, Schumann (Clara Schumann also paid a call, but only with Robert's music), Schubert, Scriabin, Johann Strauss, and Stravinsky. In later years, she added a few less classical composers: George Gershwin, Gracie Fields, Fats Waller, and John Lennon.

A record of her music, *A Musical Séance*, was released in 1970, and she told her story in three books. Scholars studied her scores, usually concluding that they were reminiscent of the attributed composers, but formally and harmonically naive.

She claimed she saw and spoke with her contacts, and even confessed to a crush on Liszt, a friendly sort who helped her shop for groceries. As she confessed, 'And if I were romantic about any of the composers who visit me — which is impossible anyway! — I think I could be as regards Liszt.' The methods of transmission varied: sometimes the composers guided her hands on the keyboard, at other times they dictated the notes. In some cases, like her two Debussy pieces, she only received part of the score, and had to fill in the harmonies.

Most critics have been interested in determining whether her music resembles its models. For me, its most striking characteristic is its similarity to other examples of channeling. Like the vast literature of written 'spiritual communications', it makes sense, but a particular kind of mild, rambling, improvisational sense. It's not surprising that her favorite composer was Liszt, whose spontaneous style was ideal for channeling.

But I suppose we can never know exactly how or why she wrote her music. If she was not a hoaxer, and if she had not actually contacted dead composers, what was she doing? I'll suggest, with, I caution, a generous spoonful of the axiomatic salt, that her ghost writers may have been summoned in the same way that children create imaginary friends. It's common enough at a certain age; perhaps she managed to do it as an adult, and it helped light up the part of her brain that made music. ☞ FIG 9 p. 219

Mediums continue to channel dead composers today. Since 1993, Melvyn Willin, of the Society for Psychical Research, has been investigating and recording them, including 'Winfred' and 'Keti', who receive Chopin, and 'Leo', an ebullient tenor who claims transmissions from Caruso.

One footnote to all this necromancy is the body of music written in imitation of earlier composers, and palmed off as genuine. Fritz Kreisler was particularly fond of this gambit, dashing off purported works by Tartini, Vivaldi, Couperin, and Boccherini, among others; Henri Casadesus also enlarged the viola repertory with concerti by Handel and C. P. E. Bach. The line between channeling and imitating a dead composer may be intrinsically thin and ambiguous.

# IV

# On Musical Ciphers

By strict linguistic standards, music is not a language, since it has no referents. It's even more tautological than speech; as Stravinsky so memorably put it, 'Music is too stupid to express anything but music.'

But it moves through time like language, with a sort of simulacrum of syntax, in which pitches and chords interact like letters and words, and melodies like sentences. And language acts like music too, since most languages are tonal, with pitch as well as phonemes. Many can be understood by pitch alone, and even whistled to carry further. The more monotonous European languages reserve pitch for emphasis, like those upward glissandi for questions and uncertainty, but are still pitched.

Here, for example, are two pitched transcriptions of speech, made by a certain F. Weber in 1891: assorted phrases, and a family in a train. ☞ FIG 1 p. 222

To make things muddier, we use language to talk about music, and give pitches and rhythms names and numbers. Indonesian music uses numbers for pitches; Byzantine, Greek letters; Japanese, syllables from the traditional pangram 'Iroha'. Scottish bagpipe notation, *Canntaireachd*, has a lexicon of syllables for both pitches and ornaments.

To our credit, we did simplify the terminology over the centuries; the Greeks called their lowest pitch *Proslambanomenos*, and we get by with 'do' or C.

The European solfeggio syllables were proposed by a Benedictine monk, Guido d'Arezzo, in the 11th century. Like the Japanese, he took them from a poem, in his case the hymn *Ut queant laxis*: ut, re, mi, fa, sol, and la. (Do and ti, or si, came later.)

His syllables use all five vowels (with an extra A), so composers eventually realized they could make a tune from a text by matching its vowels with the vowels of the solfeggio. Around 1500, Josquin Des Prez experimented with this method, eventually called *soggetto cavato*. The first was the *Missa Hercules dux Ferrariae*, probably around 1500. His patron's name, Hercules Dux Ferrariae, was reduced to E U E U E A I AE, which then became 're ut re ut re fa mi re.' This, in turn, became a *cantus firmus* around which other parts were written. He followed it with a secular piece, *Vive le roi*. V and U being interchangeable, the title produced another *cantus firmus*, 'ut mi ut re re sol mi.' Other composers followed his example, notably Cipriano de Rore, Lupus Hellinck, and

*Examples of soggetto cavato*

re ut re ut re fa mi re
Her - cu - les Dux Fer - ra - ri - e

Jacobus Vaet. If you'd like to try your hand at it, let me suggest 'Strange Attractor', which becomes 'la re la la sol.'

The practice soon sputtered out, since it was so limited. Echoes can be found, though, in later puns on solfeggio. In French, for example, 'do mi si la do re' gives *domicile adoré*, adored house, which is why that melodic snippet adorns happy homes and real estate ads. Oscar Hammerstein II pointed out that in English a doe is a female deer, and James Joyce translated from the Italian in *Finnegans Wake*: 'I give, a king, to me, she does, alone, up there, yes see, I double give.'

Words can also be converted into numbers, thanks to the ancient art of gematria, and then pressed into musical use, usually for the lengths of phrases and sections. Some Renaissance composers were mad for numerology, but it can be hard to tell if they were using gematria or some other symbolism. There's no consensus on why Jacob Obrecht used 180 in his *Missa de Sancto Johanne Baptista* (the subject does come up occasionally), but it's likely that he used 888 in his *Missa Sub tuum praesidium* because that's how 'Jesus' adds up in Greek.

Later composers preferred the letter names for the pitches, most famously Bach; since German uses B for B-flat and H for B-natural, he inserted his own name into a couple of pieces, like a Baroque tagger. His son Carl Philipp Emanuel upped the ante by spelling his second name Filippo, and writing a little 12-bar piece on C F E BACH. The most popular application seems to have been quoting names: Brahms encoded Agathe von Siebold, sort of, into his Sextet #2 as AGAHE, and Edward Elgar wrote an 'Allegretto on GEDGE' (1885) for his pupils the Gedge sisters. Other words have been used at times, 'beef' and 'cabbage', for example: John Field notated them to thank a hostess for that dish, and Nicolas Slonimsky wrote a 'Cabbage Waltz', as well as 'A Bad Egg Polka'. Robert Louis Stevenson found he could spell 'abracadabra' by using a rest for the R.

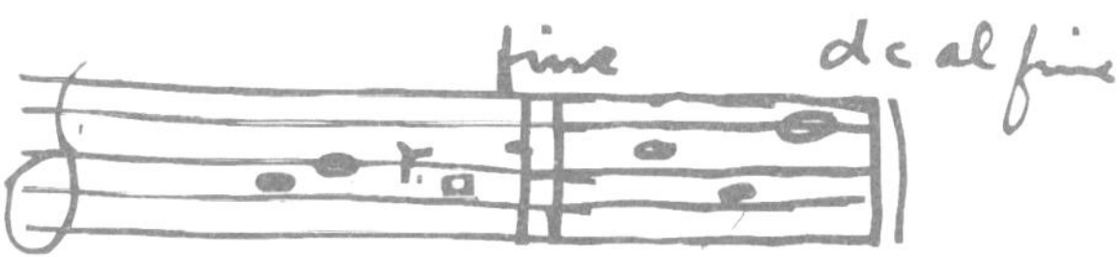


*Stevenson's 'Abracadabra*

The eccentric 19th century optician, cook, and musician William Kitchiner, to whom we owe the creation of potato chips, Wow-Wow Sauce, and eleven kinds of ketchup, went to great pains to harmonize the 'accents savage' of bubble and squeak with unusual key signatures. ☞ FIG 2 *p. 223*

There have been too many speculative theories about ciphered music to list here. As a type specimen, I give you Robert W. Padgett's argument that Beethoven encoded the word DEAF into the 'Ode to Joy' in the Ninth Symphony (that's measure 12 in the first statement of the theme). I suspect it wasn't intentional, but I do like the idea, and always think of it when that little syncopation comes around. ☞ FIG 3 *p. 224*

The idea survives in music instruction; as a child, I filled in a 'Note Speller', in which pitches spelled out words in capsule bios of canonical composers. ☟

*Note Speller*

Inevitably, our restless brains invented more formal ciphers. The familiar ones include Morse code, which assigns letters to rhythms; bugle calls, which assign military terms to brief tunes; and West African talking drums, which, like whistled languages, mimic the pitch and rhythm of speech.

Also inevitably, they've all been incorporated into music. Pop musicians particularly relish encoding Morse into their songs, Abba's 'SOS', Rush's 'YYZ', and the Alan Parsons Project's 'Lucifer', being the most conspicuous; Pearls Before Swine ('Miss Morse') and Mike Oldfield *('Amarok')* took boyish pleasure in spelling out 'fuck.' To confuse matters, some songs, like the Capris' winsome 'Morse Code of Love' and the Alberts' stirring 'Morse Code

Melody', don't use real code. However, Slim Gaillard, always a nonpareil, rose to the occasion in 'Communication', opening with the code for CQ, 'seek you', the standard ham radio call for contact, which, hooray, is also a pun.

Bugle calls have been even more popular, since they suit triadic tonality; examples include Haydn's 100th Symphony ('The Military') and George M. Cohan's 'Over There'. Talking drums enliven many songs, both by Nigerians like Sikiru Adepoju and non-Nigerians like King Crimson.

Since language feeds on itself, codes themselves become encoded. The bugle call for reveille becomes 'I hate to get up.' Morse students use familiar phrases as mnemonics, remembering that Q is 'dash dash dot dash' with 'God save the queen.'

But many more formal codes have been invented. They're generally simple substitution ciphers, assigning a pitch or short phrase to each letter. Unlike the above examples, they weren't meant to be played, just deciphered. Here, to help you pass secret messages to your allies, is a timeline of some historical methods.

One of the earliest was devised by Giovanni Battista della Porta, in his *De Furtivis Literarum Notis* (On the Secret Symbols of Letters), 1563: he simply assigned the letters to ascending whole notes and descending half notes.

The German mathematician Daniel Schwenter proposed a less obvious code in his *Steganologia et Steganographia*, published sometime around 1620. The letters A through L were given to whole notes ascending the scale, and the rest of the alphabet to descending half notes. The alphabet was also somewhat scrambled to make it less obvious.

*Della Porta's system*

*Schwenter's system*

August II, the Duke of Braunschweig-Lüneburg, also known as Gustavus Selenus, improved the model in his *Cryptomenytices et Cryptographiae libri IX*, from 1624. Each letter was ciphered with two pitches, which not only avoids a direct correlation, but provides more options for a smoother ciphertext.

| | UT | FA | SOL | MI | RE |
|---|---|---|---|---|---|
| UT | Enguiriel | Heraffiel | Sestariel | Lytarchiel | Druziel |
| SOL | Towiel | Fæxamiel | Amyriel | Haziel | Lalalala |
| FA | Statriel | Gabriel | Michaël | Hedruriel | Stefaniel |
| MI | Walfariel | Timarchiel | Donaziel | Phorchiel | Raphaël |
| RE | Lofarchiel | Segniel | Ephanael | Uriel | Ilhariel |

*Selenus's system*

Francis Godwin, under the name of Domingo Gonsales, offered snippets of a fictional lunar language in his fantasy *The Man in the Moone*, published in 1638. The moon people speak in 'tunes and strange sounds', duly notated on a staff, and inspired by his discovery that Chinese is tonal. John Wilkins, in his 1641 cryptographical treatise *Mercury, the Secret and Swifte Messenger*, revealed the key. Each pitch represents two letters, one with a half note and one with a whole note; the letter A is written with a half-note F, B with a whole-note F, and so on, descending the scale. The letters are slightly scrambled, so that 'the five vowels are represented by the Minnums [minims] on each of the five lines.' He didn't explain why that was desirable.

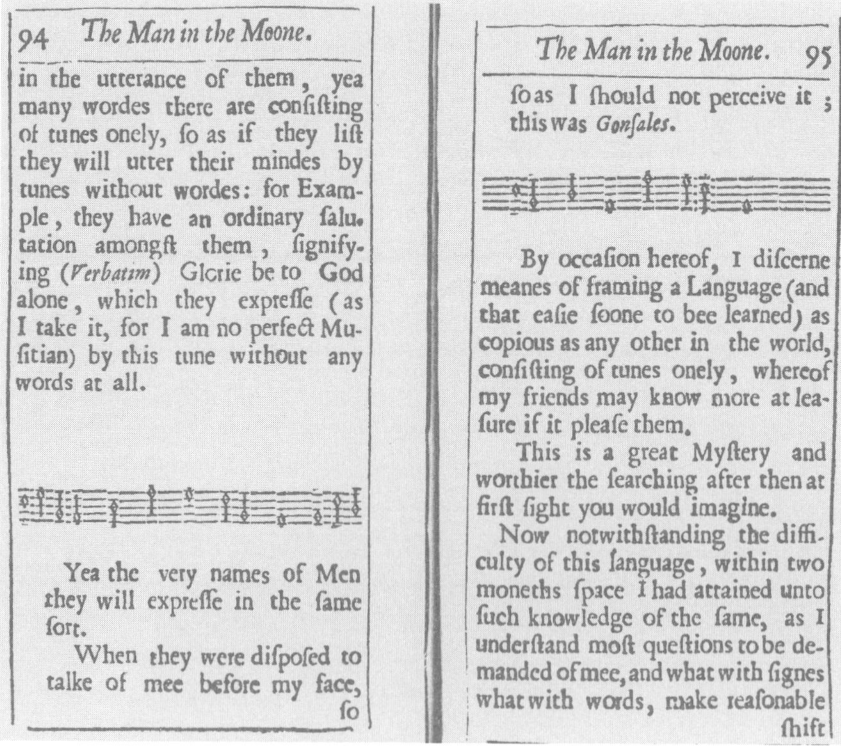

94 *The Man in the Moone.*

in the utterance of them, yea many wordes there are conſiſting of tunes onely, ſo as if they liſt they will utter their mindes by tunes without wordes: for Example, they have an ordinary ſalutation amongſt them, ſignifying (*Verbatim*) Glorie be to God alone, which they expreſſe (as I take it, for I am no perfect Muſitian) by this tune without any words at all.

Yea the very names of Men they will expreſſe in the ſame ſort.

When they were diſpoſed to talke of mee before my face, ſo

*The Man in the Moone.* 95

ſo as I ſhould not perceive it; this was *Gonſales.*

By occaſion hereof, I diſcerne meanes of framing a Language (and that eaſie ſoone to bee learned) as copious as any other in the world, conſiſting of tunes onely, whereof my friends may know more at leaſure if it pleaſe them.

This is a great Myſtery and worthier the ſearching after then at firſt ſight you would imagine.

Now notwithſtanding the difficulty of this language, within two moneths ſpace I had attained unto ſuch knowledge of the ſame, as I underſtand moſt queſtions to be demanded of mee, and what with ſignes what with words, make reaſonable ſhift

*Godwin's lunar language*

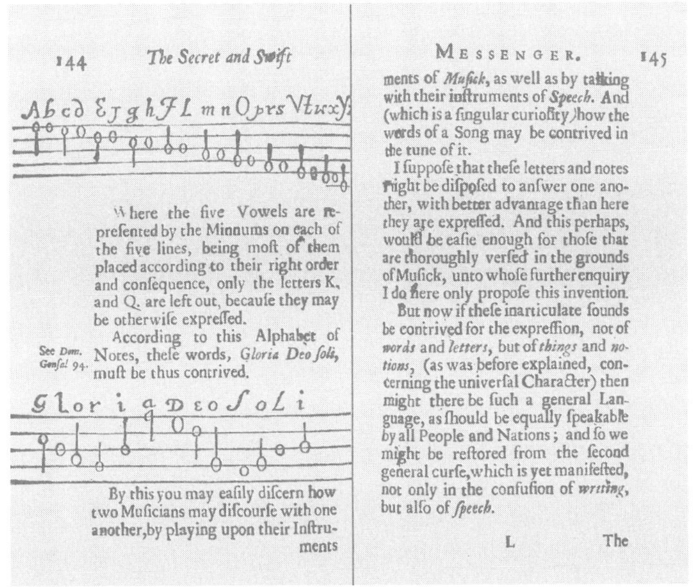

144 The Secret and Swift

Where the five Vowels are repreſented by the Minnums on each of the five lines, being moſt of them placed according to their right order and conſequence, only the letters K, and Q. are left out, becauſe they may be otherwiſe expreſſed.

According to this Alphabet of Notes, theſe words, *Gloria Deo ſoli*, muſt be thus contrived.

See Dom. Conſul. 94.

Glor i a Deo Soli

By this you may eaſily diſcern how two Muſicians may diſcourſe with one another, by playing upon their Inſtruments

MESSENGER. 145

ments of *Muſick*, as well as by talking with their inſtruments of *Speech*. And (which is a ſingular curioſity) how the words of a Song may be contrived in the tune of it.

I ſuppoſe that theſe letters and notes might be diſpoſed to anſwer one another, with better advantage than here they are expreſſed. And this perhaps, would be eaſie enough for thoſe that are thoroughly verſed in the grounds of Muſick, unto whoſe further enquiry I do here only propoſe this invention.

But now if theſe inarticulate ſounds be contrived for the expreſſion, not of *words* and *letters*, but of *things* and *notions*, (as was before explained, concerning the univerſal Character) then might there be ſuch a general Language, as ſhould be equally ſpeakable by all People and Nations; and ſo we might be reſtored from the ſecond general curſe, which is yet manifeſted, not only in the confuſion of *writing*, but alſo of *ſpeech*.

L The

*Wilkins's system*

The Italian Jesuit polymath Francesco Lana de Terzi improved the idea considerably, at least from a cipher standpoint, in his 1670 book *Prodromo all'arte Maestra* (Introduction to the Master Art). He proposed five different musical alphabets, which could be varied to make decipherment trickier. ☞ FIG 4 p. 225

The flamboyant eccentric Philip Thicknesse, the only cryptographer on our list to end his career with a position as an 'ornamental hermit', devised a 'harmonic alphabet' in his 1772 *Treatise on the Art of Decyphering and of Writing in Cypher*. Like Wilkins, he used two rhythmic values, which requires fewer pitches; he also jumbled the letters. ☟

*Thicknesse's system*

The flaw in all of these was that the ciphertexts made little musical sense. Any musically literate official who tried to hum a bit of the Thicknesse he'd intercepted might become suspicious. Johann Joseph Heinrich Bücking found one solution in his 1804 work *Anweisung zur geheimen Correspondenz systematisch entworfen* (Directions for systematically composed secret correspondence). He wrote one measure of a minuet for each letter, with extra measures to begin and end, thereby ensuring a reasonably plausible piece of music. ☞

*Bücking's system*

Josef Haydn's younger brother, Michael, is credited with an imaginative cipher in an 1808 biography by Werigand Rettensteiner. His system used accidentals, rather than the diatonic scale favored by earlier codes: ABCDE becomes G-natural, G-sharp, A-flat, A-natural, and A-sharp. Paired notes indicate letters with diacriticals, rests are used for punctuation, and a parenthesis is marked by a change to tenor clef. Unfortunately, all of those enharmonic accidentals produce an unusually incoherent ciphertext. ☞ FIG 5 *p. 226*

Here too is an example, published in *Rees's Cyclopaedia*, issued in both the US and UK from 1802 until 1820. It was described only as 'composed and published by an author of no ability in music', which is harsh but just. It follows the usual method of assigning pitches, both as half and whole notes, to the letters, but does avoid alphabetical order. I must confess I don't understand the Lento. ☞ FIG 6 p. 227

Rees's last example is also somewhat enigmatic, but is explained by a print I once found in a box of ephemera at a Manhattan flea market. The same example is given, but the full alphabet as well; among its novelties is the use of an accidental to mark a new word. It was obviously cut from an encyclopedia, but which? Was it from another edition of Rees? If not, did it swipe the example, or vice versa? An online search only yields images of my own distinctively foxed and stained copy, which I scanned and posted years ago, and which has now apparently sown its wild oats promiscuously across the internet. ☟

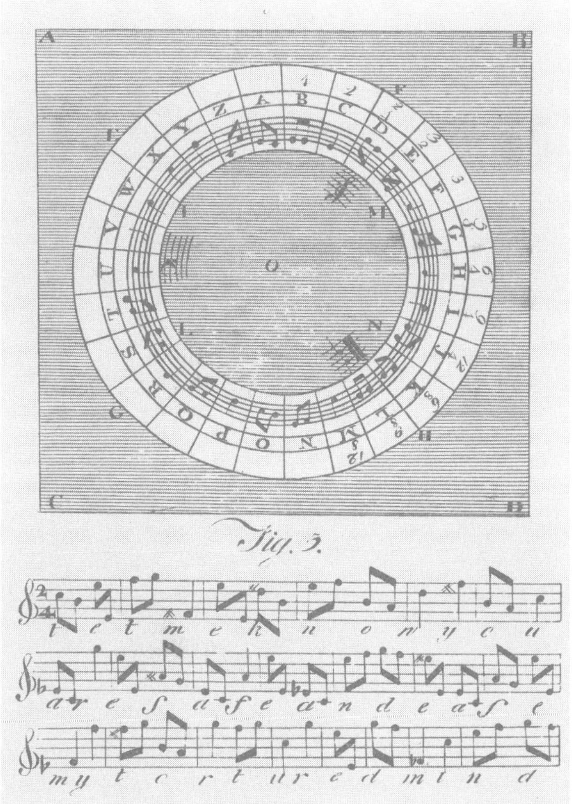


*Rees's variation*

From the 20th century, I can add an example from the prolific author, illustrator and Scoutmaster Dan 'Uncle Dan' Beard. He suggests using only rhythmic values, leaving pitches free. The same thing, obviously, could also be done with Morse code.

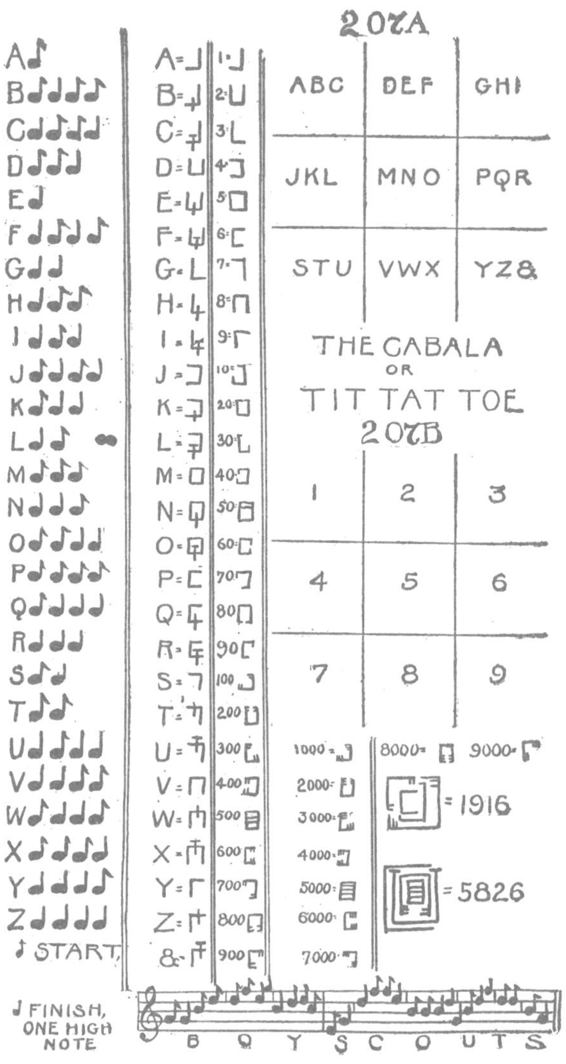


*Beard's system*

So that you can hear all of these in action, I've written out some realizations of that evocative term 'Strange Attractor.' The results vary considerably, but none sounds like music written by the usual methods. ☞ FIG 7 p. 228–229

William F. Friedman, chief cryptographer for the US National Security Agency for many years, devised many musical codes. He began his career with Elizabeth Wells Gallup, a determined woman who spent decades seeking (and, to her satisfaction, finding) Francis Bacon's biliteral cipher in early editions of Shakespeare and other Elizabethans. Unlike the dodgy ciphers claimed by other Baconians (like Ignatius Donnelly's flamboyantly incoherent numerical system), the biliteral was genuine, really described by the real Bacon in 1623. It used the alternation of two typefaces to encode a message, much like the dots and dashes of Morse, allowing a plaintext completely unrelated to the ciphertext. Although Friedman later rejected Gallup's claims, he had become besotted with the biliteral, and applied it to various binary systems, including elements of photos and drawings, and, inevitably, music: Stephen Foster's 'My Old Kentucky Home' could serve by using notes with small gaps in the stems and notes without. Here, too, is a different musical cipher, written with his family for a Christmas card in 1933. The key is provided, so you can work it out yourself. ☞ FIG 8 p. 230

A curious little piece called *Muzikalische Würfenspiele* (Musical Dice Game), published in 1792 and attributed to Mozart, invited the user to write minuets by choosing snippets of music with dice. It was almost certainly not by Mozart, and has nothing to do with our subject. However, a manuscript fragment really written by the real Mozart, now really known as K. 516f, contains a series of phrases that could be used in the same way. Mozart gave no instructions, but the musicologist Hideo Noguchi has argued persuasively (to me, anyway) that the measures were to be chosen not by dice, but from the letters of a given name, much like Bücking's cipher. It was, in other words, probably a kit for writing personalized minuets. ☞ FIG 9 p. 230

Olivier Messiaen took musical cryptography in his own idiosyncratic direction by creating his own musical alphabet, the *langage communicable*, inspired by Aquinas's speculations on angelic language. Each letter was encoded with not just a specific pitch, but a duration and timbre; he also wrote motifs for the different Latin declensions, and for such key ideas as 'to be', 'to have', and 'God.' He first used it in his 1969 organ piece, *Méditations sur le mystère de la Sainte Trinité* (Meditations on the Mystery of the Holy Trinity), to spell out passages from the *Summa Theologiae*. In the interest of brevity, he only used nouns, adjectives, and verbs, omitting all articles, pronouns, adverbs, and prepositions. ☞ FIG 10 *p. 231*

From ciphers and musical alphabets, it's a short step to a constructed language based on music. One of the first was *Pasilogie, ou la Musique considérée comme langue universelle* (Pasilogie, or Music Considered as a Universal Language), an 1806 treatise by Anne-Pierre-Jacques de Vismes. De Vismes was an interesting character, at the time the former director of the Royal Academy of Music in Paris, and the future author of *Recherches nouvelles sur l'origine et la destination des pyramides d'Égypte, suivi d'une Dissertation sur la fin du globe terrestre* (New Research on the Origin and Destination of the Pyramids of Egypt, Followed by a Dissertation on the End of the Terrestrial Globe), which was to appear only six years later.

His *Pasilogie* was not really a universal language, but simply another cipher alphabet. It was a novel one, based on a microtonal scale of 21 tones to the octave, but still a cipher. ☞ FIG 11 *p. 231*

The same could be said of *Die Instrumentalton-Sprechkunst* (The Art of Speaking with Instrumental Sound) that E. A. Weyrich published in 1930. It too had its curiosity: the alphabet was expressed with just four pitches. ☞ FIG 12 *p. 232*

All of these were rudimentary compared to Solrésol, the 'Universal Musical Language' developed by the indefatigable François Sudre in the early 19th century.

Sudre was originally a violinist and composer; his works include the songs '*Le Départ du Guerrier*' ('The Soldier's Departure') and '*Tu ne sais pas, enfant,ce que c'est que l'amour* ' ('You do not know, child, what love is'), as well as assorted nocturnes, romances, and violin solos. Around 1820 his interests turned to an auxiliary language based on pitch. His first effort was essentially a cipher alphabet, using twelve pitches. Interest from the military led him to rework it for use by bugle. Throughout the 1830s, he compiled a lexicon he called *Téléphonie*, using five notes in two octaves: do, sol, do, mi, and sol. Unfortunately, the military found it impractical in stormy weather, and saw more promise in the telegraph.

So, Sudre returned to his universal language, now called Solrésol, the word for 'language' in his system. This time, he used the seven pitches of the diatonic scale, written on a three-line staff. He spent the rest of his life writing dictionaries in eight languages, giving demonstrations in which his pupils translated messages he played on the violin, and trying to find backers. Although many people admired his ingenuity, nobody wanted to fund an invention devoid of commercial or practical potential.

In 1866, four years after his death, his widow Marie-Joséphine published his *Langue Musicale Universelle*. His other dictionaries are lost, but the French version preserves much of his work.

Sudre made a brave attempt to keep Solrésol coherent and consistent. One-pitch words were articles and conjunctions, two-pitch words were pronouns and simple concepts, and three-pitch words were the most common ideas ('God' and 'to be,' for example). My copy has several hand-written corrections for the two-pitch words, so they must have been troublesome. Four-pitch words were organized by their initial pitches: those beginning with 'do' were 'consecrated to physical and moral man, his intellectual faculties, his qualities, and his alimentation'; 're' to 'objects of toiletry, those contained in the home, housekeeping chores, and the family'; 'mi' to 'the actions of man and his faults'; 'fa' to 'the countryside, war, the sea, and travel'; 'sol' to 'the fine arts and the sciences'; 'la' to 'industry and commerce'; and 'si' to 'the city, the government, and the administration.' He barely broached the huge five-pitch vocabulary, but did establish that words starting with do-re were for animals, do-mi for plants, and do-fa for minerals. ☞ FIG 13 *p. 233*

Accents changed the same word into different parts of speech: no accent for a verb, an accent on the first syllable for an abstract noun, on the second for a concrete noun, on the third for an adjective, and on the fourth for an adverb. Verb tenses were expressed by prefixing double letters: 'do-do' for the imperfect, etc. A noun was made feminine with a macron over the article (pronounced by repeating it), and plural by an accent over the article (pronounced by prolonging it); nouns without articles took an accent on the last syllable. One oddity was that antonyms were made by reversing words: 'God' was the ascending triad do-mi-sol, so 'Satan' was sol-mi-do. (The traditional *Diabolus in Musica*, the tritone, became either 'much', fa-si, or 'little', si-fa.) He also provided an alphabet, like his predecessors, to spell names and places. Solrésol's limitation to seven symbols meant it could be spelled by any set of seven: not only syllables or pitches, but numbers, colors, or points on the hand.

Solrésol was further developed in an 1883 manual, *Théorie et pratique de la langue universelle inventée par Jean-François Sudre* (Theory and Practice of the Universal Language Invented by Jean-François Sudre), by Marie-Josephine, and a 1902 *Grammaire du Solrésol* by Boleslas Gajewski, who also created a special alphabet for it.

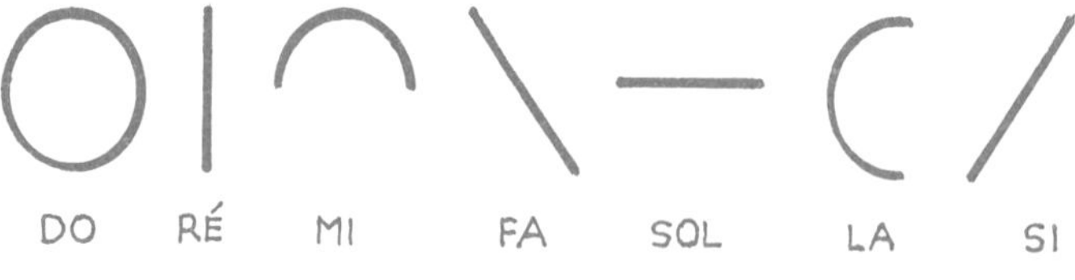


*Solrésol alphabet*

Like other *a prori* constructed languages, such as Edward Powell Foster's Ro or W. John Weilgart's aUI, Solrésol was hard to memorize. Reversing words to create antonyms conflicted with the categories for the initial letters, and was applied only sporadically: 'dictionary', sol-re-la, is not the opposite of 'lesson', la-re-sol. If musical pitches were used instead of syllables, it would be hard to tell what they were without perfect pitch or a reference. Otherwise, sol-re-sol would just sound like a perfect fourth, and could be heard as fa-do-fa (epoch) or la-mi-la (ink), which would lead to confusion (la-mi-do-sol). The accents are confusing too, and it's unclear how they could be applied with colors or points on the hand.

Solrésol has had a resurgence in recent years, prompted by Paul Collins's inclusion of it in his delightful book *Banvard's Folly*. In NYC, on January 29, 2007, the short-lived Athanasius Kircher Society, led by Joshua Foer, held its first and last meeting, which included a performance of the balcony scene from *Romeo and Juliet* in Solrésol. Introduced by Paul Collins, it was presented as solfeggio syllables, numbers, hand positions, colors, and musical notes on the clarinet and accordion. I have been unable to find the names of the actors. John Seabrook of *The New Yorker* disapproved, calling the Kircherites 'self-consciously twee New York hipsters'.

Like other constructed languages before it, Solrésol has attracted reformers. Cornelis George Boeree, for one, offered 'ses', which simplified the grammar and the cipher alphabet. I only hope it will continue to evolve, spawning rival versions and bitter feuds.

To close the chapter, I'll leave you with a more extended taste of Solrésol, in a translation of Charles Fort, who was invoked back in the introduction:

> Terrified horses, up on their hind legs, hoofing a storm of frogs. Frenzied springboks, capering their exasperations against frogs that were tickling them. Storekeepers, in London, gaping at frogs that were tapping on their window panes. We shall pick up an existence by its frogs... One measures a circle beginning anywhere. ☞

FIG 14
*p. 234*

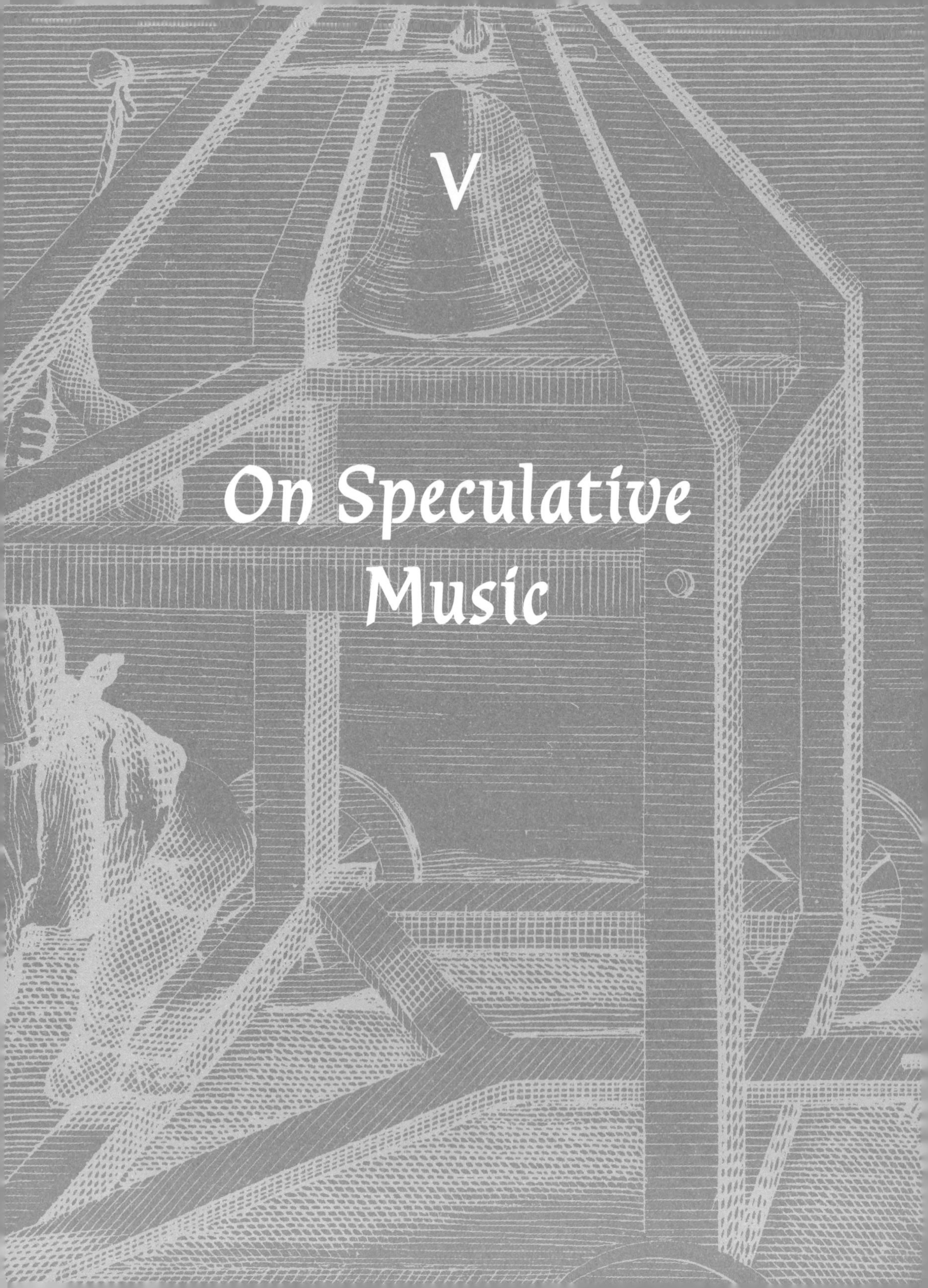

# V

# On Speculative Music

Like cryptological music, speculative music departs from standard practice not in its origin, but its intention. It's composed by normal humans, although often unusual normal humans, but is often music in name only. It's a schema or symbol, a model of the cosmos expressed in musical terms, not meant to be heard or even audiated. Sometime around 500, Boethius helpfully called it *musica mundana*, distinguishing it from human music (*musica humana*) and instrumental music (*musica instrumentis constituta*); he later added divine music (*musica divina*), which I suppose covers the celestial melodies that wafted through Chapter II.

I can offer no overarching interpretation of speculative music, no unified field theory of unified field theories, only a few type specimens and some subjective commentary. I'll observe, though, that these systems usually use both metaphor and association differently than conventional music. Perhaps the crucial difference between mathematics and numerology is that the former is based on the relations between numbers, and the latter on the relations between numbers and objects or ideas. The mathematician connects 28 to other perfect numbers; the numerologist to the number of days in the lunar cycle. The two approaches sometimes dovetail, as when St. Augustine assumed that the creation took six days because six is a perfect number. So too, the non-speculative musician associates the seven pitches of the diatonic scale with each other to create structures; the speculative musician associates them with other sets of seven elements, and folds them into the models. Once the seven pitches have been compared to the seven planets, the movements of the pitches represent the movements of the planets.

The tradition, at least in Western culture, supposedly starts with Pythagoras. The legend of his discovery of the correlation between number and harmony was told memorably in Thomas Stanley's 1687 *History of Philosophy*:

> As he past by a Smith's shop, by a happy chance he heard the iron Hammers striking upon the Anvile, and rendring sounds most consonant one to another in all combinations except one. He observed in them these three concords, the Diapason, the Diapente, and the Diatesseron; but that which was between

> the Diatesseron and the Diapente, he found to be a discord in itself, though otherwise useful for the making up of the greater of them (the Diapente). Apprehending this to come to him from God, as a most happy thing, he hasted into the shop, and by various trials, finding the difference of the sounds to be according to the weight of the Hammers… (p. 532).

If you have trouble audiating those hammers, don't despair: Pythagoras's 'various trials' have never been replicated, although many of his fans have tried.

Fortunately, he also invented the monochord, which works better. Dividing a tuned string in half produces an octave (Diapason), in two-thirds a fifth (Diapente), in three-fourths a fourth (Diatesseron), and so on, up through the harmonic series. Pythagoras's revelation was that we can hear ratios, and instinctively hear simpler ones as more consonant. To quote Stanley again, the monochord is 'an instrumental help for the Ear, solid and infallible, such as the Sight hath by a compass and a rule' (p. 532 again).

For reference, here's a picture of one, from Filippo Bonanni's 1728 Musical Cabinet. ☜

I go into all this because the monochord is the primary symbol in speculative music. The Pythagorean tradition begat Platonic idealism, which then begat many Neoplatonic curlicues. The harmonic series of a string stretched on a box became not just a metaphor, but the actual microcosm of the ordered universe.

*Monocordo, from Bonanni*

On the great chain of being, every level is a miniature of the whole, and all of it vibrates to the same harmonies. The chain itself is a monochord. We can't hear it, just as we can't hear the supramortal music of the gods. We can only describe it, or depict it in drawings and diagrams.

Probably the most enduring use of this conceit is the harmony of the spheres, developed, often in obsessive detail, throughout the centuries. One of the earliest descriptions occurs in Cicero's *Dream of Scipio*, in which his grandfather Scipio describes the universe, and with it the harmonies produced by the planets.

The universe then consisted of the solar system, conceived as nine nesting spheres. Earth squats immobile in the center; above it spin the Moon, Mercury, Venus, the Sun, Mars, Jupiter, Saturn, and the fixed stars. Each emits a pitch, producing a vast celestial harmony. Later writers varied and elaborated the design, assigning various pitches to the planets, and disagreeing about whether the Earth or the fixed stars gave the lowest tone.

The system was given its ultimate elaboration by Johannes Kepler, who jettisoned geocentrism and its perfectly circular orbits, thereby bringing the celestial harmony in line with Copernicus. In his *Mysterium Cosmographicum* (1597), he correlates musical intervals to astrological aspects, assigning the octave to opposition, the fifth to the trine, the fourth to the square, and onward. In his *Harmonices Mundi* (1619), he tackles elliptical orbits; he assigns different pitches to each planet's perihelion and aphelion, generating a range of pitches for each; he then calculates all the possible consonant combinations as the planets move through their orbits. The greatest consonant chord, he concludes, was sounded at the creation.

Many explanations have been offered for the fact that all this divine harmony is inaudible. Aristotle cited the excuse that we can't hear it because it's always there, only to dismiss the whole idea. Later theorists preferred the idea that we can only hear it with our souls, not our gross physical ears.

The connection with the monochord was made even more explicit by the prolific occultist, physician, Rosicrucian apologist, and anti-Keplerist, Robert Fludd. In *Utriusque Cosmi Maioris scilicet et Minoris Metaphysica,*

*Physica Atque Technica Historia* (Metaphysical, physical and technical history of both the greater and lesser cosmos, 1617–21), he published a plate of the 'Divine Monochord', turned by the hand of God. Fifteen pitches, from G to two octaves above it, are correlated to the chain of being from earth to heaven: Earth, Water, Air, Fire, Moon, Mercury, Venus, Sun (at the octave, in the center), Mars, Jupiter, Saturn, Fixed Stars, and the Empyrean realms: Acclamations, Voices, and Apparitions. This picture has been widely reproduced, most conspicuously on the cover of Harry Smith's iconic *Anthology of American Folk Music*. The connection between Fludd's cosmology and rural fiddlers remains one of Smith's many mysteries.

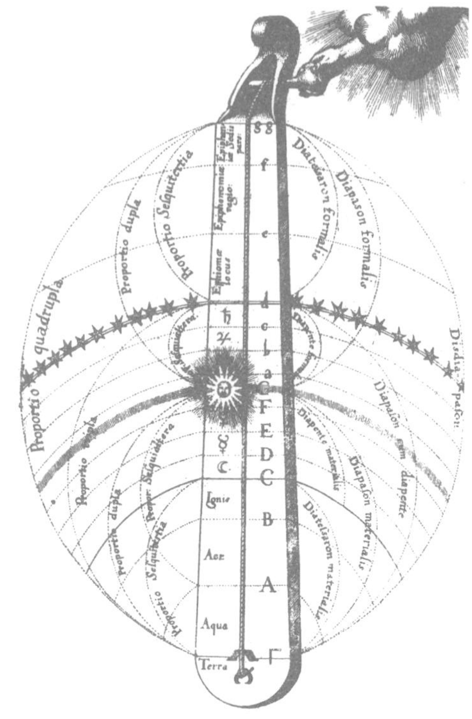


*Fludd's monochord*

Fludd elaborated the metaphor in several monochords, tuning it to the elemental realm, the human body, and the macrocosm in man. His definitive version, in *Anatomiæ amphitheatrum effigie triplici, more et conditione varia, designatum* (Anatomical amphitheater designed in three different ways and conditions, 1621), was a Great Monochord of seven octaves, assigning places to the planets, elements, angels, animals, vegetables, stones, letters of the Tetragrammaton, and divisions of the tabernacle of Moses.

The inexhaustible Jesuit polymath Athanasius Kircher expanded the conceit by multiplying the strings. In his massive *Musurgia Universalis* (1650), he imagines the universe not as one monochord, but as ten nine-stringed harps, all tuned to the same pitches. Each harp represents a different realm: the angelic world, heavenly bodies, metals, stones, plants, trees, aquatic creatures, birds, quadrupeds, and colors.

On each harp the pitches descend the ladder of being. So, on the heavenly bodies harp the nine strings are the Firmament, Saturn, Jupiter, Mars, Sun, Venus, Mercury, Moon, and Earth. On the quadrupeds harp, the strings are Panther, Ass & Bear, Elephant, Wolf, Lion, Stag, Dog, Cat, and Insects. The advantage of the harps over the monochord is that their strings vibrate in sympathy with one another. If the Sun string on the second harp is plucked, the Lion string on the ninth harp will ring out, as will the strings that match Virtues, Gold, Garnet, the Sunflower, the Lotus and Laurel, the Dolphin, the Cock, and the color Gold.

The diatonic scale becomes a metaphor for everything in the universe; I assume, and certainly hope, that we're not expected to audiate Fludd's massive monochords or Kircher's orchestra of harps. We can only admire or deplore the scope and complexity of the scheme, and the model of an internally consistent and harmonious universe, without quite understanding what to do with it.

Later practitioners adjusted these chains of associations to meet their own idiosyncratic criteria. One of the most imaginative was Joseph Alexandre Saint-Yves d'Alveydre (1842–1909), whose rich contribution to the genre deserves a closer look. It also included music that can actually be played.

D'Alveydre was born into a Catholic family in Paris; his father was the head doctor at the mental hospital Charenton. He was rebellious enough to earn stints in a reform colony and the military, and then wandered around awhile, teaching science and reading widely. In 1877, he married a wealthy Countess, and was able to devote himself to his scattered interests. He studied Sanskrit, wrote poetry, and promoted the industrial uses of seaweed. He also promoted a utopian scheme called Synarchy, which, in the interest of brevity, we can call a sort of globalist theocracy.

More to our present musical focus, at the age of 20 he decided to become the 'Pythagoras of Christianity.' To that end, he spent years elaborating a complex system of correspondences he called the Archéomètre, published only after his death.

He never finished it, but it may have been unfinishable. His notes were collected and edited by Gérard Encausse (also known as Papus) and

*The Archéomètre*

a group of his friends in 1912. As published, it's incomplete, and includes extra material by the friends. It's not always clear who wrote what, or how much of it was meant for the final work. Still, it gives us a glimmer of what he wanted.

Like all good Gallic things, it's divided into three parts: '*La sagesse vraie*' (True Wisdom), '*Description et étude de l'Archéomètre*' (Description and Study of the Archéomètre), and '*Les Adaptations de l'Archéomètre*'.

The first section is a diatribe against the individualism of pagan Greece and Rome, and its resurgence in the Humanism of the Renaissance. D'Alveydre preferred the ordered and dogmatic systems of ancient India and Egypt, and praised Pythagoras as an exception to the Greek free-for-all.

The second part explains the Archéomètre itself, a detailed diagram of the correspondences between the signs of the zodiac, the planets, the Hebrew alphabet, the Vattan alphabet, the pitches of the scale, the

*Couronne musicale Cosmologique*

colors of the spectrum, and their numerical values. Vattan (or Watan), according to d'Alveydre, was an early form of Sanskrit, although it seems to have escaped the attention of more conventional linguists. The Archéomètre recalls Fludd's monochords and Kircher's harps, but is set in a circle, divided into areas or zones.

He defines it as 'a precision instrument, cyclic protractor, cosmological code of high religious, scientific, and artistic studies' (p. 280), named after *archês métron*, Greek for 'measure of principle.' This second section includes not only his exposition of the correspondences, but a primer on astrology (written by 'A Friend of Saint-Yves'), lists of combinations of letters and their meanings in various languages, a glossary of Sanskrit, and a few appendices on scattered subjects.

The various areas of the Archéomètre he calls crowns, triangles, and stars. The musical part is the 'Cosmological Musical Crown.' To explain all of its workings would require a map at least as large as the territory, so

I'll simply point out that the given pitches are correlated to two-letter combinations in Vattan.

The third section is more explicitly about music. It's somewhat of a miscellany, largely due to Charles Gougy, who drew the architectural renderings, and Joseph Jemain, a professor at the Schola Cantorum.

Given d'Alveydre's veneration of Pythagoras, it was only natural that he design his own Archéometric monochord. He called it the Étalon (the standard), and filed a patent application for it in 1903.

Unlike earlier monochords, the Étalon is tuned to G, and based on the number 144,000, that being 'the one St. John assigns to the celestial musical system as his arithmological seal.' (p. 286). The relevant verses, incidentally, are Revelation 7:3–8 and 14:1–5, if you want to check your Gideon. Consequently, it was one meter and 44 centimeters long. ☞

Also unlike earlier monochords, the Étalon was outfitted with five rulers: one metric, one with Archéometric correspondences, and the others with the Pythagorean, Ptolemaic, and tempered scales.

Its main application was generating numerical and musical values for names, particularly holy names. As d'Alveydre demonstrates, Marie, or MRE, yields the numbers 40, 200, and 8, and the pitches D, C, and A. Gougy draws plans for cathedrals using those proportions, and d'Alveydre himself demonstrates the pitches with a setting of the Ave Maria. Since the product of all of these calculations and correspondences is either simple integers or diatonic pitches, I suspect simpler methods would work just as well. The complexity is obviously its own reward, since, to its creator, 'There is nothing that is not concordant, logical, harmonic, from the whole to the smallest detail' (p. 287).

This last section also includes designs for chalices, pitches derived from the dimensions of Biblical temples,

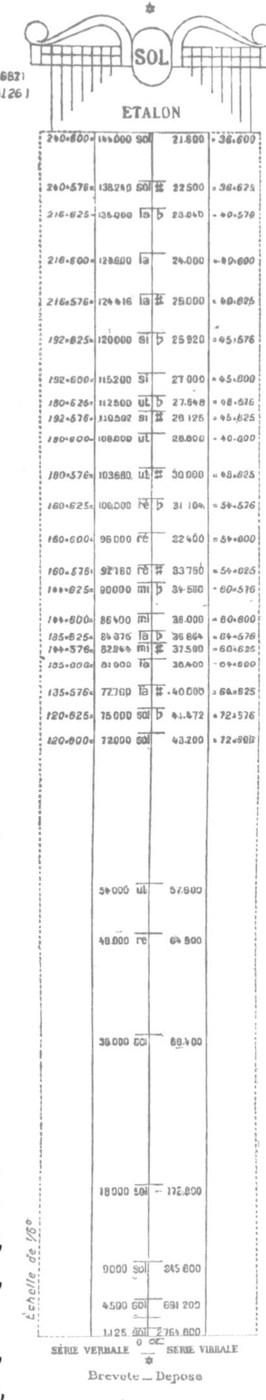


*Étalon*

and a couple of musical diagrams: diatonic scales set into squares, and the Étalon expanded into a drafting triangle.

A second volume soon followed, *L'Archéomètre Musical*, subtitled *Modes mélodiques et harmoniques*. It consists entirely of Archéometric music, and is quite a curious collection.

There are five sections. The first proposes notation on a seven-line staff, placing notes without accidentals on the spaces, and notes with accidentals on the lines, thus eliminating clefs and key signatures. The seven octaves of the system (there must be seven) are specified by Roman numerals. He gives three examples; here's one of them. ☞ FIG 1 p. 236

The next section is by far the most developed. He calls it *Diatonie Archéométrique*, with the further subtitles 'Flatted Diatonic Series — Hymnology — Conjoined Degrees and Intervals.'

Like Mérovak, he writes in C-flat. In his case it seems not to be a penchant for the black keys, but the first step in a larger design to go through all the keys. None of the music is written in his proposed new notation.

His first 'Hymnology' harmonizes a Mixolydian scale ☞, from G-flat to G-flat, ascending and descending, first with the scale in the treble, then in the bass. Six more sections follow, each a short musical phrase harmonized with the melody in the treble and then in the bass. Each is devoted to an interval with an enigmatic modifier: Tonal Seconds, Modal Thirds, Chronal Fourths, Verbal Fifths, Conjoined Sixths, and Amplexal Sevenths. The eighth section is 'Conjoined Degrees Continued' (again, a melody harmonized twice), and the ninth a similar but untitled example. The last, 'Transitive', uses an 8-note scale, G-flat to G-flat, with an added G-natural. Again, the ascending and descending scale is harmonized, first in the treble, then in the bass. FIG 2 p. 237

The function of the stated intervals is unclear, at least to me; the tunes certainly use them, but not systematically. Nor does he explain why seconds are tonal and thirds modal.

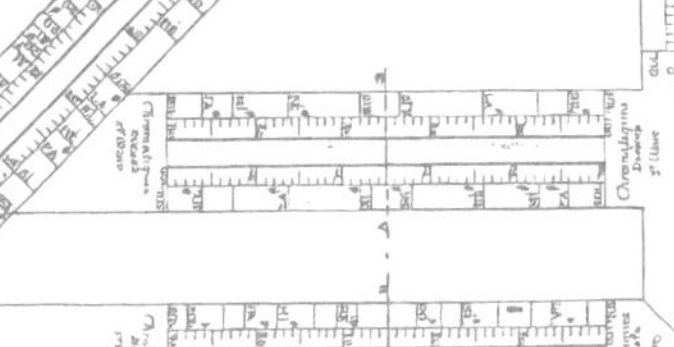

*Équerre Archéométrique*

He repeats these ten sections for the other six modes ☞, except for the scale starting on B-flat (the troublesome Locrian), which is only worked out in the 'transitive.' FIG 3 p. 238

Three more sections hint at his final design, which was to include non-diatonic scales. The first, 'First Verbal Series', uses a nine-note scale notated with flats: G, A-flat, B-flat, C-flat, C-natural, D, E-flat, F, and G-flat, which is harmonized starting on each note, except C-flat and G-flat. The next section, 'Physical Series', does the same for a nine-note scale notated with sharps: C, C-sharp, D, E, F, G, G-sharp, A, B, and C, which is harmonized on every note except C-sharp and G-sharp. The final section, 'Second Verbal Series', uses an eleven-note scale: a chromatic scale without D-flat, which is again harmonized, this time with A-flat and G-flat omitted.

All of this is based on his Archéometric standards. He counted the unison and the octave as two pitches, so for him the seven notes were eight, the nine were ten, and the eleven were twelve. He therefore had to omit one note from the standard chromatic scale to get the twelve pitches he needed for his network of correspondences.

The music itself is surprising in another way. Given his polemic against individuality, one might expect it to be conservative and severe. Instead, it's floridly Romantic, with Lisztian figurations and chromatic harmonies, and studded with expressive markings.

In 1901 and 1902, d'Alveydre published three piano pieces unrelated to the Archéomètre, all showing solid technique: 'Amrita', '*L'Étoile des Mages*', and 'Isola Bella'. He had obviously studied music seriously, but was compelled to rework music theory to fit his personal system.

It's hard to imagine how or where the *Archéomètre Musical* would be performed. It's essentially a private meditation, a combinatorial devotion like ringing changes on handbells, or like the algebraic volvelles of the Catalan visionary Ramon Lull. Like the Archéomètre itself, it's a personal diagram of the divine, fully accessible only to its creator.

Not all speculative musicians have pursued astronomical metaphors. Michael Maier's *Atalanta Fugiens* (*Atalanta Fleeing*, 1618) used music for alchemical allegory.

Maier was a baffling figure in many ways. He straddled the 16th and 17th centuries (1568–1622), and was variously a physician, alchemist, and apologist for the Rosicrucians, although he never claimed to be one. He was also a composer, and naturally combined that interest with his others.

It's always foolhardy to define alchemy. It began as simply chemistry, but by the 17th century had inspired a literary genre more interested in symbolism and metaphor than in the laboratory. Like other alchemical allegories, *Atalanta Fugiens* was based on mythology, in this case the story of Hippomenes and Atalanta: Hippomenes raced Atalanta to win her in marriage; Aphrodite gave him three golden apples to toss before her and delay her.

For Maier, Atalanta was mercury, Hippomenes sulfur, and the golden apple salt, those being the three principles of Paracelsian alchemy. I suppose this means that sulfur catches mercury by throwing out salt, although I don't know how that works, especially since Paracelsian mercury, sulfur, and salt are not the usual substances we know and love, but symbols for chemical forces.

He worked out his allegory in fifty chapters, each with a verse in Latin and German, a musical setting of the verse, an illustration, and a discourse.

He calls his settings 'fugues', thus making them metaphors for Hippomenes chasing Atalanta. They're actually brief canons, with Atalanta/mercury as counter-tenor, Hippomenes/sulfur following on tenor, and the golden apple as a ground in the bass. Counterpoint, mythology, and alchemical principles all symbolize one another, supplemented by the verse, illustration, and discourse. Who could ask for anything more?

The fifty canons call on all the tricks of imitative counterpoint, with the same bass ground in each. They are, to put it politely, of varying quality. Some are perfectly fine, others are filled with beginner's blunders, including tritone leaps and parallel fifths and octaves.

The explanation didn't come until 2015, when musicologist Loren Ludwig discovered that forty of Maier's canons were lifted from *The Divers and Sundry Waies of Two Parts in One Uppon One Playn Song*, a 1591 collection by the English madrigalist John Farmer. Maier simply changed some of the rhythms to fit his verses. The other ten, the odd-numbered ones from 1 to 19, were not taken from Farmer, and may have been Maier's own handiwork.

It's possible he didn't think it mattered. In speculative music, the metaphor is more important than the notes, and he may have simply filled out his scheme with the canons he had at hand. If he did write the remaining ten, we can wince at his mistakes, but the network of symbolism remains intact. He used a similar idea in his last work, *Cantilenae Intelectuales de Phoenice Redivivo* (Intellectual Songs of the Rebirth of the Phoenix), published shortly before his death in 1622. Again, there are three parts, the counter-tenor portraying Venus, the tenor a crab, and the bass a lion. But there's no music: the idea of the music is enough, and can be audiated as the reader likes.

Here is one of the *Atalanta Fugiens* canons not written by Farmer, with the original score, transcription in modern notation, and illustration: Fuga I. ☞

FIG 4
*p. 239–240*

As a coda, I'll mention a few pieces that are not strictly speculative, but do have hermetic associations. Many occultists have dabbled with music, like Ingres with his violin. Robert Fludd wrote some conventional pavans and allemands, innocent of monochords. Gurdjieff enjoyed noodling on the harmonium, as who doesn't, and his efforts were recorded and transcribed by his student Thomas De Hartmann; they're charming in their own way, but not flagrantly esoteric. The theatrical Satanist Anton LaVey claimed a history as carnival organist and strip show pianist, and recorded tunes like 'Satan Takes a Holiday'. It is, perhaps, of doctrinal significance that he identified the quintessential Satanic musician as Al Jolson.

The outstanding magical society of the Victorian occult revival, The Hermetic Order of the Golden Dawn, seems to have shunned music. Nevertheless, two of its leading lights, Florence Farr (*Sapientia Sapienti Dono Data*) and William Butler Yeats (*Demon Est Deus Inversus*), wrote songs together, although with only a tangential connection to magic. Both were inspired by the bardic tradition, or at least their own Celtic Twilight version of it, and developed a style of chanting verses that was not quite song. After trying harp, violin, piano, organ, and a one-string 'Montenegrin lute' (probably a gusle) as accompaniment, they contacted the luthier Arnold Dolmetsch. He made them a psaltery with 26 strings, a chromatic scale from G to G, with each note doubled at the octave. He also helped them with their settings.

*Excerpt from* Atalanta Fugiens ☞

Farr gave recitals with her psaltery, chanting poems by AE, Blake, Shelley, Swinburne, and Yeats, mostly to her own tunes, with a few by Yeats and Dolmetsch. Her nieces Dorothy and Helen Paget sometimes joined her on simpler Dolmetsch psalteries, as did Yeats. She apparently used the instrument to double her voice, rather than to add harmony. George Bernard Shaw, never one to mince invective, dismissed the entire enterprise as 'a nerve-destroying crooning like the maunderings of an idiot-banshee.' Unfortunately, she never recorded, and her psaltery now sits mute in the National Library of Ireland.

Here's one of Farr's chants, to Yeats's poem 'The Wind Blows out of the Gates of the Day'. ☞

Fig 5 p. 241

Some occult music remains doggedly occulted, although it may have been partly speculative. There is, for example, a curious little tune in *Magia Sexualis*, attributed to one of the more startling figures of the 19th century, the Black Spiritualist, doctor, abolitionist, and Rosicrucian Paschal Beverly Randolph. Among his activities were founding the Fraternitas Rosae Crucis in California, promoting sex magic, and, as we saw in Chapter III, touting the Davenports. The book survives only in a French translation published in 1931 by the Russian Satanist and magician Maria de Naglowska. Much of her text has been traced to other writings by Randolph, but the astrological parts may be hers alone.

In a chapter on astrological perfumes, colors, and sounds, she presents a 'magical melody' for enhancing magical operations. Like most speculative music, it's based on planetary correspondences. Although she provides pitches for the planets, the pitches in the tune are based, somehow, on a scale formed by ranking the planetary influences in a given horoscope. I'll add that the F-flat in the 17th measure is puzzling, since it's the same as the E-natural before and after it; it would make more sense if the melody were in bass clef, making it an A-flat. At any rate, here, with all its puzzles, is the only astrological sex magic tune I know. ☞

*Sex Magic tune*

I mentioned the Count of Saint Germain in Chapter II, since he was promoted to the rank of Venusian organist by Guy and Edna Ballard. He was, however, a real Earthling, and, at least early in his career, a musical one. He first attracted notice in London in 1745, as a violinist and

composer who kept his real identity secret. He then dazzled the court of Louis XV in the 1750s, by chatting in several languages and hinting he was older than he seemed. He was rumored to be an alchemist, a Rosicrucian, or the Wandering Jew.

In later years, he confessed himself the illegitimate son of Prince Francis Rákóczy of Transylvania, which is possible. He ended up living with Carl of Hesse-Kassel, where he tinkered with herbal remedies and dyes, and eventually died, probably in his 80s.

He had, however, created a legend, which kept fermenting after his death. Other people impersonated or imitated him, and he also became confused with other people named Saint Germain. By the 20th century, H. P. Blavatsky and her Theosophists had appropriated him as an Ascended Master, and Guy and Edna Ballard then transmuted him into an alien.

Nevertheless, he did actually write music: six trio sonatas, seven solos for violin, four English songs, and forty-two Italian arias. Fittingly, he was sometimes confused with a composer named Giovannini, who was, in turn, confused with J. S. Bach. One of Anna Magdalena Bach's notebooks contains an aria, '*Willst du dein Herz mir Schenken*?' ('Will you pour out your heart to me?'), marked as an aria by Giovannini, which some scholars assumed was a pet name for Johann.

I offer here one of the English songs, 'Gentle Love'. As a warning to musicologists, I mention that another English song, 'The Maid That's Made for Love', was misread by French biographer Paul Chacornac as 'The Maid That's Made for Dove', which he dutifully translated as *La servante changée en colombe* ('The servant girl changed into a dove'). ☞ FIG 6 *p. 242*

And, speaking of mistranslations, and doves, we now turn to the language of the birds.

notis musicis

Gallicinium

Cuculicu Cuculicu Cuculicu

A

Vox Cuculi

Gucu gucu gucu & gucu

E

Vox Coturnicis

Bikebik bike

D

# VI

# On the Language of the Birds

We share the earth not only with dubious ultraterrestrials, extraterrestrials, and ex-terrestrials, but with creatures of other species. Like all children of nature, we usually interact with them by slaughtering them, for food or recreation. But birds, those strange non-featherless bipeds, also inform and influence our music. Although many animals make sounds, we have always found birds the most musical.

The nightingale has long been our favorite songbird. Greek mythology gave it a repellent backstory. Tereus, the king of Thrace, raped his wife's sister, Philomela, and cut out her tongue. The wife, Procne, retaliated by serving Tereus his own son for dinner, at which Tereus tried to kill both her and Philomela. The gods finally stepped in and turned them all into birds, which we can only hope improved them. In Ovid's *Metamorphoses* (Book 6), Tereus became a hoopoe, Procne a swallow, and Philomela a nightingale. Other versions made Procne the nightingale. In either case, the birdsong is assumed to be sorrowful and female. In fact, only the male nightingale sings, probably either to attract a mate or defend his territory. Or so say human scientists, in the papers they publish to attract mates and defend their territories.

Perhaps we hear birdsong as musical because the discrete pitches remind us of our own singing, whereas the glissandi in other animal cries sound like our speech. Lucretius claimed that our singing began with attempts to imitate birds:

> Thro all the Woods they heard the charming noise
> Of chirping birds, and try'd to frame their voice,
> And *imitate*. Thus *Birds* instructed *Man*,
> And taught them *Songs*, before their *Art* began.

Whether Lucretius was correct or not (he was not infallible), we have a long and complicated history with both birdsong and imitation. For centuries, we've tried both to notate and learn it, and to teach birds our own speech and song. And, predictably, we've often been puzzled that their music isn't like ours.

The 16th century theologian Jean Bodin noted that birdsong sounds harmonious, but lacks the mathematical ratios we think are crucial:

> Also the most dissimilar songs of birds, blended by no ratio, produce a most pleasing delight for the ears. Plato thought it strange that no dissonance is perceived in the song of birds, however much it is joined with men's voices or lyres.

I have, by the way, failed to trace that bit of Plato. Maybe he was thinking of someone else.

Erik Satie satirized this attitude, again invoking the nightingale:

> As for the nightingale, always cited, its musical knowledge makes its most ignorant listeners shrug their shoulders. Not only is its voice improperly placed, but it has no understanding of either keys, tonality, modality, or tempo. Perhaps it has talent? It's possible; it's even certain. But we can affirm that its artistic education is unequal to its natural gifts, and that its voice, of which it is so proud, is only an instrument quite inferior and useless in itself.

The urge to mimic birds goes back to at least 6000 BCE, the presumed date of the earliest instrument found in China, the *gudi*, a vertical flute made from the wing bone of a red-crowned crane. Historians assume it was a game call.

Attempts to notate birdsong don't go back quite as far. As recently as 414 BCE, Aristophanes included a few in *The Birds*. He used the letters of the alphabet: the hoopoe sings 'Epopopoi popoi popopopoi popoi' and calls a flamingo with 'Torotix, torotix.' The hoopoe's name in Ancient Greek was *epops*, so its song was its own onomatopoeic name. The nightingale is represented not by language, but by music, either on the flute or the aulos. Since the hoopoe in the play is king Tereus, we already have a human actor portraying a bird that was once a man.

Unfortunately, Aristophanes didn't write out the nightingale part, and even his choice of instrument is disputed. Later notations used the standard Western system, with dots spotted on a staff. Since it was developed for diatonic tunes in duple meters, it's ideal for the tunes that we primates chant and march around to, but not for the microtones and irregular rhythms of birds. An early experiment was made by Athanasius Kircher, in his *Musurgia Universalis* in 1650. He wrote down the calls of a nightingale, cuckoo, cock, hen, and quail, as well as a parrot saying 'hello' in Ancient Greek. I cannot account for its refusal to quote Aristophanes. ☞ FIG 1 *p. 244*

Kircher was often maligned in later centuries for his effort, but he did take pains with the rhythms, even if the pitches were doomed to imprecision. His successors tried numerous combinations of letters and notes, with varying degrees of ingenuity and success. A few core samples will show their techniques.

The German naturalist Johann Matthäus Bechstein used Aristophanes's alphabetic approach in 1795. Here, to compare and contrast, is his version of the nightingale, which I recommend reading aloud:

Tiuu tiuu tiuu tiuu,
Spe tiu zqua,

Tio tio tio tio tio tio tio tix;
Qutio qutio qutio qutio,

Zquo zquo zquo zquo;
Tzü tzü tzü tzü tzü tzü tzü tzü tzü tzi,
Quorror tiu zqua pipiqui.
Zozozozozozozozozozozozo Zirrhading!
Tsisisi tsisisisisisisisi,
Zorre zorre zorre zorre hi;
Tzatn tzatn tzatn tzatn tzatn tzatn tzatn zi,
Dlo dlo dlo dlo dlo dlo dlo dlo dlo dlo
Quio tr rrrrrrrr itz.
Lü lü lü lü ly ly ly ly li li li li.
Quio didl li lülyli.
Ha gürr gürr qui quipio!
Qui qui qui qui qi qi qi qi gi gi gi gi;
Gollgollgollgoll gia hadadoi,
Quigi horr ha diadiadillsi!
Hezezezezezezezezezezezezezezezeze quarrhozehoi;

Quia quia quia quia quia quia quia quia ti:
Qi qi qi io io io ioioioio qi -
Lü ly li le lä la lö lo didl io quia,
Higaigaigaigaigaigaigai giagaigaigai
Quior ziozio pi.

The alphabetic approach has its limitations; we get the lyrics, but no melody.

The English composer William Gardiner returned to spots on the staff in a sprawling *Musurgia*-like miscellany from 1832, with the splendid title *The Music of Nature; Or, An Attempt to Prove that what is Passionate and Pleasing in the Art of Singing, Speaking, and Performing Upon Musical Instruments, is Derived from the Sounds of the Animated World.* He also enlarged on Lucretius by finding musical inspiration not only from birds, but from cattle, horses, tigers, dogs, elephants, sheep, pigs, and such human utterances as coughing, laughter, sighing, yawning, and the crying of infants, all of which he scrupulously notated. He was also unique in not always identifying his birds, sometimes simply tagging a tune as 'bird' or 'small bird.'

Gardiner's other musical activities included hymns, biography (*The Lives of Haydn and Mozart*, 1818), and the promotion of Beethoven in England. His 496 pages discussed not only bird and animal cries, but the anatomy of the ear, speech, notable singers, ornaments, dynamics, psalmody, national anthems, musical forms, London street cries, and much more. Despite his avowed interest in 'the animated world', he also transcribed a wheelbarrow and a stocking-frame.

Here's the song of the throstle as a sample of his handiwork. ☞ FIG 2 *p. 245*

Some of his ideas were echoed by Simeon Pease Cheney, a choir director and bird enthusiast who tramped through New England in search of birdsong, armed with music paper and a pitch pipe. After his death, his notes were edited by his son, John Vance Cheney, and published in 1892 as *Wood Notes Wild: Notations of Bird Music.*

Like Gardiner, the elder Cheney firmly believed that everything in nature is musical; he also insisted that it conforms to human music theory: 'The trombone blasts of the peacock are in melodic steps, the horse uses both the diatonic and chromatic scale, and the ass jerks out his frightful salute in perfect octaves.' He too transcribed other animals and objects; here's his rendition of water dripping into a bucket. ☞ FIG 3 p. 245

Birds, he was convinced, sing in major and minor scales, and he echoed Lucretius by finding the originals of human songs in birds, claiming he had heard a chewink warble 'Rock of Ages', and arguing that 'Old Dan Tucker' copied the clucking of a hen.

He noted his grandfather's alphabetic rendition of the bobolink, which sounds quaintly American compared to Bechstein's extravagant German:

Queer, queer, ker chube
Ker dingle-dongle swingle
Serangle kalamy kalamy
Whoa boys, whoa boys
Wicklemerlick wicklemerlick steeple
Steeple stoot steere
Queer queer temp, temp!

But he preferred musical notation, sometimes with lyrics. Here are his graphic innovations for the goldfinch, partridge, and screech owl. ☞ FIG 4 p. 246–247

Cheney assumed he was a pioneer, and acknowledged only a few precursors, including Bechstein. His son, who tactfully characterized his father as 'simple-hearted', was far more scholarly, and stuffed the second half of the book with copious notes from other naturalists and a 12-page bibliography. He added notations from ten of his father's predecessors, including Kircher and Gardiner.

Soon after the Cheneys came Charles A. Witchell, who not only wrote such works as *The Fauna and Flora of Gloucestershire* (1892), but a pastiche of Pope and a defense of eugenics. In *The Evolution of Bird-Song* (1906), he follows Cheney in adapting birdsong to classical notation. Some of his choices of meter are provocative: the cock crows in 3/16, the thrush sings in 9/8. ☞ FIG 5 p. 248

F. Schuyler Mathews mounted a more sustained assault on the problem in *Wild Birds and Their Music* in 1904. He was primarily a painter, best known for his illustrated field guides. For this book, he

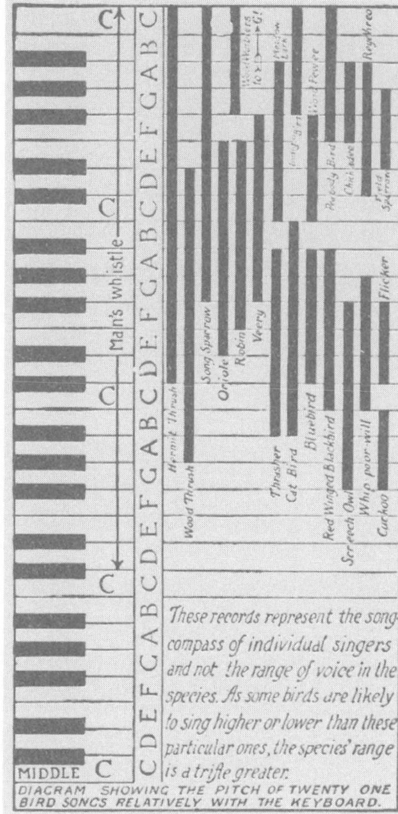


*Keyboard chart*

offered not only paintings of birds, but notations for the calls of 127 of them. ☞ He also composed piano accompaniments for many of them. Like the aulos, it was probably not the ideal instrument for birdsong, but he did recommend that the songs be whistled. And he did provide a helpful chart correlating birds to the keyboard.

FIG 6 *p. 249*

The ornithologist Hans Stadler and the composer Cornel Schmitt tried a fresh approach in their article 'The Study of Bird-Notes', in the January 1915 issue of *British Birds.* They proposed reducing the traditional staff to three lines, for C3, C4, and C6. Calls are to be written within the proper octave, but with only relative pitch. They explained that pitch was not only hard to pinpoint in the upper registers, but didn't correspond to the tempered scale. They also proposed three new markings: a note with a wavy line for a trill, a note with a line through it for a pitch with 'non-musical sounds', and a note canceled with an x for a non-pitched sound. They also suggested that researchers carry a set of eight small organ pipes to test the higher pitches. Cheney's simple pitch pipe was no longer sufficient. ☞

FIG 7 *p. 249*

One of the last in the field was Aretas A. Saunders, with his 1929 book *Bird Song.* Like Stadler and Schmitt, he gave only approximate pitches, relying on idiosyncratic graphic scores with lyrics. His method avoided the pitfalls of the tempered scale, but was still hobbled by our stubbornly non-phonetic alphabet. ☞

FIG 8 *p. 250–253*

Stadler and Schmitt had groused about having to write down birdsong at all. As they remarked,

> When once the phonograph, assisted by photographic registering, can be employed scientifically in the field of ornithology, we shall have birds sing from the apparatus with all the shades of timbre, tone, and sound, as we hear at present more or less good musical productions of our own species.

And in fact, recording soon made all the spots and squiggles obsolete. The first effort dates to 1889, when young Ludwig Koch cut a cylinder of an Indian Shama at the Frankfurt zoo. Not surprisingly, the first commercial disc featured the nightingale, marketed by Victor in 1910 as 'Song of a Nightingale, Made by a Captive Nightingale in the possession of Herr Reich, Bremen.' Records of birds became common, some compiling calls for birdwatchers, some adding human instrumental accompaniment to improve them. The vagaries of pen and ink were no longer needed.

The only thing more musical than birdsong to the human ear is a fellow human imitating it. Many of us are like the Emperor of China in Hans Christian Andersen's 1843 story *Nattergalen* (The Nightingale), who loses interest in the real bird when he receives a mechanical one.

Quoting birdsong in musical compositions started early. The cuckoo's two-note call was especially appealing to composers, since it was easy to notate and recognize. As early as the 13th century, singers were mimicking it, as we know from 'Sumer is icumen in', in which the cuccoo is urged to lhude sing. Nevertheless, those two pitches have seldom been the same. Giovanni Andrea Bontempi, a 17th century castrato, composer, and theorist, observed that the cuckoo sang a fourth in Italy, and in other countries a minor third, or, less often, a major third. It was the fourth that Bontempi himself used in his 'Bird Trio', which also has the peculiarity of quoting birdsong in the bass. ☞ FIG 9 *p. 251–253*

The cuckoo sings a major third in Beethoven's *Pastoral Symphony* and Saint-Saëns' *Carnival of the Animals*, and a minor third in the *Toy Symphony* attributed to Leopold Mozart. Cheney had objected to all of this, insisting that 'the cuckoo of New England never sings a third of any kind', adding that it usually stuck to one pitch, with an occasional minor second.

Both the nightingale and cuckoo appear in Clément Janequin's iconic 16th century choral number, *'Le Chant des oiseaux'*, as do the thrush and blackbird. His cuckoo sings not only a fourth, a major third, and a minor third, but a major second. Jean-Philippe Rameau, the long-suffering uncle of the troublesome nephew we admired in Chapter O, imitated a hen on the harpsichord in *'La Poule'.* Some composers have unlocked the whole aviary, most notably Boccherini, in his string quintet *L'Uccelliera*; Vivaldi stuck to the goldfinch in his flute concerto *Il Gardellino*.

Special mention must be made of Helen Phillips Eddy, for her 1919 collection *Tree Top Tunes for Tiny Tots*. She composed twenty brief songs based on bird calls, notating both pitch and lyrics. The oven-bird calls 'teacher, teacher', the robin 'cheer up!', the chickadee and phoebe announce their own names, and the owl and crow sound their traditional 'whoo' and 'caw.' Even the woodpecker is given a song, although the performer mimics it by singing 'tap, tippy, tap, tap', rather than knocking on wood. Here are the last two, the Maryland Yellowthroat ('witchery, witchery') and thrush ('eohlay!'). ☞

FIG 10
*p. 254–255*

Eddy's most illustrious disciple, at least in Europe, was Olivier Messiaen, whose musical cipher we examined in Chapter IV. Inspired by Saint Francis, he spent decades working birdsong into his pieces. One of the most ambitious is the *Catalogue d'oiseaux*, written from 1956 to 1958. His chosen instrument was the piano. Again, it may seem unsuitable, but not to Messiaen:

> Since the piano's register is extensive and its attack immediate, it is an excellent instrument for the mimicry — from the point of time as well as range — of the great bird virtuosos such as the woodlark, skylark, garden-warbler, blackcap, nightingale, song-thrush, sedge warbler, and reed-warbler.

Messiaen's technique is nothing if not idiosyncratic; quoting birds with loud dissonant piano chords and thundering bass notes would have baffled Kircher and upset Cheney.

The classical Chinese approach is more obviously mimetic. The preferred instrument is no longer the *gudi*, but the *dizi*, a small bamboo flute with a kazoo-like membrane, or the two-string fiddle, the *erhu*. The dizi does well with trills and piping; the erhu can chirp quite convincingly.

One of the standards of the erhu repertory, 'Birds Singing on a Deserted Mountain' *(Kōng Shān Niǎo Yǔ)*, certainly sounds like birds. It's one of only 14 pieces by the virtuoso Liu Tianhua, who died in 1932 at only 37. ☞ FIG 11 *p. 256–257*

We not only imitate birds by musical instruments, but, following the example of the birds themselves, with our unassisted anatomy. There has always been an audience for personable entertainers who mount the stage empty-handed and make animal noises. Although Joseph Pujol, *Le Pétomane*, the legendary 'fartiste' of the Moulin Rouge in the 1890s, reportedly imitated a cock, owl, bluebird, and duck, the usual orifice is the mouth.

Whistling was the favorite method. The first black recording star, George W. Johnson, whistled 'Listen to the Mockingbird' for Edison in 1896. The whistlers Sybil Sanderson Fagan, Margaret McKee, and Charles Kellogg all performed and recorded extensively.

But there were other methods. In the heyday of vaudeville, every ventriloquist was expected to round out his act with imitations of animals and musical instruments.

Robert Ganthony's manual *Practical Ventriloquism* offers some pointers for non-whistling birds. For cocks and parrots, he recommends the Punch voice. For ducks, he sensibly remarks, 'In imitating ducks you must not say "quack," because a duck, having no lips, does not say quack… use your mouth as a duck does its upper and lower bill, opening it as wide as you can and making the exaggerated action the bird does.'

Arthur Prince, in *The Whole Art of Ventriloquism*, gives a few others, like the hen: 'This is made through or by the top back of the throat, "Uck, uck, uck-er-ka". The last 'dek'ka' is harder than the beginning of the syllable.' And he adds, 'There are one or two other birds you can imitate, using the above methods, such as the crow (say "Caw-caw").'

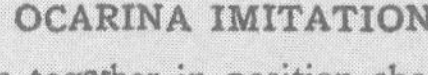

OCARINA IMITATION

Place hands together in position shown in accompanying cut, being careful to fit the right hand into the left, in order that the fingers of the left hand are en-

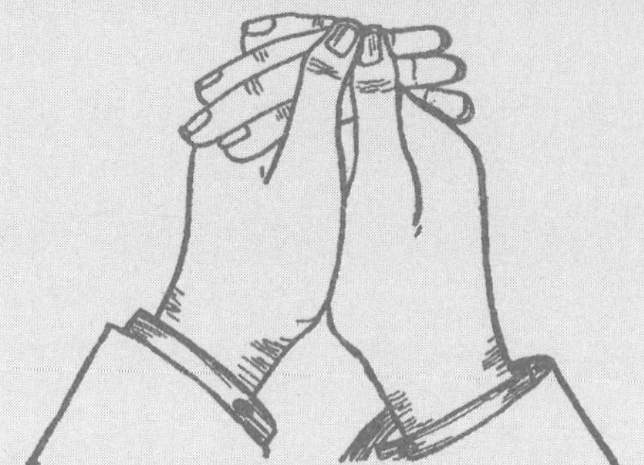

Position of Hands for Flute or Ocarina Imitation

tirely free, as they act on the same principle as the valves of a cornet. Allow the thumbs to fall naturally into position, with the nails just touching, causing an opening between the thumbs; then place lips over the thumb joints, being careful to leave opening under the lips, between the thumbs, to permit the sound to escape. By blowing into the cavity so formed you will accomplish the desired result. To ascend the scale, gradually move fingers of left hand outward; to descend, close them. A little practice will of course be required, in order to make each tone perfect.

*The hand ocarina*

George (Steamboat) Stewart, who earned his nickname for his rendition of a boat whistle, describes a technique for the canary in *The Stewart Simplified Method of Mimicry and Parlor Amusement:*

> To imitate the voice of the canary bird compress lips and draw air into left corner of mouth. Practice then will give you all the notes of the canary. To make effect louder, place left hand lightly over the opening between the lips. By varying the compression of the lips and the position of the hand, you accomplish imitations of the quail, sparrow, lark, kingfisher, snipe, and other varieties of birds.

He gives detailed instructions for another method, the 'hand whistle', for the dove and screech owl.

Stewart also tells us how to make a 'Ventrilo', which, oddly enough, has nothing to do with ventriloquism. You simply scraped away part of a leek leaf, leaving a thin membrane. You then soaked it in water, and blew it as a single reed. If you didn't want to scrape a leek, you

**Boys! Boys! Boys! Learn Ventriloquism and Apparently**

**THROW YOUR VOICE**

**Into a trunk, under the bed, under a table, back of the door, into a desk at school,** or anywhere. You get lots of fun fooling the teacher, policeman, peddlers, and surprise and fool all your friends besides.

**THE VENTRILO**

is a little instrument that fits in the mouth out of sight. Cannot be detected. It is used in connection with the above, and with the aid of this wonderful **DOUBLE THROAT or VENTRILO,** you can imitate many kinds of birds, animals, etc. Remember you get everything for only ten cents—the book which gives you instructions on how to become a Ventriloquist and the Double Throat or Ventrilo, besides.

**No. 3461. PRICE OF COMPLETE OUTFIT, ONLY........ 10c**

*Ventrilo Ad*

could buy a commercial Ventrilo, usually a piece of sausage casing mounted in a leather holder, and routinely pitched in tiny ads in comic books and pulp magazines.

A similar device, the swazzle, was long a trade secret of Punch and Judy professors, who routinely swallowed it in the pursuit of their art. Another variation is 'The Wonderful Double Throat of Swiss Warbler Bird Call, Only Original Bird Call and Prairie Whistle', which is still available. I have no idea what makes it Swiss.

The same type of free-beating reed is the basis of many game calls, including the duck, crow, and goose. Whistles serve for doves and curlews, as well as for the flocks of birds that inspire samba whistles in Brazil. A few tweaks to the design produce the tinamou, guam, dove,

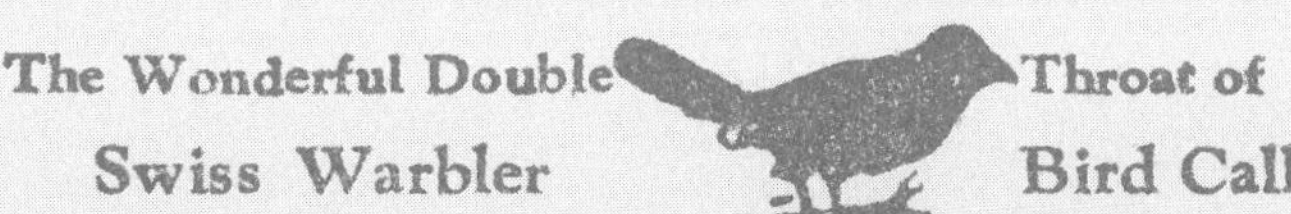


**Only Original Bird Call and Prairie Whistle**

*Direction For Use* — Soak in water until throughly saturated, then place on your tongue with read nearest the teeth and fimished side of leather upwards and hiss gently at first keep increasing the hiss for a lounder sound in giving imitations of Birds and Beasts, you make variations with the tongue and lips. Any person following these directions we will guarantee they can imitade any Bird or Animal in a few minute.

*Swiss Warbler*

and seed-eater. Some whistle calls also use water; New Yorkers may remember an elderly pitchman who used to demonstrate plastic water calls in Herald Square in the '90s. The outliers in the genre are the turkey call, which works by friction, either by scraping a wooden box, or rubbing glass or slate with a stick, and the Audubon Bird Call, which uses a rod of rosined pewter inside a wooden cylinder.

Thanks to recent technology, the British artist Marcus Coates was able to attain the ideal of bird imitation, after all those centuries of approximation. For his 2007 video work *Dawn Chorus*, he recorded bird songs, slowed them down to the range of the human voice, and then taught them to singers. When filmed and sped up, the singers trilled and chirped with remarkable fidelity.

We also turn the tables on all this mimicry by training birds to imitate us. Human hubris inspired a catalogue of tune-books that teach birds how to whistle properly. The determined bird keeper sat before the cage with a miniature recorder called a bird flageolet, and repeated the tunes until his student obeyed.

*The Bird-Fancyer's Delight*, published by both Richard Meares and John Walsh in 1717, gave tunes for the bullfinch, canary, linnet, woodlark, skylark, starling, parrot, sparrow, mynah, and throstle. And, despite the accolades for the nightingale that punctuate this chapter, two tunes are even supplied for its improvement. ☞ FIG 12 *p. 258*

Mozart, too, owned birds; his letters to his sister Nannerl ask about their various canaries, tomtits, and robins. On May 27, 1784, he bought a starling, and proudly noted a scrap of melody it could whistle, adding 'It was beautiful!' The little tune has puzzled Mozartologists, because it resembles the theme of the third movement of his Piano Concerto No. 17 in G, K. 453. The concerto was finished on April 12 and first performed on June 13, so it's likely he taught the bird the theme in the interim. However, it's also possible that the bird taught it to him, either in the shop before he finally broke down and paid 34 kreutzer for it, or before the premiere. Whatever the case, the starling sang a G sharp in the second measure, and Mozart used a G natural. We have no way of knowing if Mozart corrected the starling, or it corrected him. ☞ FIG 13 *p. 258*

We also have a compulsion to teach birds to talk. Several birds mimic speech, including the mynah, the starling, the parakeet, and the aptly named mockingbird.

Perhaps the most famous was Charles Dickens's raven Grip, whom he wrote into *Barnaby Rudge*, and who inspired Poe's poem 'The Raven'. We can only regret that Poe opted for the portentous 'Nevermore', rather than Grip's favorite expression, 'Halloa old girl.'

The parrot, though, is our favorite student. One of the side effects of this is our compulsion to imitate parrots imitating us. Illustrious parrotists include Vivian Stanshall ('Mr. Slater's Parrot') and Dr. Horatio Q. Birdbath (Purv Pullen), who mimicked parrots and other birds for Spike Jones. Pullen also voiced the animatronic parrot Pierre in the Tiki Room at Disneyland, which would have enraptured Andersen's Emperor; as the show has been updated, other voice artists have imitated Dr. Birdbath's imitation. In 1859, the idiosyncratic composer Charles-Valentin Alkan wrote a funeral march for a parrot, *Marcia funèbre, Sulla morte d'un Pappagallo*. Four vocalists sing '*As-tu déjeuné Jacquot? Et de quoi?*' (Did you have lunch, Jacquot? And what was it?), the equivalent of 'Polly want a cracker', but Alkan did not specify the parrot's distinctive timbre. Alkan's idea may be unique, although Georg Philipp Telemann and Lord Berners both wrote funeral marches for canaries: the former, *'Cantate oder Trauer-Musik eines kunsterfahrenen Canarien-Vogels, als derselbe zum größten Leiwesen seines Herrn Possesseris verstorben'* (Cantata of Funeral Music for an Artistically Trained Canary-Bird Whose Demise Brought the Greatest Sorrow to His Master Possessoris), 1732; the latter, the second of his *'Trois Petites Marches Funèbres'* (Three Little Funeral Marches), 1914.

The other side effect is a backlog of jokes about talking parrots. Just as we puzzle over birds that spin out melodies without theory, we're confounded by parrots that talk without knowing what they say. We assume that when a parrot says 'Hello' (or, in Kircher's case, 'Khaire') it means 'Hello.' A common trope is a parrot that innocently says something dirty, usually learned from a former owner. The fullest flowering of the conceit may be Jean-Baptiste-Louis Gresset's 1734 poem *'Ver-Vert'*, a thirty-page epic about a parrot who shocks a convent by swearing like a sailor. The usual variation is a parrot that understands what it's saying, but, like Saki's talking cat Tobermory, ignores human discretion. This generated many jokes in which a recently acquired parrot recognizes the husband or wife from its former life in a whorehouse (in the fantasy world of jokelore, all brothels have parrots), or insults the guests. Perhaps its greatest iteration is John Skelton's poem 'Speke Parrot', c. 1521, in which the titular bird apparently has the license to say rude things about Cardinal Wolsey.

In a category of its own is Claude Sosthène Grasset d'Orcet's 1888 story *Le Perroquet virtuose* (The Virtuoso Parrot), in which a parrot hides in the prompter's box to sing opera.

Some bird lovers have also treated the calls as language, and tried to master it. According to legend, Melampus, Aesop, Anaximander, and Apollonius of Tyana all spoke with birds. Pliny cited Democritus's claim that serpents can be generated from birds' blood, and that eating the serpent reveals the birds' language.

Other linguists tried other methods. One of the most persistent was Pierre Samuel du Pont de Nemours, who in 1807 compiled a lexicon of the crows. Here's a sample:

> I will probably see some of my respectable colleagues, and those I hold most dear, smile at what I have to say about the dialogues of the crows, of which they know only a rather unpleasant cry.

I wanted to live with them in the fields, to enlighten myself by their lights, and also to study them far from the village, in a rough shelter, quite immobile, quite silent, my eye watchful, my ear attentive, a pencil and a little white book in hand, neither crows nor other animals fear books... It is a long labor. Crows cost me two winters, and cold hands and feet. This is what I have collected of their cry, which is thought to be always the same, when heard infrequently and distractedly.

> Cra, Cré, Cro, Crou, Crouou
> Grass, Gress, Gross, Grouss, Grououss
> Craé, Créa, Croa, Croua, Grouass
> Crao, Créé, Croé, Croué, Groues
> Craou, Créo, Croo, Crouo, Grouoss

> There are twenty-five words, their similarity is quite grammatical... Their twenty-five words are enough to express 'here, there, right, left, forward, stop, food, warning, man with gun, cold, hot, leave, I love you, me too, nest', and ten or so others that they can draw upon according to their needs.

They are quite reasonable and educated about what concerns them. The reason and education of man are more valuable.

A little later (1888), Charles Frederick Holder wrote a brief 'dictionary of the domestic fowl language':

> *Ur-ka-do-dle-do-o-o.* Challenge of male.
> *Tuck, tuck, tuck.* Food call of male.
> *K-a-r-r-e.* Announcing presence of hawk.
> *Cut, cut, ca-da-cut.* Announcement of egg-laying.
> *Cluck, cluck, cluck.* Call of young.
> *Kerr, kerr, kerr.* Song of contentment of hen.
> *C-r-a-w-z-z-e.* Quieting young chicks.
> *W-h-o-o-i-e* (whistle). Expression of apprehension at night.
> *C-r-a-i-a-i-o-u.* Terror and protest at capture.

The pragmatic vocabulary of crows and chickens was excluded from the 'language of the birds' expounded by some French occultists. It was described by the aforementioned Claude Sosthène Grasset d'Orcet, in a series of articles in *La Revue Britannique* and *La Nouvelle Revue*, and adopted by the pseudonymous alchemist Fulcanelli and his followers, principally Eugène Canseliet. D'Orcet defined it as a phonetic cabala that hides correspondences and multiple meanings in puns, rebuses, and anagrams. He found it in the Latin poetry of the medieval Goliards, in Rabelais, and in later Rosicrucians and Freemasons. It was called 'the language of the birds' from the Ringing Island in Rabelais's apocryphal Fifth Book, where Pantagruel visited a community of birds ruled by a parrot. D'Orcet thought the Fifth Book was written by or for Henri II's mistress, Diane de Poitiers, and symbolized a secret society of Goliards, with the parrot, the *papegault*, a Goliard pope. The secrets of alchemy, the Golden Fleece Jason sought in the Argo, were encrypted in Goliard poetry (*art gault)*, Gothic cathedrals (*art goth*), and the slang and jargon of artisans (*argot*). The unwritten language, the language of song, is the key to nature. To *résonner* (echo, resonate) is to *raisonner* (reason).

The same principle led Raymond Roussel, whose imaginary instruments we audiated in Chapter 0, to use puns to suggest plots and images. Inevitably, he was rumored either to know Fulcanelli or to belong to a group that wrote the works collectively, and a dubious acrostic of d'Orcet (dubious because it's actually d'Oncet) was even unearthed in his poem '*La Meule*' (The Millstone).

Jean-Pierre Brisset, a railroad employee and language teacher who became a favorite of the Surrealists, took punning in a different direction. As he said in his 1900 flyer *La Grande Nouvelle* (The Great News): 'All ideas that can be expressed with the same sound, or a sequence of similar sounds, have the same origin and present a certain connection between them, more or less evident, about things that have always existed or have previously existed in a continuous or accidental manner.'

He credited these connections to frogs, rather than birds, since humans had evolved from frogs, and our language had developed from theirs. Our *prêtres* (priests) were the frogs' *pré-êtres* (meadow creatures).

Frogs inspire our music less than birds, despite the fact that Aristophanes also pioneered transcriptions of them. Darwin, in *The Expression of Emotion in Man and Animals*, argued that the gibbon was one of the most musical animals: 'An ape, one of the Gibbons, produces an exact octave of musical sounds, ascending and descending the scale by half-tones; so that this monkey alone of brute mammals may be said to sing.'

More recently, zoologists have slowed down recordings of mice, as Marcus Coates did with birds, and found them just as complex. Sadly, this discovery blunts the premise of Kafka's singing mouse Josephine, but does suggest that future research may further blur distinctions between the music of humans and other animals.

In the heyday of 19th-century transcription outlined above, many researchers followed William Gardiner in writing non-avian animal cries. Here, from 1887, are Dr. F. Weber's notations of the wind, a cow, a dog, a donkey, and a cat. ☞ FIG 14 *p. 259*

And from 1891, an insect concert from Anna Hinrichs. ☞ FIG 15 *p. 260*

None of these has particularly inspired composers. In recent years, the nightingale's prime contender has been the whale. In the late 1960s, biologists Scott McVay and Roger Payne started recording them, and in 1970 released an LP, *Songs of the Humpback Whale*. Latter-day Janequins promptly appropriated whalesong. George Crumb imitated whales on flute, cello, and piano (*Vox Balaenae*, 1971); Alan Hovhaness wrote an orchestral accompaniment for them (*And God Created Great Whales*, 1970).

However, whales may have inspired human music long before that. In the Blasket Islands, off Ireland, 19th century sailors sometimes heard eerie music floating over the waves. Naturally, they assumed it came from fairies or spirits. Just as naturally, they learned it, and turned it into a traditional tune called *'Port na bPúcai'*, 'The Song of the Spirits'. After whale recordings became available, some listeners recognized the melody in a song by a humpback whale. ☞ FIG 16 *p. 261*

So, the same tune was interpreted variously as the song of ultraterrestrials, ex-terrestrials, or aquaterrestrials. Natural sounds may also explain some of the music in earlier chapters, although whales probably didn't dance at night on Irish meadows.

The fairy music Morgan Gwillim heard at Cylepsta Waterfall might have been birdsong, strained through his cultural filters. It's also possible that it was another non-human sound. In 1881, the organist Eugene Thayer heard music in the roar of Niagara Falls, and notated it as the harmonic series based on G, although, curiously, he omitted a partial. If Gwillim heard what Thayer did, he may have picked out some of the higher overtones. A background in organ pipes or in Welsh fairylore may determine what one hears in the white noise of rushing water. ☞ FIG 17 *p. 262*

# VII

# On Music From Dreams

Some of the music in the preceding chapters might have originated in dreams. Celestial hymns could have drifted through those impressionable states that bookend sleep, the hypnagogic while dozing off, or the hypnopompic while waking. In many of the reports in Chapter I, witnesses meet their ultraterrestrials late at night, or while napping. Our brains can generate sounds and images so vivid that they seem real, especially when provoked by suggestions from outside, like rain, running water, or birdsong. Sleep deprivation and carbon monoxide poisoning can also trigger powerful hallucinations. I confess myself baffled by the evolutionary advantage of this.

Seasoned anomalists have read their Sextus Empiricus and Bishop Berkeley, and appreciate the folly of separating subjective impressions and objective reality. The 1972 Philip experiment, in which a group of investigators in Toronto invented a spirit and then summoned him in séances, is a case in point. Aleister Crowley fretted over whether the hobgoblins he materialized came to him from within or without. But it doesn't matter here; witnesses still report music they didn't consciously create, whatever its origin.

To my surprise, there has been little study of music in dreams. One of the few surveys I've found was conducted by Valeria Uga of the University of Florence in 2006. She wanted to find out if musicians dream about music more than non-musicians. She found that 'musicians dream of music more than twice as much as non-musicians... Nearly half of all recalled music was non-standard, suggesting that original music can be created in dreams.'

The paucity of the literature may be due to music's unusual characteristics. Dreams have been interpreted in many ways throughout history: as prophecy, religious epiphany, allegory, or irrelevant nonsense. Freud argued they were wish fulfillment, in his *Interpretation of Dreams.*

Music doesn't fit any of these explanations, since, to cite Stravinsky again, it's too stupid. It can prophesy nothing but more music, is not religious in itself, is (Maier notwithstanding) unsuitable for allegory, and makes its own kind of sense. Nor does it fit into Freud's schema, unless the dreamer wants to hear a specific tune. But then, Freud was famously averse to music, barring it from his home, and covering his ears if he heard it in public. Perhaps if his parents had sprung for piano lessons he would have turned out better.

Many of us dream about what we did when awake. Freud himself analyzed his own dreams of examining patients, Niels Bohr dreamed of atoms, Jack Nicklaus corrected his golf swing.

So, not surprisingly, musicians dream about music. Their brains keep working after hours, reviewing and recombining the music they made in the day.

Valeria Uga's finding that nearly half of recalled music is 'non-standard' may need a footnote. Non-musicians may not realize how much of common-practice composition entails reshuffling and varying prior material. The symphonies of Haydn and Mozart were not written from the ground up, but within established four-movement patterns, with tonal, harmonic, melodic and instrumental conventions. All blues songs use the same chord sequence, with occasional variations. The popular music of a given time and place can be so generic that it's hard to tell one song from another, and it takes a dedicated specialist to identify a given Irish fiddle or Chinese guzheng tune. And even if composers are avoiding established genres, their work will be based on their own earlier pieces. The dream state, by reshuffling and varying memories and impressions, sometimes just continues the process.

Many pieces have been composed about dreams. The idea was popular enough in Renaissance England for Robert Fludd to write a trio called 'Robert Fludd's Dreame', and Giles Farnaby to write 'Giles Farnaby's Dreame' for the virginals. Later additions to the Western concert repertory were more explicitly drowsy: Schumann's *'Träumerei'*, Liszt's *'Liebesträume'*, Fauré's *'Après un rêve'*, Debussy's *'Rêverie'*, and John Cage's 'Dream.' By the late 19th century, songs about dreams had become so popular that Harry Dacre (or, to give him his real name, Frank Dean) parodied them in his 1891 'humorous ditty with waltz chorus', 'I Dreamt That I Was Dreaming.' Although Dacre wrote such hits as 'Bicycle Built for Two', this number never caught on. It's never too late, though, so here it is, salvaged from oblivion. ☞

FIG 1
*p. 264–266*

None of these, to my knowledge, was drawn from an actual dream. But many musicians have claimed direct inspiration. One of the best-known specimens is Giuseppe Tartini's *Devil's Trill Sonata*, inspired by a dream he had in 1713. The devil appeared before him, and sawed diabolically on the violin. When Tartini awoke, he tried to write it down, but admitted that his rendition was only approximate.

George Antheil was also disappointed when he tried to recapture his dream music. As he later recalled:

> I found myself walking along a pathway of small residential buildings. Out of each of them, came the music of a symphony orchestra playing—my music! But it was not music similar to anything I had written or, indeed, to anything I had known... I woke up, and as I have a very retentive, almost 'photographic' ear, I immediately snatched a piece of blank music paper and, for the next two hours, wrestled with the problem of getting down as many fragments of the music as I could remember. These, as I discovered the following morning, were very unsatisfactory; they were but chords, pieces of melodies, a few rhythms I had never heard awake, and some rapid orchestral sketches.

He added that several of his pieces, including *Airplane Sonata*, *Sonata Sauvage*, *Death of the Machine*, and *Mechanisms*, were based on those elusive scraps.

Stravinsky's *Sacre du Printemps* was also sparked by a dream, but not a musical one. He wrote that he saw a young woman dancing herself to death before a group of elders, as a sacrifice to spring. However, he also claimed more explicitly musical dreams: portions of *L'Histoire du Soldat* were taken from a gypsy fiddler he heard in a dream.

In the last chapter, I mentioned the collaborations between W. B. Yeats, Florence Farr, and Arnold Dolmetsch, so let me add the contributions of Maud Gonne. Fittingly, she enters this chapter for her participation in the play *Cathleen Ni Houlihan*, by Yeats and Lady Gregory, which Yeats said was inspired by a dream. Gonne played the Old Woman, and chanted a few of Yeats's verses. In Volume Four of the Shakespeare Head edition of his works, Yeats writes, 'The tune beginning "Do not make a great keening" and "They shall be remembered for ever" are said or sung to an air heard by one of the players in a dream.' However, in Volume Three, he attributes them to Florence Farr, who was not in that play. Whether dreamed by Gonne or Farr, they were apparently dreamed, so here they are. ☞ Fig 2 p. 267

Commercial pop music provides more examples. Luckily for our topic, we can cite one of the most familiar, Paul McCartney's 'Yesterday'. McCartney often told how he dreamed the tune, and then, when he woke up, gave it the placeholder lyrics, 'Scrambled eggs, oh you've got such lovely legs', or, in another version, 'Scrambled eggs, oh my baby how I love your legs.' Unlike some of the composers above, he remembered the tune; also unlike some of them, he assumed it wasn't his own, but that his brain was offering unconscious plagiarism. Once assured that nobody recognized it, he tinkered with it awhile before recording it, adding blander lyrics, and, perhaps, changing the melody as well. He claimed another song, 'No Values', also came to him in a dream. Again, he assumed he was remembering what someone else had written; in the dream, it was played by the Rolling Stones.

Other songs inspired by dreams include Prince's 'Purple Rain' and Sting's 'Every Breath You Take'. For Prince, the inspiration was an image of purple haze, and for Sting the title. Neither claimed he dreamed the music.

One potentially useful approach to this subject is to analyze the music from my own dreams. I apologize; nobody is more sickened by the current narcissistic obsession with memoirs and monologues that is the bitter fruit of the weed of anti-intellectualism than I. But because I was the one who heard it, I can examine it more closely.

I've observed a few things about it. One is that I experience it differently if I hear it or if I play it. In some dreams, I've heard music that I don't recognize, playing from a radio. I listen with interest, sometimes disappointed that I can't preserve it. In some cases, the music is mine — not music I actually wrote when awake, but mine in the narrative of the dream.

In one dream, I found an LP of some orchestral music I had written in high school. I did spend much of my troublesome teen years writing music, and did write pieces for the school orchestra. And my proud parents did record my first attempts at orchestration as they sat in the auditorium. The tapes didn't survive, but that may be the backstory for the dream. I don't think the music on the record was one of the pieces I wrote, though.

In another dream, I was preparing some music I had written in my student days for performance by a student orchestra in the present. I saw the score, but, again, didn't recognize it.

In both cases, I didn't remember the music when I woke up. I only remember music when I'm playing it. I've also noticed that the music itself, although it seems mine at the time, is usually a distorted memory of something I already know. Sometimes I can trace it to pieces by other people, sometimes to my own.

In the first example below, I was performing outdoors, with other performers, in a sort of improvisatory happening that traveled through the countryside. I mention as an aside that this doesn't match any show I've done. As I trudged down a path and over a small hill, I sang the word 'Gargantua' to this four-note phrase. I held the last note as long as I could, then fell face forward — not because I was exhausted, but because it was part of the show. Other performers walked past me as I lay there, and who can blame them.

When I woke up, I remembered the phrase. I had seen a poster in the subway for the Ringling Brothers Circus, reproducing an old one for a gorilla named Gargantua. I assumed that was what provoked the word. The music seemed familiar, but I didn't recognize it. Months later, I realized that it was a distorted recollection of the final phrase of Charles Ives's song 'Grantchester', a 1920 setting of Rupert Brooke, which I'd read through in the privacy of my studio. My sleeping brain had changed Ives's octave to a ninth, and rewrote 'In Grantchester' as 'Gargantua'. Neither was an improvement.

In the second example, I sang this tune as I pushed two carts, loaded with my possessions, down a street. The street was deserted, and I was lost. The words for the first two measures were 'Winnow the tale, winnow the goose bump.' I have no idea what they mean. 'Tail' might make slightly more sense, but it was definitely 'tale.' I think the words were probably repeated for measures 3 and 4, 9 and 10, and 11 and 12, but I can't be sure. I don't remember any other words.

The scenario may have derived from an 1897 painting by Grass-Mick, showing Erik Satie moving his furniture through the streets of Paris, reproduced in a book I have. In the painting, though, the street is full of people, and his friends are helping him.

I kept repeating the tune in my head as I woke up, revising and remembering it. The final drop to the minor felt quite momentous in that state, like a plunge from a cliff. The tune doesn't remind me of any I already knew, although there may be one locked in my head somewhere.

In the third example, I played these four measures on a toy piano onstage, as part of a show. No doubt the show in question was *The Harlequin Studies* by Bill Irwin, for which I wrote the music, and which had a run at the Signature Theater in NYC in 2003. I did use a toy piano briefly in the score, and some of the other performers appeared in the dream. For some reason, my sleeping brain revisited it five years later. The music in the dream, following the usual drill, was not from the real show. Again, I repeated it and reworked it in my head as I woke up.

In the fourth example, I had written a piano piece based on this repeated quartal phrase. However, it was not in standard notation; each note was represented by a color cartoon of a monkey, against a bright orange background. I showed it to a pianist, and explained that I could easily rewrite it in conventional notation, but thought it was more fun to look at like that.

Again, I think I can identify the ingredients. The music is reminiscent of a dance score I wrote for the choreographer Virginia Mathews, back in San Francisco in 1978. The monkeys on the orange background remind me of two old children's card games I have: one with pictures of monkeys, and one with cowboys and cattle against a vivid orange background. The idea of using a children's card game springs, I suspect, from an anthology of Cornelius Cardew's 'Scratch Music'. One of Christopher May's graphic scores consists of four cards from a children's game. These unrelated bits were mixed together by my sleeping brain, which apparently had nothing better to do.

In the fifth example, I woke up with this fragment, complete with words, running through my head. I didn't recognize it, so I expanded it and used it in a string quartet.

The sixth example also became lodged in my head equipped with lyrics. The tune reminds me of the brief last movement of John Cage's Suite for Toy Piano. Perhaps toy pianos are particularly appealing to my dream mechanism. The phrase 'at the gasoline station' is probably lifted from the old Tampa Red song 'Ducks Yas Yas': 'Down on Morgan there's a good location, right there next to a gasoline station.' I've used this song teaching ukulele classes, despite students' complaints about the bar chords, so it's lodged in my memory, ready to pop out when not invited.

I've also had dreams in which I play instruments that I can't play when awake. I once dreamed I played trombone, which I must admit inspired me to buy a used one and start practicing lip slurs. I also dreamed that I played the double bass. In that case, I later recognized the music as bits of the 'cello part of a string quartet I was writing. I don't play the 'cello much anymore (the days just fly by at my age), but I do visualize the hand positions when writing double stops, to make sure they're feasible. I probably recycled those mental images in the dream. ☞

FIG 3
*p. 268–269*

# AFTERWORD

As you sink into a fitful doze, with the snippets of my dream tunes fading into your own, let me murmur a few closing remarks.

As I said at the outset, I've collected this material for years, and have occasionally presented it in concerts and lectures. Reactions have been varied, but all too often rooted in belief: the crucial point for many listeners is whether the music is paranormal or not, so they can decide whether to upbraid me for being too skeptical or too credulous.

I try to stress that music need not be paranormal to be abnormal. A piece of 'music from elsewhere' may in fact come from inside the human brain, but not in the usual way. All 'normal' music is written for human motivations: to make money, to be fashionable, to trigger emotions, to shock mommy and daddy, to show off, to conform, to compete. It's contaminated with the whole catalogue of human faults.

Music that seems to come from other sources, whether it does or not, and whether it's paranormal or not, often escapes all that. It's fundamentally disinterested; it simply arrives, ringing through the air, unsummoned and uncalculated. That gives it a certain *quidditas*, a whatness, to cite Joyce famously citing Aquinas. A few notes heard in a waterfall may not be musically arresting, but their lack of human intention sets them apart from other strings of pitches.

I started gathering this material because I like music and enjoy the unusual. After all, beauty is always bizarre, to bring in Baudelaire. As I discovered, though, and as this collection shows, 'music from elsewhere' is surprisingly common. People have been hearing it for centuries. It may have piquant touches of the bizarre here and there, but for me its most appealing quality is that it's anti-social. It wasn't made for other people; it has no place in society, and it's usually bracingly uncommercial.

Listen! My, what a welcome change!

# NOTES AND FURTHER READING

## INTRODUCTION

Charles Fort's letter to Theodore Dreiser is quoted in *Charles Fort: The Man who Invented the Supernatural*, by Jim Steinmeyer, Jeremy P. Tarcher, NY, 2008, p. 195.

'Ella Ree' is discussed in *American Folk Songs: A Regional Encyclopedia*, by Norm Cohen, Greenwood Press, Westport, CN, 2008, Vol. 1, pp. 266–267, and in the *Traditional Ballad Index*, by Robert B. Waltz and David G. Engle, online at fresnostate.edu.

The quotation from Theodore Dreiser is from 'My Brother Paul', originally the third chapter of *Twelve Men* (Boni and Liveright, NY, 1919), reprinted in Haldeman-Julius Little Blue Book 660, *My Brother Paul, and W. L. S.* (c. 1924), and revised as the preface to *The Songs of Paul Dresser* (Boni and Liveright, NY, 1927).

'Ella Ree' is from the online collection of the Library of Congress.

'Juanita' is from the *New York State College Songbook*, John Worley Company, Boston, MA, 1917.

'On the Banks of the Wabash, Far Away' is from *The Songs of Paul Dresser.*

## CHAPTER ZERO

The most comprehensive work I know about blank and silent works, musical and otherwise, is *No Medium*, Craig Dworkin, MIT Press, Cambridge, MA, 2013. I also recommend Kyle Gann's delightful and exhaustive study of John Cage's *4'33"*, *No Such Thing as Silence*, Yale University Press, New Haven and London, 2010.

Alphonse Allais's contributions to the Arts Incohérents are documented in *Alphonse Allais*, François Caradec, Belfond, Paris, 1994, pp. 427–434. The *Album Primo-Avrilesque* is reprinted in the fifth volume of Allais's complete works, *Œuvres Posthumes II*, La Table Ronde, Paris, 1966. I reproduce here the one-page edition of the *Marche funèbre*, p. 381. I've translated several of Allais's books for Black Scat Books, for the benefit of anglophones.

Erwin Schulhoff's *'Fünf Pittoresken'* were published by Jatho Verlag, Berlin, n. d.

Yves Klein's score for *'Symphonie-Monoton-Silence'* is posted at yvesklein.com.

Mike Batt's confession that the Peters lawsuit was a publicity stunt was reported in the BBC News article 'Wombles composer Mike Batt's silence legal row 'a great scam'' on Dec. 8, 2010.

The Divje Babe flute is proudly defended at www.divje-babe.si.

The Hohle Fels flute is displayed at the Urgeschichtliches Museum in Blaubeuren: www.urmu.de.

Suzanne Haïk-Vantoura's *La musique de la Bible révelée* was published in 1976 by Dessain et Tolra, Paris, and was followed by numerous revisions, scores, and recordings. An English edition, *The Music of the Bible Revealed*, translated by Dennis Weber and edited by John Wheeler, was published by BIBAL Press, North Richland Hills, TX, 1991.

I quote Marsilio Ficino from Charles Boer's translation of *De Vita Triplici: The Book of Life*, Spring Publications, University of Dallas, Irving, TX, 1980. There is also much ado about Ficino's music in *Spiritual and Demonic Magic from Ficino to Campanella*, D. P. Walker, Pennsylvania University Press, University Park, PA, 2000, Chapter 1, and in *Music in Renaissance*

*Magic*, Gary Tomlinson, University of Chicago Press, Chicago and London, 1993, Chapter 4.

Leonardo da Vinci's performances and musical inventions are documented in many places; the most comprehensive is *Leonardo da Vinci as a Musician*, Emanuel Winternitz, Yale University Press, New Haven and London, 1982.

Jean-François Rameau's lost harpsichord collection is documented in *Rameau le Neveu: Textes et documents*, edited by André Magnan, CNRS Éditions, 1993, pp. 75–86, 89–90, 168.

Robert Benchley's essay 'Mind's Eye Trouble' appeared in *Bookman* 72, Dec. 1930, and was reprinted in *No Poems, or Around the World Backwards and Sideways*, Harper & Brothers, NY, 1932, pp. 234–244.

Alphonse Allais's story *Dressage* was first published in *Le Journal*, March 3, 1894, and reprinted in no fewer than three collections: *2 + 2 = 5* (Paul Ollendorff, Paris, 1895), *On n'est pas des bœufs* (Ollendorff, 1896), and *Le Captain Cap* (Félix Juven, Paris, 1902). My translation of *Captain Cap* was published by Black Scat Books in 2013.

Satie's cephalophones can be found in his *Écrits*, edited by Ornella Volta, Éditions Champ Libre, Paris, 1981, p. 187.

The theatrical version of Raymond Roussel's *Impressions d'Afrique* is discussed in *Raymond Roussel*, François Caradec, Fayard, Paris, 1997, pp. 135–139 and 149–157, and in *Raymond Roussel and the Republic of Dreams*, Mark Ford, Cornell University Press, Ithaca, NY, 2001, pp. 114–117 and 118–120. The surviving script is published in Roussel's *Œuvres Théâtrales*, edited by Annie Le Brun and Patrick Besnier, Pauvert/Fayard, Paris, 2013, pp. 21–171.

The version of *Quan Lou Bouyé* I transcribe here is from the collection *La Chanson du pays*, Imprimerie Nationale, Paris, 1953.

*A Chantar* is taken from partitionsdechansons.com, which seems as good as any.

## CHAPTER ONE

John Keel's definition of 'ultraterrestrial' is taken from his unpublished UFO dictionary, in my possession.

Jacques Vallee compares fairy and alien reports in *Passport to Magonia*, Henry Regnery, Chicago, IL, 1969.

Thomas Wood's fairy music can be found in his autobiography, *True Thomas*, Jonathan Cape, 1936. I take the score from *Fortean Times* 321, p. 48.

Samuel Drew's quotation is taken from *The History of Cornwall*, William Penaluna, London, 1824, Volume 1, p. 98.

Morgan Gwillim's tune can be found in *Fairy Legends and Traditions of the South of Ireland*, Thomas Crofton Croker, John Murray, London, 1828, Part III, p. 214.

Wirt Sikes's *British Goblins: Welsh Folk-Lore, Fairy Mythology, Legends and Traditions* was published by William Clowes and Sons, London, 1880. Sikes misquotes Gwillim on p. 98, transcribes *'Dowch, dowch'* on p. 99, and gives Ned Pugh's tune on p. 102. *'Toriad y Dydd'* can be found on p. 126.

*'Ffarwel Ned Pugh'* is taken from *Musical and Poetical Relicks of Welsh Bards*, Edward Jones, Third Edition, Printed for the author, London, 1808, p. 148.

'Largo's Fairy Reel' appeared in Nathaniel Gow's *Fifth Collection of Strathspey Reels*, Gow and Shepherd, Edinburgh, 1809. I've taken a version from the Traditional Tune Archive, at tunearch.org.

'Fairy Dance' is taken from *Irish Wonders: The Ghosts, Giants, Pookas, Demons, Leprechawns, Banshees, Fairies, Witches, Widows, Old Maids, and Other Marvels of the Emerald Isle*, David Russell McAnally, Jr., Houghton, Mifflin, and Company, Boston and New York, 1888, p. 97.

The story of Lusmore is found in many places; I used the version from *More Celtic Fairy Tales*, Joseph Jacobs, David Nutt, London, 1894, pp. 156–163.

'The Gold Ring' is from *Dance Music of Ireland: 1001 Gems*, Francis O'Neill, Lyon and Healy, Chicago, IL, 1907, p. 19.

McAnally transcribes the wail of the banshee on p. 100 of *Irish Wonders*.

The second cry of the banshee is from *Ireland, Its Scenery, Character, Etc.*, Volume III, Samuel Carter Hall and Anna Maria Hall, Jeremiah How, London, 1843, p. 106.

The third cry is from *Irish Fairy Tales*, W. B. Yeats, T. Fisher Unwin, London, 1892, p. 232.

*'Oran Talaidh na Mna-Sidhe'* is from the *Journal of the Folk-Song Society*, Volume 4, No. 16, pp. 174–175. The two water-horse songs are from the same journal, pp. 160 and 161.

Thomas Keightley's description of the trow comes from *The Fairy Mythology*, George Bell and Sons, London, 1892, p. 165.

The trowie tunes are well known, at least to trow buffs. I've taken them from the Traditional Tune Archive at tunearch.org. 'Winyadepla', 'Hylta Dance', and 'Aith Rant' are preserved in the second volume of the *Shetland Folk Book*, from the Shetland Folk Society, Shetland Times, Lerwick, Shetland, 1951. 'Garster's Dream' can be found in *Da Mirrie Dancers*, edited by Tom Anderson, published by the Shetland Folk Society in 1970.

The two versions of *'Yn Bollan Bane'* are from *Manx Ballads and Music*, Arthur William Moore, G & R Johnson, Douglas, Isle of Man, 1896, pp. 224–226.

Heinrich Meyer's letter was translated and published in *The New Musical Times*, August 1, 1882, p. 433.

The two versions of the troll tune are from Ludvig Mathias Lindeman's 1841 collection *Norske Fjeldmelodier*, No. 124, as *Underjordisk Musik*; and Andreas Peter Berggreen's 1861 *Norske Folke-Sange og Melodier*, No. 68, as *Norsk Troldmusik*.

The citation about the Huldrafolk is from the aforementioned Keightley, p. 79.

'Hulder-Laat' is also from Lindeman, No. 68.

The Swedish tune is from *Mythologie Der Germanen*, Elard Hugo Meyer, from the 1903 edition, Karl J. Trübner, Straszburg, 1903.

## CHAPTER TWO

Both *Cives apostolorum et domestici* and *Regina caeli* laetare are taken from the archive at gregorien.info.

*NAD: A Study of Some Unusual 'Other World' Experiences*, D. Scott Rogo, University Books, NY, 1970, has been republished as *A Casebook of Otherworldly Music*, Anomalist Books, San Antonio, TX and Jefferson Valley, NY, 2005.

Ernest Legouvé's account of Christian Urhan is taken from the *Gazette de France*, November 21, 1835.

*Unveiled Mysteries* was published in 1934 by the Saint Germain Press, Chicago, IL. The passages I quote are from pp. 99–100 and 249–250.

*The Magic Presence* was published in 1935, again by the Saint Germain Press in Chicago. The songs I listed are mentioned on pp. 76, 121, 248, 249, 250, 295, and 381.

The 1938 edition of *'I AM' Songs* was published by the Saint Germain Press in Chicago. 'I Come on the Wings of Light' is on p. 131, 'Beloved Leto' on p. 23.

The 'Goddess of Music's Discourse', which Edna Ballard delivered to the Chicago Class on January 16, 1944, was printed in *The Voice of the 'I AM'*, March 1944. The quotations are from pp. 10, 18, and 12.

The Ballards' trials for mail fraud eventually reached the Supreme Court; they're documented in Chapter 6 of *The Lustre of Our Country: The*

*American Experience of Religious Freedom*, John T. Noonan, Jr., University of California Press, Berkeley, CA, 1998. Virginia LaFerrera's testimony is on p. 152.

The latest edition of the *'I AM' Songbook* was published in 2014. The Saint Germain Press is now in Schaumburg, IL.

Vivenus's book *Vivenus: Starchild* was published by Global Communications, NYC, 1982. The *Oakland Tribune* clipping is on p. 61.

Howard Menger told his story in *From Outer Space to You*, Saucerian Books, Clarksburg, WV, 1959. The quotations are from pp. 117 and 118.

Eugenio Siragusa's claims can be pondered at eugeniosiragusa.it.

Recordings and videos of Claude Vorilhon's music are available at rael.org.

The quotations from Philip Rodgers are from *Alien Meetings*, Brad Steiger, Ace Books, NYC, 1978, pp. 204 and 205.

The score of Philip Rodgers's music is from *The Flying Saucer Menace*, Brad Steiger, Award Books, NY, Tandem Books, London, 1967, p. 34.

George Hunt Williamson describes his experiments with alien contact and the language Solex Mal in *Other Tongues—Other Flesh*, Amherst Press, Amherst, WI, 1953 and *The Saucers Speak*, New Age Publishing Company, Los Angeles, 1954; revised edition, Neville Spearman, London, 1967.

The history of the STAR Fellowship is recounted in Philip Heselton's article '"Skyways and Landmarks" and the STAR Fellowship', *Journal of Geomancy*, Vol. 4 No. 2, Jan. 1980.

Sir Patrick Moore discusses Bernard Byron's appearance on 'Can You Speak Venusian?' in the 1972 book of the same name. 'Anya Ray' was printed in the newsletter of the STAR Fellowship, *Amskaya*, #57, Jan. 2004.

## CHAPTER THREE

The story of the Drummer of Tedworth is told in many places; pride of place goes to *A Blow at Modern Sadducism, In Some Philosophical Considerations about Witchcraft*, Joseph Glanvill, 1668, and its 1681 revision *Saducismus Triumphatus: or, Full and Plain Evidence Concerning Witches and Apparitions*. I took the basic story from Charles Mackay's always enjoyable *Memoirs of Extraordinary Popular Delusions and the Madness of Crowds*, Volume II, pp. 224–227, my copy being from the Office of the National Illustrated Library, London, 1852; and from 'New Light on the 'Drummer of Tedworth': conflicting narratives of witchcraft in Restoration England', Michael Hunter, *Historical Research*, Vol, 78, Issue 201, pp. 311–353. The excerpts from Mompesson are taken from the latter.

The Shaker melodies are from *The Gift to be Simple: Songs, Dances, and Rituals of the American Shakers*, Edward Deming Andrews, J. J. Augustin, 1940.

Ann Leah Underhill (formerly both Fox and Fish, serially) describes the writing of 'The Haunted Ground' in *The Missing Link in Modern Spiritualism*, Thomas R. Knox & Co., NY, 1885, pp. 415–420.

*The Davenport Brothers, The World-Renowned Spiritual Mediums; Their Biography, and Adventures in Europe and America*, anonymous, but attributed to Paschal Beverly Randolph, was published in 1869 by William White & Company, Banner of Light Office, Boston. The quotations are from pp. 122 and 123.

*Modern American Spiritualism*, by Emma Hardinge (not yet Britten), was published by the author, NY, 1870. Chapter 30 is devoted to Koons and Tippie; the quotes are from pp. 308, 317, and 318.

The Jonathan Koons 'spiritual machine' is presented in *Scientific American*, Feb. 3, 1855, p. 162.

Hereward Carrington is quoted from *The Physical Phenomena of Spiritualism: Fraudulent and Genuine*, third edition, Dodd, Mead, and Co., NY, 1920, p. 249.

Emma Hardinge Britten's unfinished *Autobiography* was edited by her sister, Mrs. Margaret Wilkinson, and published by John Heywood, London, 1900. Chapter VI is devoted to 'The Song of the Stars.' Britten's quotation is on p. 65, the opinion of the *N. Y. Herald* on p. 67, and the program and libretto on pp. 70–72.

Gustav Brabbée's 'Dirge of Hard-working Prime Numbers' is reproduced in the booklet to *Okkulte Stimmen*, a collection of mediumistic recordings compiled by Andreas Fischer and Thomas Knoefel, supposé, Berlin, 2007.

*The Spirit Harp: A Gift, Presenting the Poetical Beauties of the Harmonial Philosophy*, compiled by Maria F. Chandler, was published by R. P. Ambler, Springfield, Mass., 1851.

*Spirit Voices: Odes, Dictated by Spirits of the Second Sphere, for the Use of Harmonial Circles*, by Esther C. Henck, was published by Henck herself in Philadelphia, 1853.

*The Spirit Minstrel; A Collection of Hymns and Music for the use of Spiritualists, in their circles and public meetings*, by J. B. Packard and J. S. Loveland, Bela March, Boston, 1856. The introduction is on p. 1, 'Light' on p. 11.

Gaston Méry's first article on Mérovak appeared in *L'Écho du Merveilleux*, No. 24, Jan. 1, 1898. *Les Improvisations de Mérovak* was in the next issue, No. 25, Jan. 15, 1898. The quotations I translated are on pp. 27 and 28, the *Chant des Immortels* is on pp. 29–32. The quotes from Mérovak and Adolphe Brisson are from No. 28, March 1, 1898, p. 95.

Mérovak's carillon gig for the Exposition is documented in *L'Exposition de Paris (1900)*, Librairie Illustrée, Montgredien, Paris, 1900, p. 97.

*An Adventure*, by Charlotte Moberly and Eleanor Jourdain, was first published pseudonymously in 1911, and in revised editions in 1913, 1924, and 1931. I have here the 5th edition, edited by Joan Evans, Faber and Faber, London, 1955. Jourdain's description of the music is on p. 47. The music was published in *The Music of 'An Adventure'*, Ian Parrott, Regency Press, London, 1966. The debate about the music can be found in the *Journal of the Society for Psychical Research*, London, Dec. 1967, March 1968, and June 1968.

James Edward Holroyd's remark can be found in 'Versailles Revisited', *Blackwood's Magazine*, No. 1752, Volume 290, Oct. 1961, pp. 289–294.

The most extended study of Jesse Shepard/Francis Grierson that I know is 'The Illusioned Ear: Disembodied Sound and the Musical Séances of Francis Grierson', by Matt Marble, which is at earwaveevent.org.

Much about Jorge Rizzini, including the score of 'Glória a Kardec', can be found at jorge-rizzini.blogspot.com.

Rosemary Brown's three books are *Unfinished Symphonies: Voices from the Beyond*, William Morrow and Company, NY, 1971; *Immortals at My Elbow*, Bachman & Turner, London, 1974; and *Look Beyond Today*, Bantam Press, NY and London, 1986. *A Musical Séance* was released by Philips in 1970. The quotation about Liszt is from p. 99 of *Unfinished Symphonies*.

Melvyn Willin's studies of channeled music include his 1999 Ph.D. thesis for the University of Sheffield, *Paramusicology: An Investigation of Music and Paranormal Phenomena, and Music, Witchcraft, and the Paranormal*, Melrose Books, Cambridgeshire, UK, 2005.

## CHAPTER FOUR

Stravinsky was quoted in an article by C. Stanley Wise, 'American Music Is True Art', *New York Tribune*, Jan. 15, 1916. Wise gave the statement in its original French: *'La musique est trop bête pour exprimer autre chose que la musique.'*

Weber's transcriptions are from his article 'On Melody in Speech', *Longman's Magazine*, Feb. 1887, pp. 405 and 406.

C. P. E. Bach's cipher is found in the Fughetta in F Major, H. 285.

'A Bad Egg Polka' and 'Cabbage Waltz' are numbers 39 and 40 in Nicolas Slonimsky's *51 Minitudes for Piano*, G. Schirmer, New York and London, 1979.

Robert Louis Stevenson's musical cipher was unearthed by John F. M. Russell in *The Music Manuscripts of Robert Louis Stevenson in Historical Order*, 2017, which can be read at robert-louis-stevenson.org. Stevenson noted his abracadabra in a letter to his cousin Bob Stevenson, on Aug. 1, 1886.

'Bubble and Squeak' is reproduced from *The Cook's Oracle*, William Kitchiner, Fifth Edition, A. Constable & Co., Edinburgh, 1823, p. 364. Some editions prudently remove this experiment.

Robert W. Padgett offers his theory about Beethoven in 'Beethoven Ninth DEAF Cipher', elgarsenigmasexposed.org, Nov. 24, 2014.

Michael Haydn's cipher is from *Biographische Skizze von Michael Haydn*, Werigand Rettensteiner, Salzburg, 1808, p. 61.

Dan Beard's cipher is in *The American Boys' Book of Signs, Signals, and Symbols*, Dan Beard, J. B. Lippincott Company, Philadelphia and London, 1918, p. 85.

Francis Bacon introduced his biliteral cipher in *De Dignitate & Augmentis Scientiarum*, 1623. Elizabeth Wells Gallup applied it to Baconism in *The Bi-literal Cypher of Sir Francis Bacon*, Howard Publishing Co., Detroit, MI, 1901. Her work is critiqued in *The Shakespearean Ciphers Examined*, William F. and Elizebeth S. Friedman, Cambridge University Press, London, 1957, Chapters 13–18.

Hideo Noguchi's article 'Mozart—Musical Game in C K. 516F' is available at www.asahi-net.or.jp/~rb5h-ngc/e/k516f.htm.

Olivier Messiaen described his musical language in *Technique de mon langage musical*, Leduc, Paris, 1944.

I've consulted my own tattered copy of *Langue Musicale Universelle inventée par François Sudre*, 2nd Edition, G. Flaxland, Paris, 1866.

Paul Collins discusses François Sudre and Solrésol in *Banvard's Folly*, Picador, NY, 2001, Chapter 5, and in 'The Prophet of Sound', *Fortean Times* 145, April 2001, pp. 40–45.

John Seabrook vented his disapproval in 'Kooky! Dept.: Wonder Boys', *New Yorker*, Jan. 29, 2007.

## CHAPTER FIVE

The ninth section of Thomas Stanley's *The History of Philosophy* (1687), devoted to Pythagoras, was published in facsimile by The Philosophical Research Society, Los Angeles, CA, 1970.

Filippo Bonanni's *Gabinetto Armonico* was published in Rome in 1723. The plates, by Arnold van Westerhout, were reprinted by Dover Publications in 1964.

Robert Fludd's monochords have been described in many books, including monographs by Serge Hutin (Omnium Littéraire, Paris, 1971), Joscelyn Godwin (Thames and Hudson, London, 1979), and William Huffman (North Atlantic Books, Berkeley, CA, 2001). A hefty slice of Fludd's *Mosaical Philosophy*, edited by

Adam McLean, was published in the Magnum Opus Hermetic Sourceworks Series in 1979.

Athanasius Kircher's description of the harps, from *Musurgia Univeralis*, is included in Joscelyn Godwin's *Music, Mysticism, and Magic: A Sourcebook*, Penguin Books, London, England, 1987, pp. 154–160.

*L'Archéomètre: Clef de toutes les religions & de toutes les sciences de l'antiquité. Réforme Synthétique de Tous les Arts Contemporains*, by Joseph Alexandre Saint-Yves d'Alveydre, was published by Dorlon-Aîné in Paris. There's no date of publication, but the introduction is dated 1911. I used the scan available online on Gallica, from the Bibliothèque Nationale de France.

D'Alveydre announced his desire to be the 'Pythagoras of Christianity' in *L'Archéomètre*, p. 9.

*L'Archèomètre Musical* is also undated, but bears a copyright of 1909, the year of d'Alveydre's death. I thank Joscelyn Godwin for giving me a photocopy of it, and of d'Alveydre's three piano pieces. He and his son Ariel Godwin have translated and edited an English edition of the *Archéomètre*, published in 2008 by the Sacred Science Translation Society, which I haven't seen.

The edition of Michael Maier's *Atalanta Fugiens* that I use is the French translation by Etienne Perrot, Librairie de Médicis, Paris, 1969, which reproduces the music from the original 1618 edition. The transcription of the music given here is mine. Joscelyn Godwin edited and translated an edition of the emblems, fugues, and epigrams (but no discourses), published by Phanes Press in 1990.

Loren Ludwig announced his discovery that Maier used Farmer's canons in a presentation by Donna Bilak, 'The Art of Encryption: Music-Language-Text in Michael Maier's Alchemical Emblem Book, *Atalanta Fugiens* (1618)', given April 15, 2015 at the Bard Graduate Center, which I watched spellbound on YouTube.

Maier's *Cantilenae Intelectuales de Phoenice Redivivo* was published in Latin and French translation (by Jean-Baptiste Le Mascrier) by Debure l'aîné in Paris in 1758. A scan is available on Google Books.

The Yeats and Farr collaboration is documented in a number of works, including the first volume of R. F. Foster's *W. B. Yeats: A Life* (1997) and Ronald Schuchard's *The Last Minstrels: Yeats and the Revival of the Bardic Arts* (2008), as well as Schuchard's earlier lecture 'The Countess Cathleen and the Revival of the Bardic Arts' (*South Carolina Review*, 32:1, Fall 1999). Yeats gave his own account in his essay 'Speaking to the Psaltery', originally published in the *Monthly Review*, and collected in *Ideas of Good and Evil* (1903). Shaw's insult was quoted by Foster, p. 257. Farr's chant is taken from Volume Three of the 1908 Shakespeare Head Press edition of Yeats's works.

*Magia Sexualis*, by Paschal Beverly Randolph, edited and translated by Maria de Naglowska, was published by Robert Télin, Paris, 1931. There have been many editions; the most recent English translation, by Donald Traxler, was published by Inner Traditions, Rochester, VT, 2012.

There have been many books about the Count of Saint Germain, of varying sensationalism. The most comprehensive account of his music is in Jean Overton Fuller's monograph *The Comte de Saint-Germain: Last Scion of the House of Rákóczy*, East-West Publications, London, 1988. Paul Chacornac's mistranslation can be found in his book *Le Comte de Saint-Germain*, Éditions Traditionnelles, Paris, 1977, p. 46. Some of the music (the arias for the opera *L'Incostanza Delusa* and the continuo parts for six sonatas for two violins) was published in facsimile by the Philosophical Research Society, Los Angeles, CA, 1981. I can also direct insatiable readers to my article 'The Immortal Count', in the *Fortean Times* 146, May 2001

(June in the US), which traces the development of his legend into the 20th century. 'Gentle Love' is taken from *Amaryllis: Consisting of such Songs as are most esteemed for Composition and Delicacy, and sung, at the Public Theatres or Gardens; All chosen from the works of the Best Masters*, J. Tyther, London, c. 1750. Facsimile by Benjamin Blom, NY, 1968.

## CHAPTER SIX

Lucretius is quoted from Book 5 of *De Rerum Natura*, in Thomas Creech's equally authoritative translation from 1682.

Jean Bodin is quoted from *Colloquium Heptaplomeros*, 1588, translated by Marion Leathers Daniels Kuntz, and cited in *The Harmony of the Spheres: A Sourcebook of the Pythagorean Tradition in Music*, Joscelyn Godwin, Inner Traditions International, Rochester, VT, 1993, p. 216.

Erik Satie is quoted from *L'intelligence et la Musique chez les Animaux*, in *S. I. M.* (the monthly magazine of the Société Internationale de Musique), February 1, 1914, collected in *Écrits*, edited by Ornella Volta, Éditions Champ Libre, Paris, 1981, p. 24.

*Naturgeschichte der Stubenvögel*, by Johann Matthäus Bechstein was first published in 1795. I quote from the 1840 edition, Halle, pp. 321–322.

*The Music of Nature; Or, An Attempt to Prove that what is Passionate and Pleasing in the Art of Singing, Speaking, and Performing Upon Musical Instruments, is Derived from the Sounds of the Animated World*, by William Gardiner, was first published in 1832. I consulted the third edition, Longman, Brown, Green, and Longmans, London, 1849. The song of the throstle is taken from p. 222.

*Wood Notes Wild: Notations of Bird Music*, by Simeon Pease Cheney, edited by John Vance Cheney, Lee and Shepard, Boston, 1892. 'The trombone blasts...' is from p. 192, the bucket from p. 3, his grandfather's bobolink from p. 192, the goldfinch from p. 39, the partridge from. p. 94, the screech owl from p. 102.

*The Evolution of Bird-Song*, by Charles A. Witchell, was published by Adam and Charles Black, London, 1896; the selection is from p. 244.

*Field Book of Wild Birds and Their Music*, by Ferdinand Schuyler Mathews, was published by G. Putnam's Sons, NY and London, 1904. The chart is from p. xxviii, the grosbeak from p. 136.

Hans Stadler and Cornel Schmitt's article 'The Study of Bird-Notes' appeared in the January 1915 issue of *British Birds*, pp. 2–8. The musical examples are from pp. 6 and 7, the quotation from p. 5.

Aretas A. Saunder's *Bird Song* was published by the University of the State of New York, Albany, NY, 1929. The example is from p. 169.

Bontempi's *Trio d'Oiseaux* can be found in Jean-Baptiste Weckerlin's *Dernier Musiciana*, Garnier Frères, Paris, 1899, pp. 129–131.

Cheney's observation on the cuckoo is from *Wood Notes Wild*, op. cit, p. 2.

*Tree Top Tunes for Tiny Tots*, Helen Phillips Eddy, Oliver Ditson Company, Boston, MA, 1919. The selections are from pp. 42 and 43.

Messiaen is quoted from the liner notes to Yvonne Loriod's recording of *Catalogue d'Oiseaux*, The Musical Heritage Society, 1423/4/5/6, 1973.

The duck instructions are taken from *Practical Ventriloquism*, Robert Ganthony, Frederick J. Drake, Chicago, IL, 1904, p. 101.

The hen is invoked in *The Whole Art of Ventriloquism*, Arthur Prince, Will Goldston, Limited, London, 1921, p. 44.

George Stewart is cited from *The Stewart Simplified Method of Mimicry and Parlor Amusement*, self-published, NY, 1918. The canary is on p. 12, the hand whistle on pp. 9 and 10.

The full title of *The Bird Fancyer's Delight* is *The Bird Fancyer's Delight, or Choice Observations and Directions Concerning ye Teaching of all Sorts of Singing-Birds, after ye Flageolet & Flute, if rightly made as to Size & tone, with a Method of fixing ye wett Air, in a Spung or Cotton, with Lessons properly Composed, within ye Compass & faculty of each Bird, Viz. for ye Wood-lark, Black-bird, Throustill, House-sparrow, Canary-bird, Black-thorn-linnet, Garden-Bull-finch, and Starling.* It was published in London in 1717 by both Richard Meares and John Walsh, with a few different tunes; the 1954 Schott and Co. edition combines the two collections. The nightingale's tunes are on pp. 19 and 20.

*Le Perroquet virtuose*, by Claude Sosthène Grasset d'Orcet, first appeared in *La Revue Britannique*, Dec. 1888.

The language of the crows is taken from *Quelques mémoires sur différens sujets, la pluspart d'Histoire naturelle, ou de Physique générale et particulière*, Pierre Samuel du Pont de Nemours, Seconde Édition, A. Belin, Paris, 1813, pp. 176–177.

The domestic fowls are in *A Strange Company: Wonder-Wings, Mullingongs, Colossi, Etc.* Charles Frederick Holder, D. Lothrop Company, Boston, 1888, p. 238.

I've summarized Grasset d'Orcet's ideas from his articles *Les Gouliards* (*La Revue Britannique*, Dec., 1880) and *Le Cinquième Livre de Pantagruel* (*La Nouvelle Revue*, May 15, 1885).

Raymond Roussel explained his compositional methods in his posthumous book *Comment j'ai écrit certains de mes livres*, Lemerre, Paris, 1935; *La Meule* can be found on pp. 122 and 123 of the 10/18 paperback, which is what I have here.

Jean-Pierre Brisset published *La Grande Nouvelle* himself, in Paris in 1900. The quotation is from p. 1.

Darwin is quoted from *The Expression of Emotion in Man and Animals*, John Murray, London, 1872, p. 87.

Dr. Weber's examples are from his article 'On Melody in Speech', *Longman's Magazine*, Feb. 1887, pp. 399 and 400.

Anna Hinrich's article 'Summer's Natural Orchestra' appeared in *Popular Science News*, Sept. 1891. The notations are taken from Cheney, op. cit., p. 226.

I've taken *'Port na bPúcaí'* from the Traditional Tune Archive, at tunearch.org.

Eugene Thayer's article 'The Music of Niagara' appeared in *Scribner's Monthly*, Vol. xxi, No. 4, Feb. 1881, p. 583–586.

## CHAPTER SEVEN

The Philip experiment is documented in *Conjuring up Philip: An Adventure in Psychokinesis*, Iris Owen, Harper & Row, NY, 1976.

Aleister Crowley ponders the objectivity of magical phenomena in his essay 'The Initiated Interpretation of Ceremonial Magic', in *The Lesser Key of Solomon: GOETIA, The Book of Evil Spirits*, pp. 9–14 in my probably pirated and certainly undated De Laurence edition.

'Music in Dreams', by Valeria Uga, Maria Chiara Lemut, Chiara Zampi, Iole Zilli, and Piero Salzarulo, appeared in *Consciousness and Cognition*, Volume 15, Issue 2, July 2006, pp. 351–357.

Antheil's dream is quoted from his memoir *Bad Boy of Music*, Doubleday, Doran, & Company, NY, 1945, p. 20.

'Do not make a great keening' and 'They shall be remembered for ever', by some combination of William Butler Yeats, Maud Gonne, and Florence Farr, are taken from Volume Three of the 1908 Shakespeare Head edition of Yeats's complete works, p. 233. Yeat's description of its origin in dreams is from Volume Four, p. 242.

# INDEX

# Musical Notation

## Introduction

*THE FOLLOWING MUSICAL SELECTIONS are inevitably of varying graphic quality, although every effort was made to clean them up. The author copied a few pages himself, particularly traditional tunes, but hopes the reader will appreciate the many original notations for their historic value. All of the pieces given here are either in the public domain, or are brief excerpts for the sake of example.*

**FIG 1**

*Juanita, p. 11*

FIG 2

*On the Banks of the Wabash 1/3, p. 11*

# On The Banks Of The Wabash, Far Away

Words and Music by
PAUL DRESSER

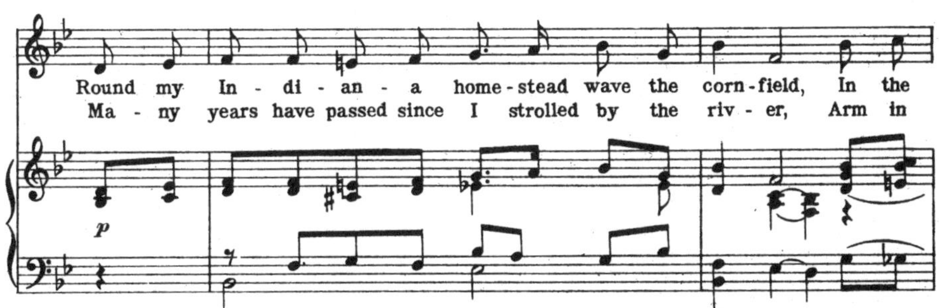

## Fig 2

*On the Banks of the Wabash 2/3, p. 11*

## FIG 2

*On the Banks of the Wabash 3/3, p. 11*

FIG 3

*Ella Ree 1/3, p. 12*

# ELLA REE.

WORDS BY C.E. STEUART. MUSIC BY JAMES W. PORTER.

## Fig 3

*Ella Ree 2/3, p. 12*

carry me back to Ten_nes_see, Dar let me live and die, A_
mong de fields ob yal_ler corn, And de land whar El_la lie.
CHORUS.
AIR.
Carry me back to Tennessee, Dar let me lib and die, A_
1st TENOR.
Carry me back to Tennessee, Dar let me lib and die, A_
ALTO.
Carry me back to Tennessee, Dar let me lib and die, A_
BASS.
Carry me back to Tennessee, Dar let me lib and die, A_
PIANO FORTE.
Ella Ree, 4.

## FIG 3

*Ella Ree 3/3, p. 12*

_mong de fields ob yal_ler corn, And de land whar El_la lie.
_mong de fields ob yal_ler corn, And de land whar El_la lie.
_mong de fields ob yal_ler corn, And de land whar El_la lie.
_mong de fields ob yal_ler corn, And de land whar El_la lie.
THIRD VERSE.
De summer moon will rise and set, And de night birds thrill dar lay, And de
possum and coon so soft_ly step, Round de grave of El_la Ree, Den
carry me back to Tennes_see, Dar let me lib and die, A_
_mong de fields ob yal_ler corn, And de land whar El_la lie. (CHORUS.)
Ella Ree, 4.

0

# Musical Notation

## On Music That Isn't There

## FIG 1

*In Futurum, p. 18*

## Fig 2

*Quan lou bouyé, p. 30*

## Fig 3

*A chantar m'er, p. 31*

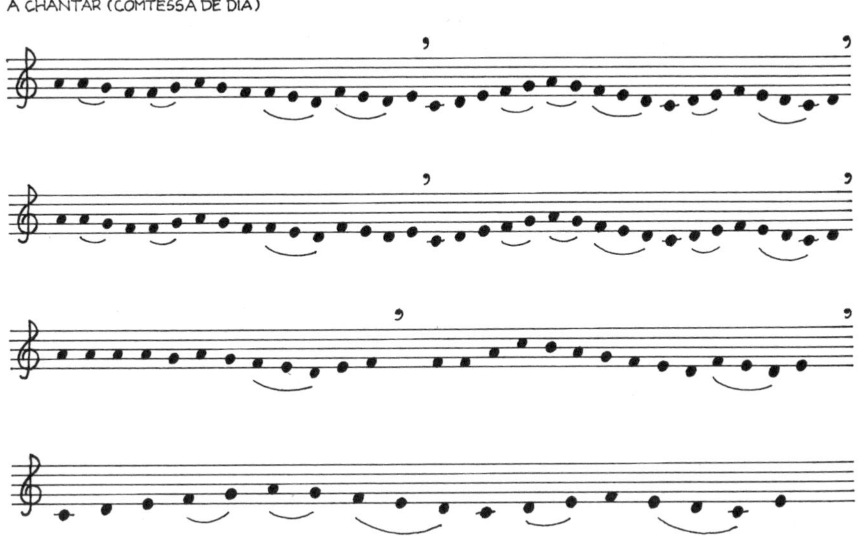

# I

# Musical Notation

## On the Music of the Ultraterrestrials

FIG 1

*Iolo ap Hugh tune, p. 38*

FIG 2

*Ffarwel Ned Puw, the 1784 version, p. 38*

# Ffarwel Ned Puw

## Ned Pugh's Farewell

*Air*

**Maestoso**

## Fig 3

*Toriad y Dydd, p. 38*

## Fig 4

*Dawns y Tylwyth Teg, p. 39*

## FIG 5

*Fairy Dance, p. 39*

FAIRY DANCE.
As played by a Connaught Piper, who learned it from "the Good People."
FINE.
D.C.

## Fig 6

*Dé Luain, Dé Màirt, p. 40*

FIG 7

*The Gold Ring, p. 40*

FIG 8

*Banshee 1/3, p. 40*

SONG OF THE BANSHEE.

FIG 9

*Banshee 2/3, p. 40*

FIG 10

*Banshee 3/3, p. 40*

FIG 11

*Oran Talaidh na Mna-Sidhe 1/2, p. 41*

FIG 11

*Oran Talaidh na Mna-Sidhe 2/2, p. 41*

FIG 12

*The Lullaby of the Water-Horse (The Lament of the Water-Horse), p. 41*

## 5.—ORAN TÀLAIDH AN EICH-UISGE.

(THE LULLABY OF THE WATER-HORSE.)

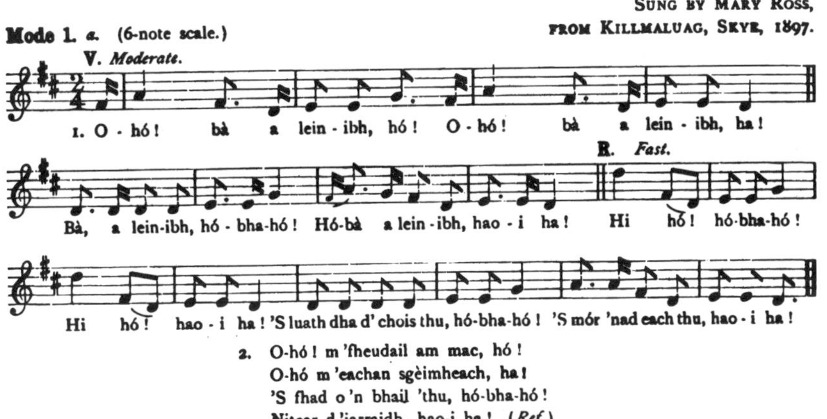

SUNG BY MARY ROSS,
FROM KILLMALUAG, SKYE, 1897.
Mode 3. a. b [with ♭7th]. (7-note scale.)
1. Och, Och - an 's mi dìr - eadh, Och, Och - an 's mi teàrn - adh; Och,
Och - an 's mi dìr - eadh a caoidh na rinn m 'fhàg - ail! A
Mode 1. a. (6-note scale.)
V. Moderate.
1. O - hó! bà a lein - ibh, hó! O - hó! bà a lein - ibh, ha!
R. Fast.
Bà, a lein-ibh, hó - bha-hó! Hó-bà a lein - ibh, hao - i ha! Hi hó! hó-bha-hó!
Hi hó! hao - i ha! 'S luath dha d' chois thu, hó-bha-hó! 'S mór 'nad each thu, hao - i ha!
2. O-hó! m 'fheudail am mac, hó!
O-hó m 'eachan sgèimheach, ha!
'S fhad o'n bhail 'thu, hó-bha-hó!
Nitear d 'iarraidh, hao-i ha! (Ref.)

## 6.—CAOIDH AN EICH-UISGE.

(LAMENT OF THE WATER-HORSE.)

dìr - eadh 's a teàrn - adh, A teàrn-adh 's a dìr - eadh; A dìr - eadh 's a teàrn - adh, 'S mi
caoidh na rinn m 'fhàg - ail. 2. A Mhór thoir a bhruth-ach ort, A

Mhór, thoir an gleann ort! A Mhór nach freag-air thu 'n fhead? A Mhór - ag bheag nan gamh-na!

## FIG 13

*Winyadepla, p. 42*

WINYADEPLA

## FIG 14

*Hylta Dance, p. 42*

## Fig 15

*Aith Rant, p. 42*

## Fig 16

*Garster's Dream, p. 42*

FIG 17

*Bollan Bane 1/3, p. 43*

## Fig 17

*Bollan Bane 2/3, p. 43*

FIG 17

*Bollan Bane 3/3, p. 43*

# Yn Bollan Bane (The White Wort).

(DOUGLAS).

FIG 18

*The Underground Cliff Concert in Norway, p. 43*

Etwas Neues unter der Sonnen!

oder

Das Unterirrdische

Klippen=Concert

im Norwegen /

aus glaubwürdigen Urkunden

auf Begehren angezeiget,

von

Mattheson.

---

Felsenlied unsichtbarer Geschöpffe.

---

HAMBURG, im Brachmonath, 1740.

Gedruckt bey seel. Thomas von Wierings Erben, im güldnen A. B. C.

## FIG 19

*Lindeman and Berggreen & Norsk Troldmusik 1/2 p. 44*

FIG 19

*Lindeman and Berggreen & Norsk Troldmusik 2/2 p. 44*

## Fig 20

*Hulder-Laatt 1/2, p. 44*

FIG 20

*Hulder-Laatt 2/2, p. 44*

## FIG 21

*Meyer's Swedish tune, p. 44*

# II

# Musical Notation

## On the Music of the Sky People

FIG 1

*Cives apostolorum et domestici, p. 47*

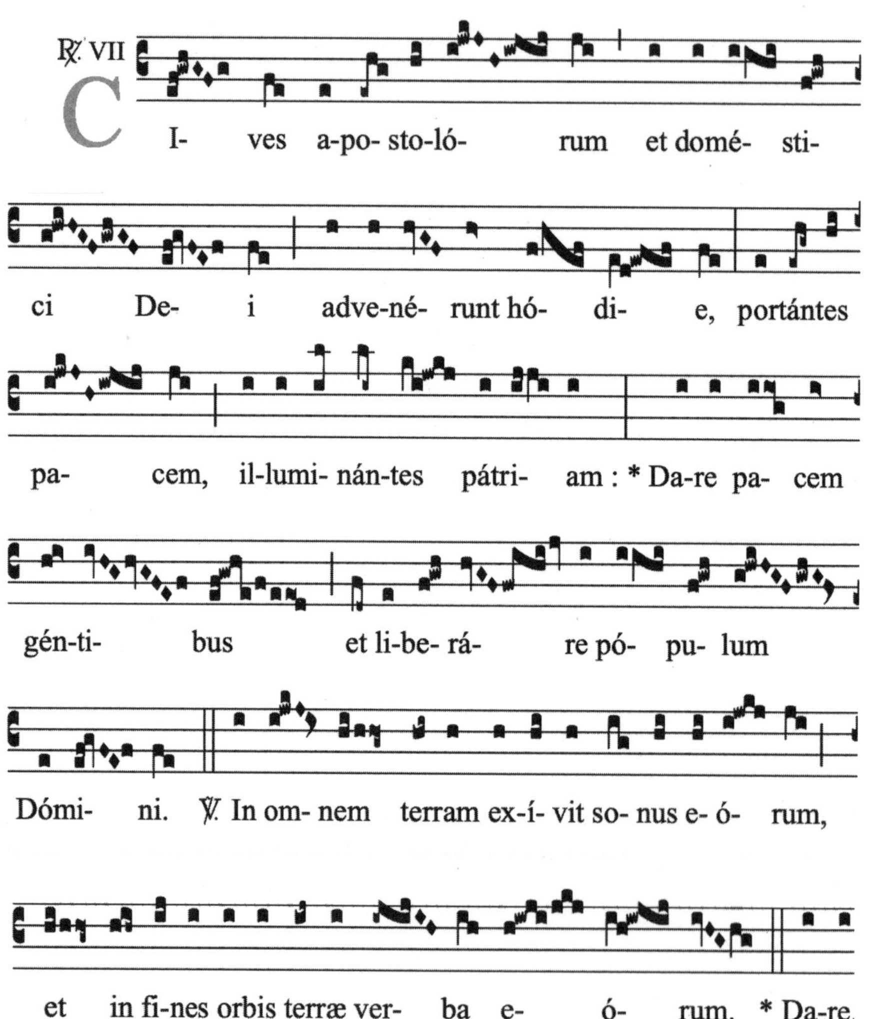

FIG 2

*L'Ange et l'enfant 1/9, p. 49*

# L'ANGE ET L'ENFANT

Mon ami! ecrivez ce que je vous ai fait entendre.

J'OBEIS.

Ce petit dialogue eut lieu dans le bois de Boulogne

près Paris moi étant seul le 20 Août 1835.

## Fig 2

*L'Ange et l'enfant 2/9, p. 49*

## FIG 2

*L'Ange et l'enfant 3/9, p. 49*

## Fig 2

*L'Ange et l'enfant 4/9, p. 49*

FIG 2

*L'Ange et l'enfant 5/9, p. 49*

## Fig 2

*L'Ange et l'enfant 6/9 p. 49*

Non, non, dans les champs- de l'es-
pa- - - - -ce A-vec moi tu vas t'en-vo-ler La
pro- - - - -vi- -den- -ce te fait gra- - - - - - - -ce Des
jours que tu de-vais cou-ler Que per- -

FIG 2

*L'Ange et l'enfant 7/9 p. 49*

## FIG 2

*L'Ange et l'enfant 8/9 p. 49*

## Fig 2

*L'Ange et l'enfant 9/9 p. 49*

FIG 3

*Schumann's last theme, p. 50*

# Thema (Es dur)

**für das Pianoforte**

**von**

ROBERT SCHUMANN.

FIG 4

*Rodgers's music, p. 55*

## Fig 5

*Anya Ray, p. 56*

# III

# Musical Notation

## On the Music of the Dear Departed

## Fig 1

*Mother Ann's Song, p. 63*

Vum vi - ve vum vi - ve vum vum vo, Ve vum vi - ve vum vi - ve vum vum vo,
Vum vi - ve vum vi - ve vum vum vo, Ve vum vi - ve vo ve vum vum vo.
Vum vi - ve vum vi - ve vum vum vo, Vi - ve vi - ve vi - ve vi - ve vum vum vo,
Vum vi - ve vum vi - ve vum vum vo, Ve vum vi - ve vum ve vum vum vo.

## Fig 2

*From the Moon, p. 63*

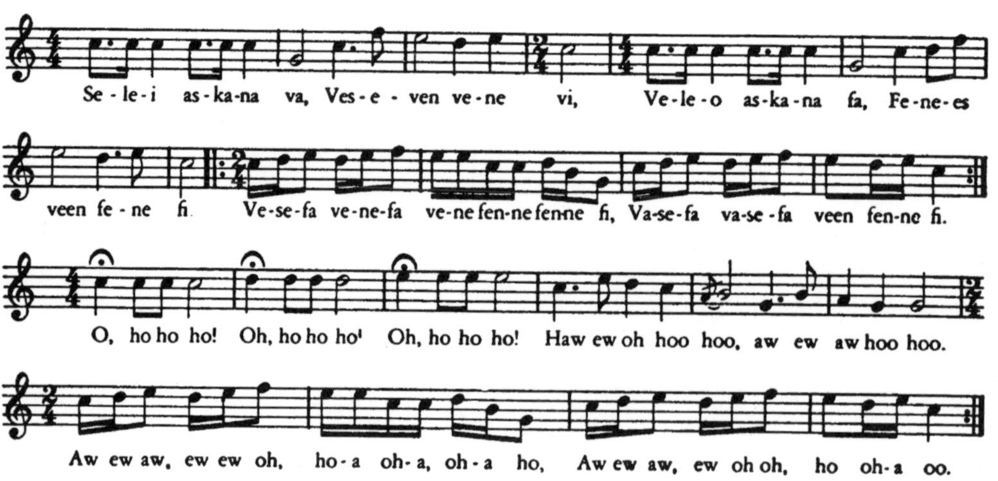

Se - le - i as - ka - na va, Ves - e - ven ve - ne vi, Ve - le - o as - ka - na fa, Fe - ne - es
veen fe - ne fi Ve - se - fa ve - ne - fa ve - ne fen - ne fen - ne fi, Va - se - fa va - se - fa veen fen - ne fi.
O, ho ho ho! Oh, ho ho ho' Oh, ho ho ho! Haw ew oh hoo hoo, aw ew aw hoo hoo.
Aw ew aw, ew ew oh, ho - a oh - a, oh - a ho, Aw ew aw, ew oh oh, ho oh - a oo.

Fig 3

*'The Haunted Ground', p. 60*

# THE HAUNTED GROUND.

Arr. by J. Jay Watson.

FIG 4

*Brabbée's 'Dirge', p. 68*

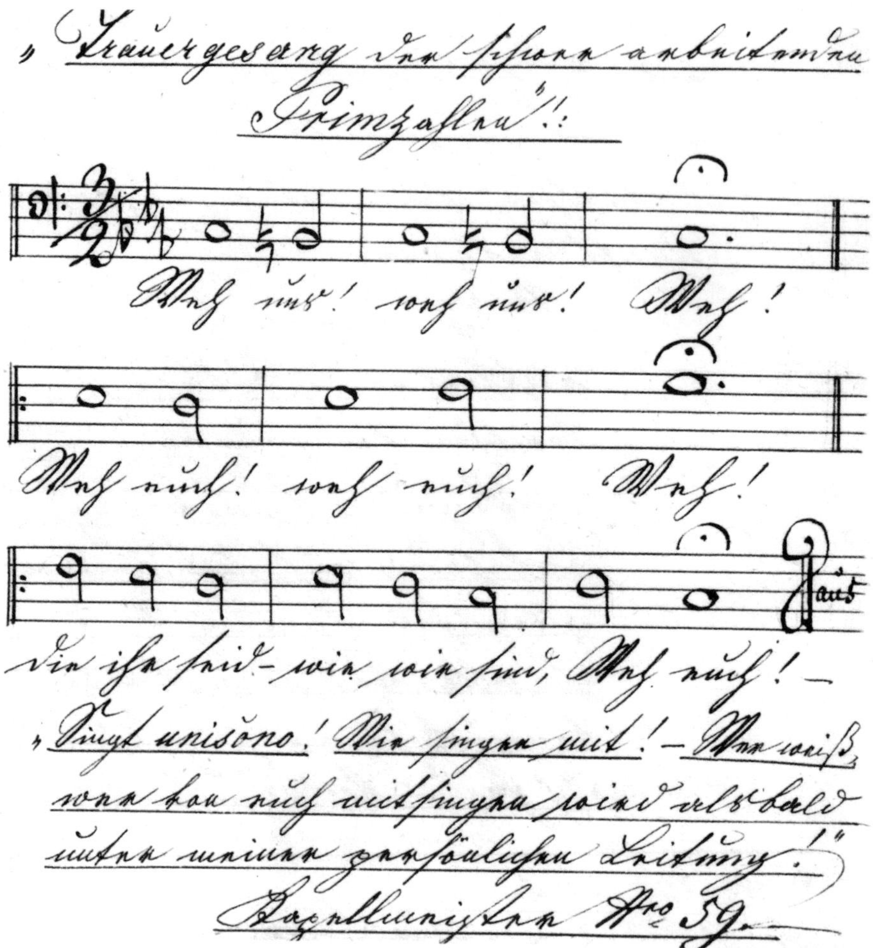

FIG 5

*Packard's 'Light', p. 69*

LIGHT
8s & 7s
B. PACKARD.
11
1. Gently o'er the senses stealing, Lute-like comes an unseen throng, Spirits, waking each a feeling With a birth-baptismal song.
2. Chalice held by fairy fingers, Seems the soul—all brimming o'er— 'Neath a fountain, still it lingers Where the living waters pour


3

Now, a mirror's disc it seemeth,
Far beneath a crystal flow,
Where the inner sun-light gleameth
As the bubbles upward go.

4

Beaming eye-light truly telleth,
In a language all its own,
That behind these glances dwelleth
Love, illuming pleasure's throne.

FIG 6

*Chant des Immortels 1/4, p. 71*

## FIG 6

*Chant des Immortels 2/4, p. 71*

## FIG 6

*Chant des Immortels 3/4, p. 71*

## Fig 6

*Chant des Immortels 4/4, p. 71*

FIG 7

*Music notated by Jourdain, p. 72*

FIG 8

*Glória a Kardec, p. 74*

FIG 9

*Song for the World, Rosemary Brown's manuscript, p. 75*

# IV

# Musical Notation

## On Musical Ciphers

FIG 1

*Weber's speech notations, p. 77*

FIG 2

*Bubble and Squeak, p. 79*

364 MADE DISHES, &c.

*Bubble and Squeak, or fried Beef and Cabbage.*—(No. 505.)

" When 'midst the frying Pan, in accents savage,
The Beef, so surly, quarrels with the Cabbage."

FIG 3

*DEAF in Beethoven, p. 79*

Fig 4

*De Terzi's system p. 83*

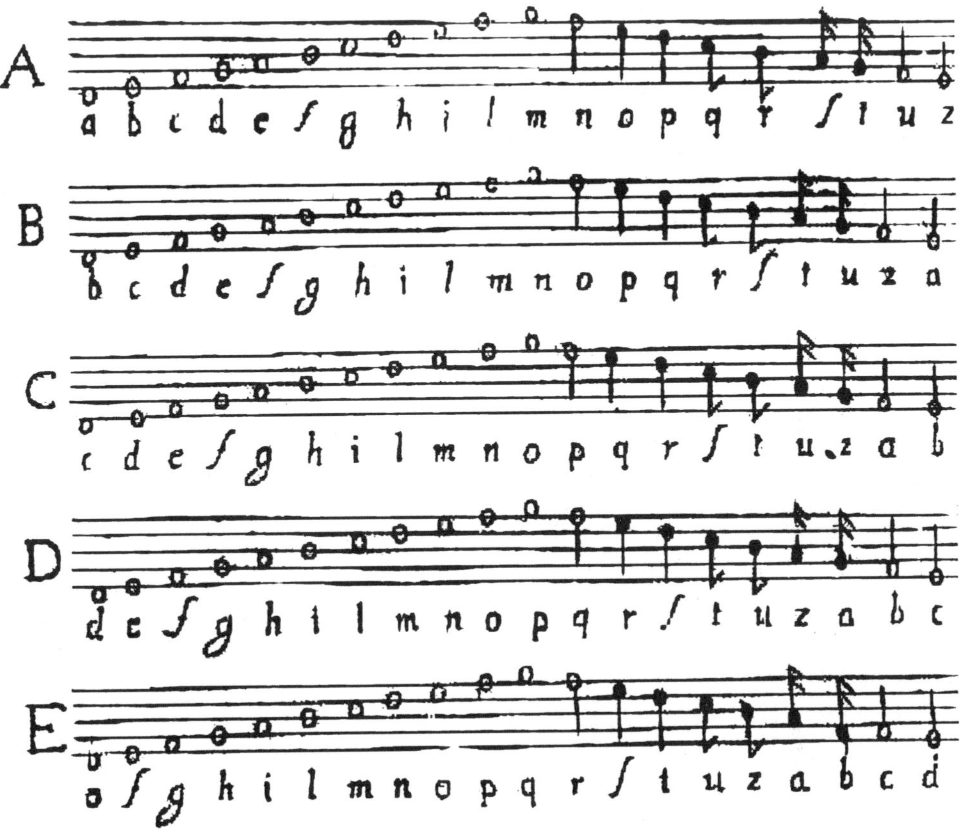

## Fig 5

*Haydn's system, p. 84*

*Rees's code, p. 85*

FIG 7

*Strange Attractor 1/2, p. 87*

## FIG 7

*Strange Attractor 2/2, p. 87*

FIG 8

*Friedman Christmas card, p. 87*

FIG 9

*K. 516f, p. 87*

FIG 10

*Messiaen's alphabet, p. 88*

FIG 11

*De Vismes's system, p. 88*

## Fig 12

*Weyrich's system, p. 88*

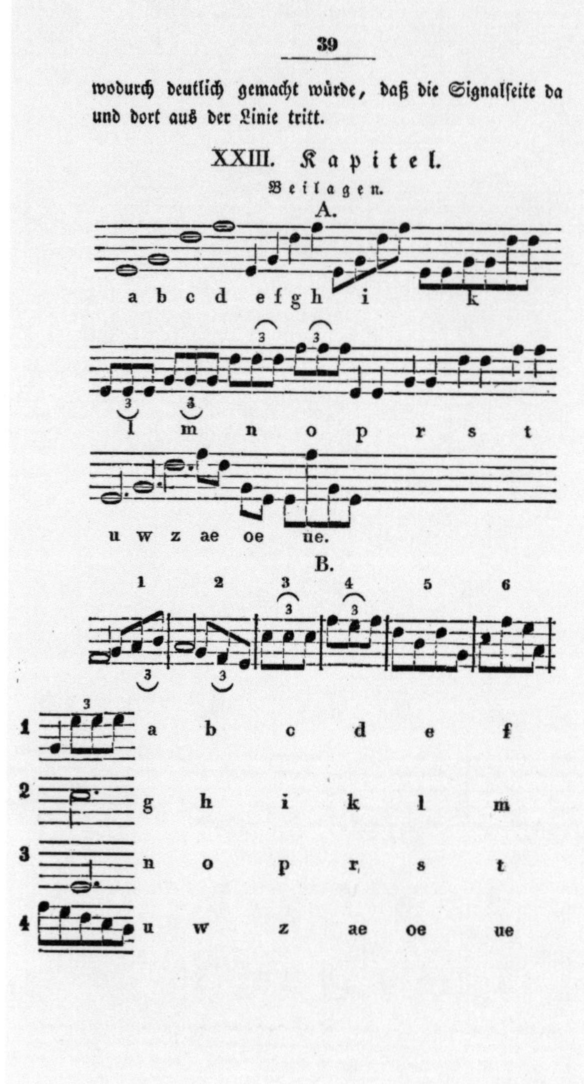

39

wodurch deutlich gemacht würde, daß die Signalseite da und dort aus der Linie tritt.

XXIII. Kapitel.

Beilagen.

A.

a b c d e f g h i k

l m n o p r s t

u w z ae oe ue.

B.

1 2 3 4 5 6

1 a b c d e f

2 g h i k l m

3 n o p r s t

4 u w z ae oe ue

# Fig 13

*Two-pitch words with corrections, p. 89*

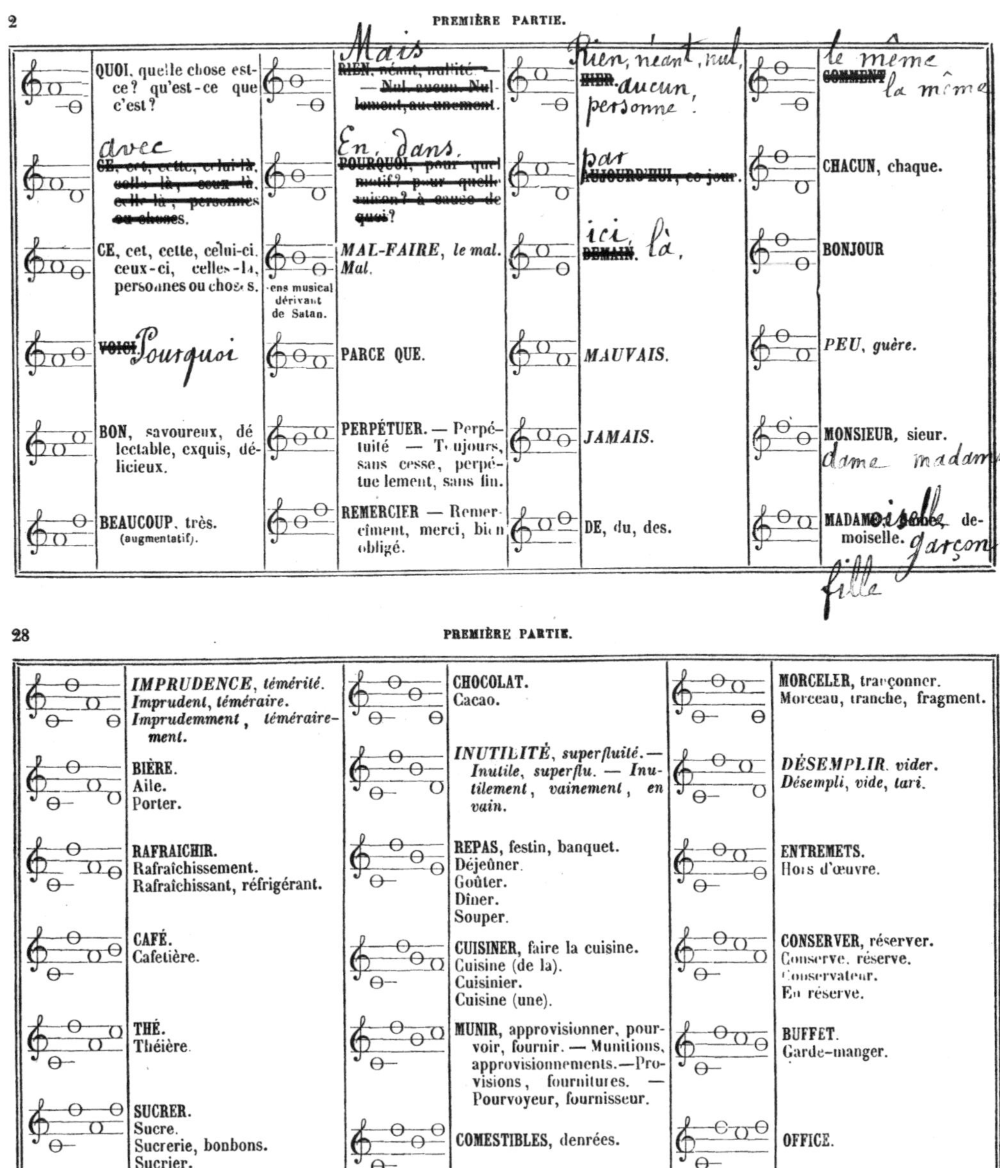

2 PREMIÈRE PARTIE.

| | | | | | | | |
|---|---|---|---|---|---|---|---|
| | QUOI, quelle chose est-ce? qu'est-ce que c'est? | | Mais ~~RIEN, néant, nullité. — Nul, aucun. Nullement, aucunement~~. | | Rien, néant, nul, ~~HIER~~. aucun, personne! | | le même ~~COMMENT~~ la même |
| | avec ~~CE, cet, cette, celui-là, celle-là, ceux-là, celle-là, personnes ou choses~~. | | En, dans. ~~POURQUOI, pour quel motif? pour quelle raison? à cause de quoi~~? | | par ~~AUJOURD'HUI, ce jour~~. | | CHACUN, chaque. |
| | CE, cet, cette, celui-ci, ceux-ci, celles-là, personnes ou choses. | ens musical dérivant de Satan. | *MAL-FAIRE, le mal. Mal.* | | ici, ~~DEMAIN~~. là, | | BONJOUR |
| | ~~VOICI~~. Pourquoi | | PARCE QUE. | | *MAUVAIS.* | | *PEU, guère.* |
| | BON, savoureux, délectable, exquis, délicieux. | | PERPÉTUER. — Perpétuité — Toujours, sans cesse, perpétuellement, sans fin. | | *JAMAIS.* | | MONSIEUR, sieur. dame madame |
| | BEAUCOUP, très. (augmentatif). | | REMERCIER — Remerciment, merci, bien obligé. | | DE, du, des. | | MADAMoiselle ~~MADAME, dame~~, demoiselle. garçon fille |

28 PREMIÈRE PARTIE.

| | | | | | |
|---|---|---|---|---|---|
| | ***IMPRUDENCE**, témérité.* *Imprudent, téméraire.* *Imprudemment, témérairement.* | | **CHOCOLAT.** Cacao. | | **MORCELER**, tronçonner. Morceau, tranche, fragment. |
| | **BIÈRE.** Aile. Porter. | | ***INUTILITÉ**, superfluité.* — *Inutile, superflu.* — *Inutilement, vainement, en vain.* | | ***DÉSEMPLIR**, vider.* *Désempli, vide, tari.* |
| | **RAFRAICHIR.** Rafraîchissement. Rafraîchissant, réfrigérant. | | **REPAS**, festin, banquet. Déjeûner. Goûter. Dîner. Souper. | | **ENTREMETS.** Hors d'œuvre. |
| | **CAFÉ.** Cafetière. | | **CUISINER**, faire la cuisine. Cuisine (de la). Cuisinier. Cuisine (une). | | **CONSERVER**, réserver. Conserve, réserve. Conservateur. En réserve. |
| | **THÉ.** Théière. | | **MUNIR**, approvisionner, pourvoir, fournir. — Munitions, approvisionnements. — Provisions, fournitures. — Pourvoyeur, fournisseur. | | **BUFFET.** Garde-manger. |
| | **SUCRER.** Sucre. Sucrerie, bonbons. Sucrier. | | **COMESTIBLES**, denrées. | | **OFFICE.** |

3 5

# FIG 14

*Fort in Solrésol, p. 91*

# V

# Musical Notation

## On Speculative Music

## Fig 1

*Andante espressivo, p. 103*

FIG 2

*Musical example, p. 103*

# MODE DE SOL

## HYMNOLOGIE

GAMME OGDACORDE

DEGRÉS CONJOINTS

Nº 1

Andante

*p*

*f*

Andante

*p*

*f*

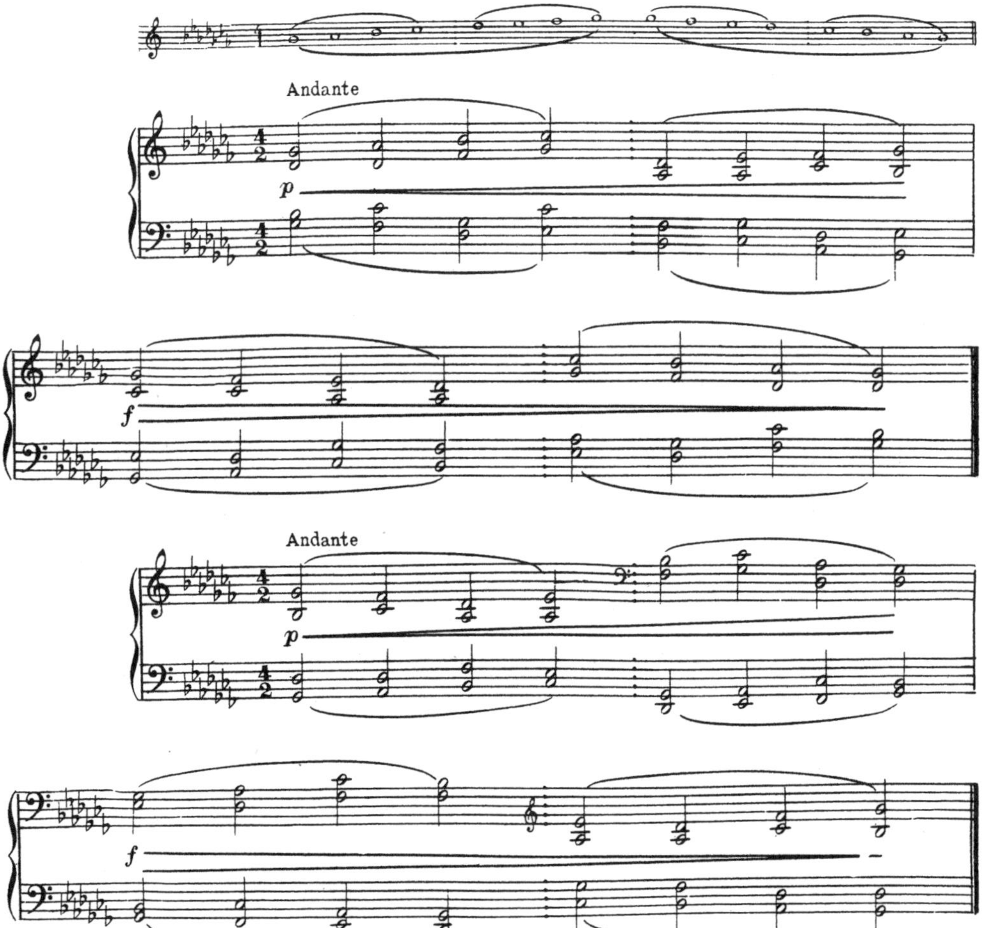

## FIG 3

*Musical example, p. 104*

FIG 4

*Excerpt from* Atalanta Fugiens *1/2, p. 106*

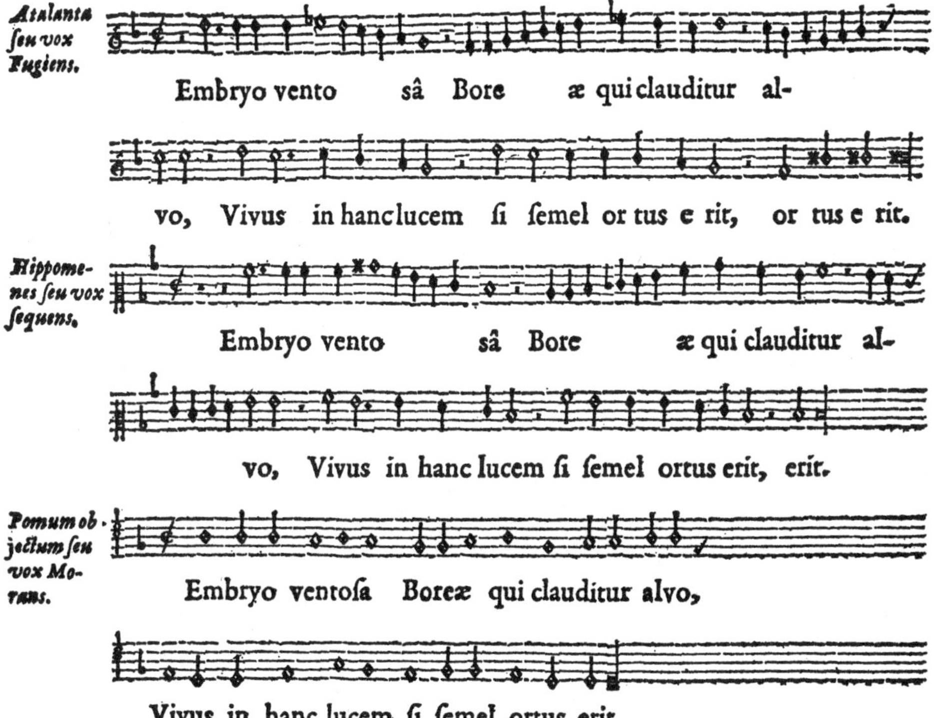

## Fig 4

*Excerpt from* Atalanta Fugiens *2/2, p. 106*

FIG 5

*A Farr chant, p. 108*

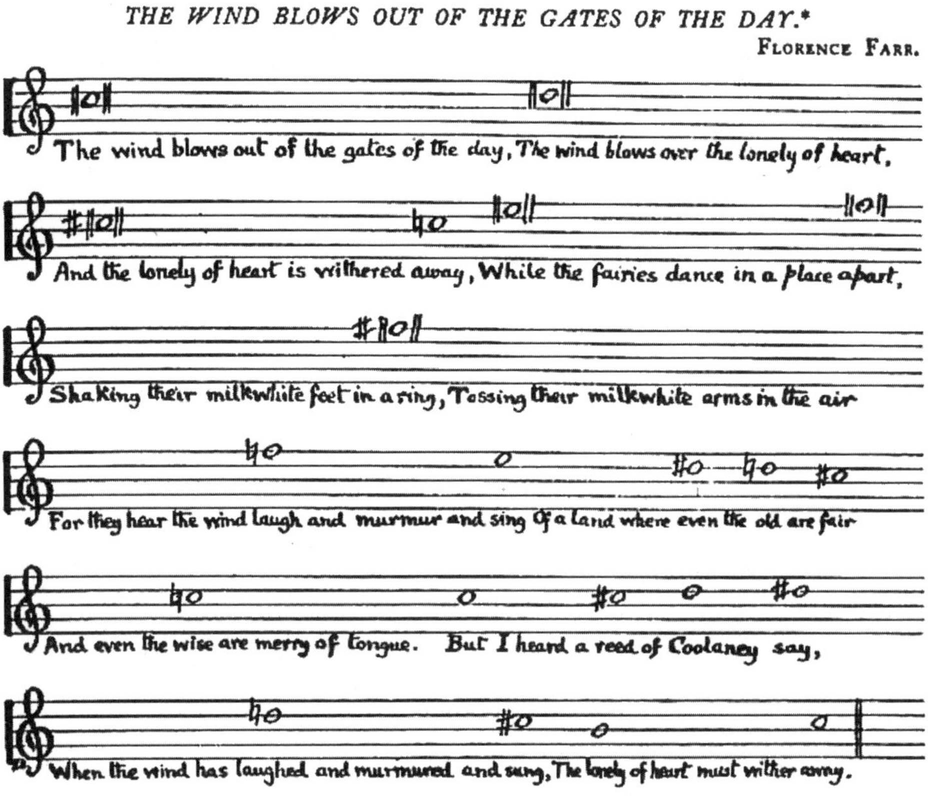

*THE WIND BLOWS OUT OF THE GATES OF THE DAY.**

FLORENCE FARR.

The wind blows out of the gates of the day, The wind blows over the lonely of heart,
And the lonely of heart is withered away, While the fairies dance in a place apart,
Shaking their milkwhite feet in a ring, Tossing their milkwhite arms in the air
For they hear the wind laugh and murmur and sing Of a land where even the old are fair
And even the wise are merry of tongue. But I heard a reed of Coolaney say,
When the wind has laughed and murmured and sung, The lonely of heart must wither away.

*Gentle Love, p. 110*

# VI

# Musical Notation

## On the Language of the Birds

FIG 1

*Kircher birdsong, p. 115*

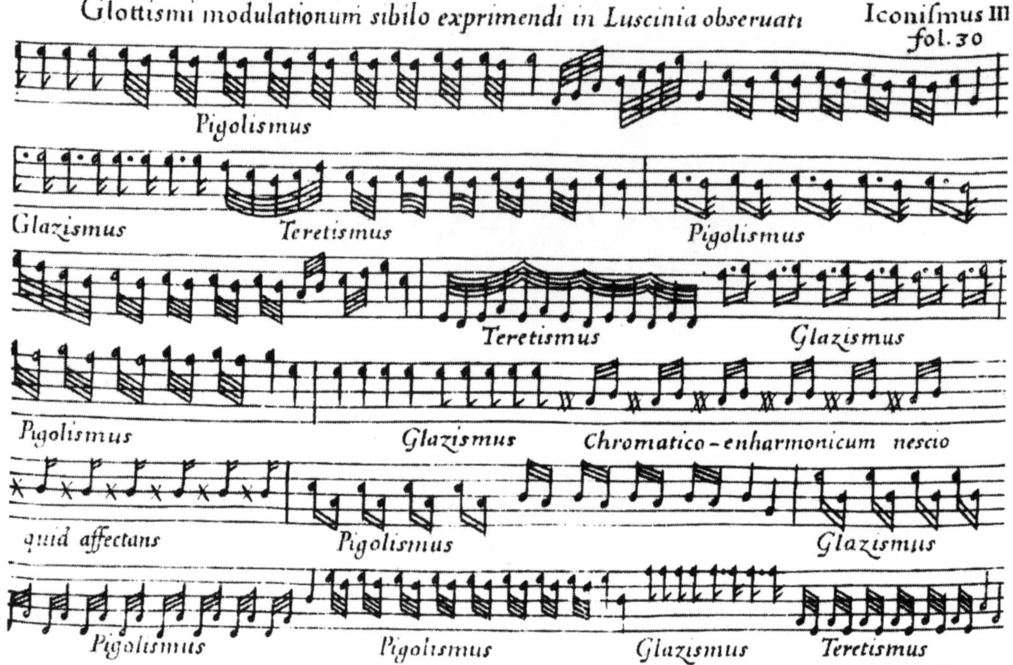

FIG 2

*Gardiner page of notation, p. 116*

FIG 3

*Cheney's bucket, p. 117*

FIG 4

*Cheney notations, 1/3 p. 117*

8va.

**With sweep and swing from crest to crest, the song runs: —**

FIG 4

*Cheney notations, 2/3 p. 117*

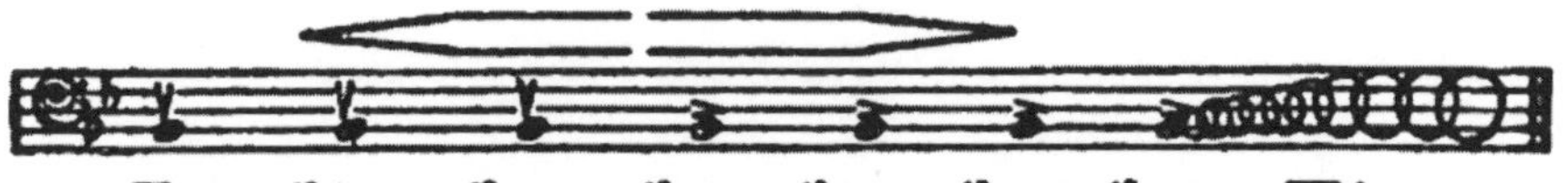
Thump, thump, thump, thump, thump, thump, thump. Whir. . . .

FIG 4

*Cheney notations, 3/3 p. 117*

FIG 5

*Witchell's thrush, p. 117*

# MUSIC OF THE THRUSH

FIG 6

*Matthews's piano arrangement of the grosbeak p. 118*

FIG 7

*Stadler and Schmitt's nightingale and wren, p. 120*

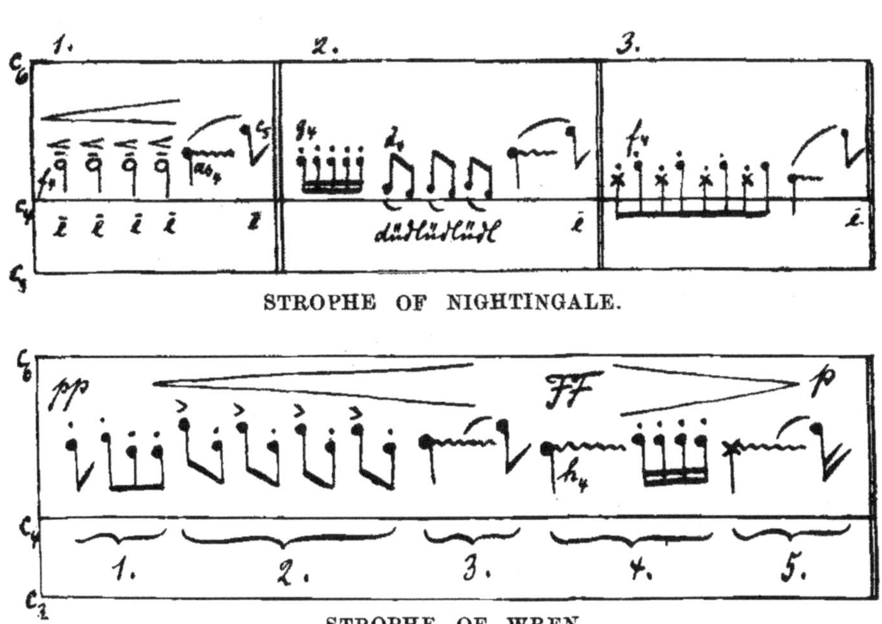

## FIG 8

*Saunders rendition of the wood pewee, p. 118*

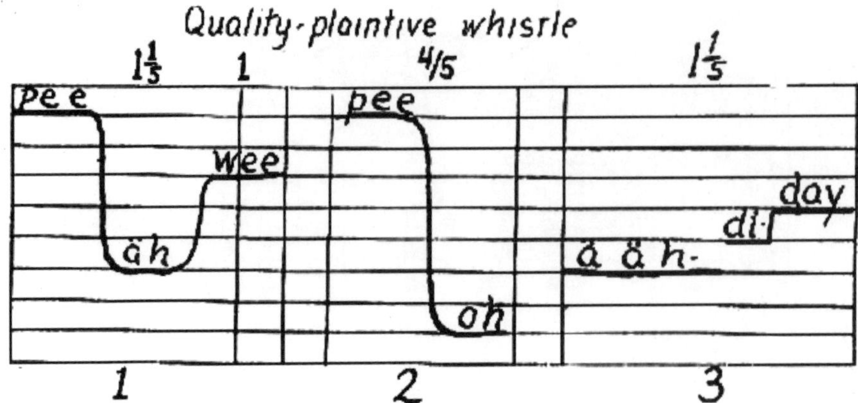


Figure 70 Twilight song of the Wood Pewee. Rate of singing 10 phrases to 15 seconds. Order of phrases. 3132313231313132313131321312313132313231321313131332132 Fairfield, Conn., June 28, 1927, about 4.30 A. M. E. S. T.

FIG 9

*Bird trio 1/3 , p. 119*

# TRIO D'OISEAUX DE BONTEMPI

## Fig 9

*Bird trio 2/3 p. 119*

## Fig 9

*Bird trio 3/3 p. 119*

## FIG 10

*Tree Top Tunes 1/2, p. 120*

## Fig 10

*Tree Top Tunes 2/2, p. 120*

## FIG 11

*Birds Singing 1/2, p. 121*

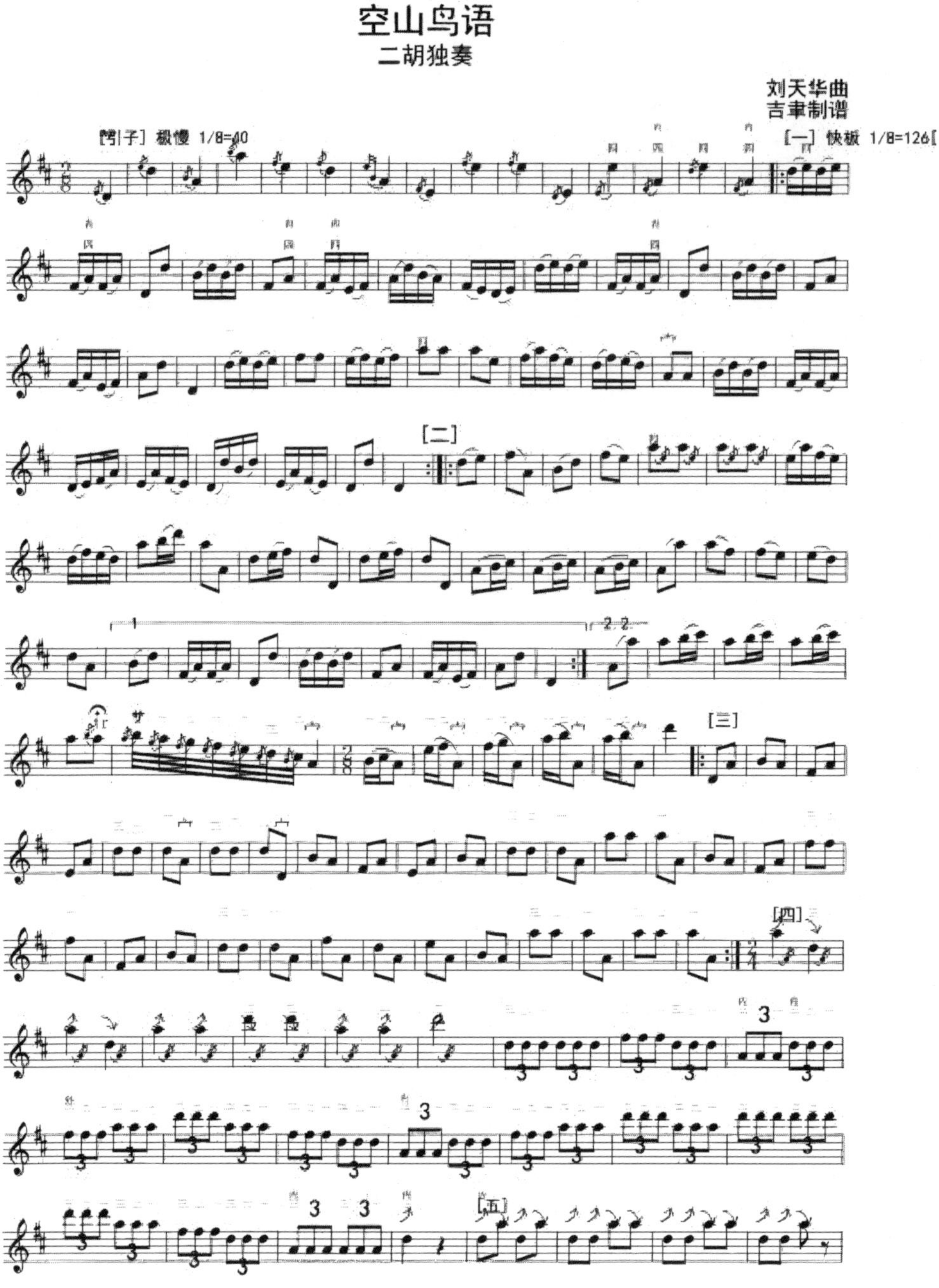

# 空山鸟语

## 二胡独奏

刘天华曲
吉聿制谱

[引子] 极慢 1/8=40

[一] 快板 1/8=126

[二]

[三]

[四]

[五]

## FIG 11

*Birds Singing 2/2, p. 121*

FIG 12

*Two tunes for the nightingale, p. 124*

FIG 13

*Mozart's starling, p. 124*

## FIG 14

*Weber's notations, p. 128*

All the animals on land, quadrupeds and bipeds, have their characteristic voices and calls in distinct intervals. Of our domestic animals the cow gives a perfect fifth and octave or tenth:

The dog barks in a fifth or fourth:

The donkey in coarse voice brays in a perfect octave:

The horse neighs in a descent on the chromatic scale:

The cat in a meek mood cries:

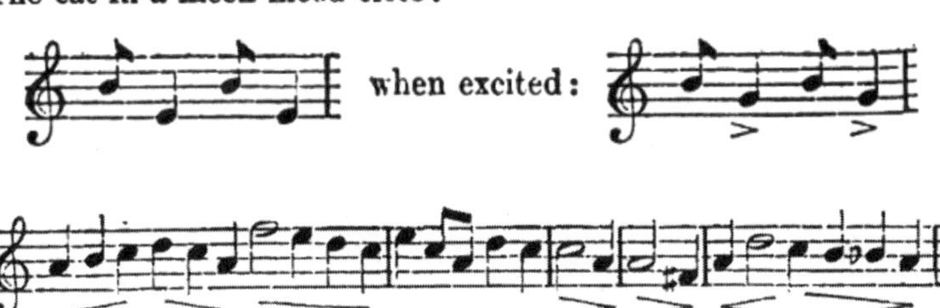

FIG 15

*Hinrichs's insects, p. 128*

# ANNA HINRICHS.

**(Summer's Natural Orchestra, in "The Popular Science News," vol. xxv. no. ix., September, 1891.)**

## Fig 16

*Port na bPúcai, p. 129*

## FIG 17

*Thayer's Niagara, p. 129*

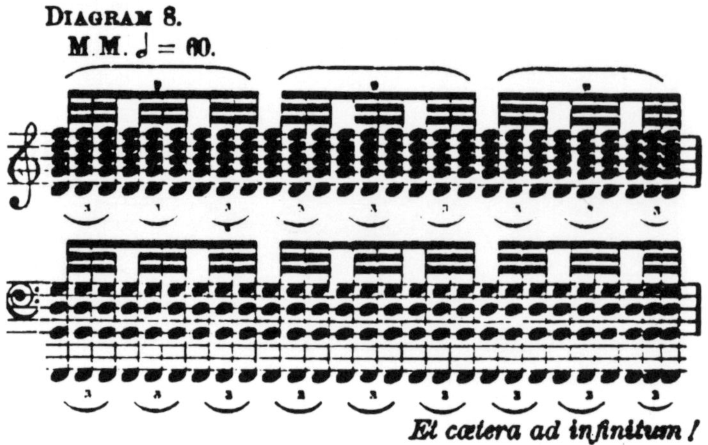

# VII

# Musical Notation

On Music
From Dreams

Fig 1

*I Dreamt That I Was Dreaming 1/3, p. 132*

# I DREAMT THAT I WAS DREAMING.

## FIG 1

*I Dreamt That I Was Dreaming 2/3, p. 132*

## FIG 1

*I Dreamt That I Was Dreaming 3/3, p. 132*

FIG 2

*Two chants from "Cathleen Ni Houlihan", p. 136*

## FIG 3

*Six examples of music from my dreams 1/2, p. 137*

## FIG 3

*Six examples of music from my dreams 2/2, p. 137*

5
OH DEAR YOU'LL NEVER UN-DER-STAND YOU'LL KEEP ON TO THAT
UNDISCOVERED LAND
6
YOU JUST FILL 'EM IN THE MORNING, YOU JUST FILL 'EM IN THE NIGHT, AT THE GASOLINE STATION,
THEN YOU KNOW THAT EVERYTHING'S ALL RIGHT.